Secrets In The Shadows

Women Of Strength Series (Book 3)

Lucy Appadoo

Copyright© 2023

Lucy Appadoo

Contents

1. PROLOGUE 1

2. REACHING OUT 4

3. A DECISION 10

4. SOUR TASTE 14

5. REUNITED 18

6. REFLECTIONS 28

7. YOUTH CLUB 34

8. GRIEF-STRICKEN 38

9. A LETTER 45

10. A DECISION 50

11. IMMERSED 56

12. A LONE JOURNEY 61

13. HONOURING MANUEL 69

14. ATTRACTION 75

15. STABBING INCIDENT   81

16. HOSPITAL VISIT   91

17. A NEW LIFE   97

18. SUSPECTED DANGER   104

19. FRIENDLY SUPPORT   109

20. A PHYSICAL THREAT   114

21. ENTRAPMENT   120

22. RESEARCH   128

23. CURIOUS VISIT   133

24. CONFLICTED   139

25. A CRIMINAL   146

26. A YOUNG MIND   152

27. AN ATTACK   158

28. MISSING   165

29. FREE AT LAST   172

30. RESPITE   179

31. A CONNECTION   186

32. SELF-DEFENCE   194

33. MESMERISED   200

34. HOSPITAL VISIT   204

35.	A LIFE TAKEN TOO SOON	212
36.	SAD NEWS	220
37.	CONDOLENCES	227
38.	SEEKING ANSWERS	235
39.	A YOUNG MIND	245
40.	INTIMACY	251
41.	INSTINCT	257
42.	A LEAD	267
43.	DOUBTS	273
44.	CAPTURED	281
45.	FEAR FOR SAFETY	289
46.	HAUNTING DISPLAY	295
47.	DRUG SHIPMENT	300
48.	FEAR OF THE UNKNOWN	306
49.	A TARGET	312
50.	BREAKING FREE	319
51.	LUCK RUNS OUT	323
52.	THE TRUTH	332
53.	TRUE LOVE	340
54.	FORCING HIS HAND	346

55. A TRACKER   353

56. A DRIVE TO SAFETY   359

57. FIGHT FOR FREEDOM   365

58. POLICE ARRIVAL   373

59. GOOD NEWS   377

60. EPILOGUE   381

ABOUT THE AUTHOR   385

ALSO BY LUCY APPADOO   387

Chapter 1

PROLOGUE

Manuel Perez extended his hand. "Here you go. The money for the hash. What's the next job?" He ignored the sweat on the back of his neck.

The other man towered over him, his wide-open shirt showing the tattoos across his chest. His empty black eyes were unnerving, and Manuel didn't want to cross a man who could be impulsive and dangerous. "Shifting ten tons of hash as soon as possible, and discreetly. The Civil Guard's watching. Or have you not noticed?"

Manuel nodded, his eyes roaming the stacked boxes of drugs in the dingy warehouse, including a surplus of hash and methamphetamine. On the floor stood open boxes of weapons and ammunition. A few of the creep's cronies stood on either side of him, holding semi-automatic pistols, their expressions stern. His hair stood on end, and his legs felt unsteady on the uneven, dusty floor. If only he could get his hands on some of those guns, but he had to play it smart. "Of course. I can liaise with the usual team, can't I?"

The big man laughed, throwing his head back. "I've made arrangements for them to focus on more important matters." The man scanned him from top to bottom, "Is there a reason you can't work on your own? You've been out of prison for a few months, and I assume you established contacts on the inside." Manuel nodded, masking his unease. "My sources tell me you have made friends with a man named Tomas." His eye twitched. "He also explained that you have a brother who is a police officer."

Oh, no! Manuel was crazy stupid to have trusted Tomas in prison. He had promised not to say anything about his brother. It was a stupid slip of the tongue. "He's a former police officer and is not in my life anymore. He left the city because the bastard didn't approve of my lifestyle. I have no idea where he is. You see, I have no ties, no family. I'm on my own." He wasn't lying about that, but he had hoped to reconnect with his brother once all this crap was over.

The man broke into his thoughts. "I want you to kill Tomas once you've shifted the product. He's become a liability and might be talking to the police." Manuel's hands shook, but he steadied them by focusing on his performance. *That* wasn't part of the plan. He couldn't kill anyone. But was it possible they could fake his death?

"Okay," he lied. Manuel's spine prickled, and he wondered if the man knew what he was truly doing. He had realised back in prison how he wanted to make a new start for himself. He had done a lot of crazy, illegal things in his life, but he had never killed anyone and didn't intend to start now.

"After you've shifted the goods, I want you to take my team with you. Make sure it's done properly with Tomas. We want his body disposed of in the usual way." Manuel realised how sorry he was for letting down his family. He missed his parents and brother, and wondered if it was too late to make amends.

"Now get out of here and do your job."

Manuel nodded, his heart racing a mile a minute. "Of course, boss."

Chapter 2

REACHING OUT

K im Mai threaded her hands through her shoulder-length, jet black hair as her yoga students strolled out of the building, waving goodbye. Her friends, Blanca and Daniela, sorted their belongings and rummaged inside their bags, chatting. Blanca's black hair framed her beauty well, highlighting her sparkling green eyes, tall and well-toned build, and well-defined features. Daniela was equally beautiful, her dark brown hair tied up in a high bun, her figure trim and taut.

Kim wiped her face, neck and upper shoulders with a towel, then retrieved her phone. Looking around the centre, at the wall-to-wall abstract paintings and displays of positive affirmations lining the walls, she noted that the linoleum flooring needed a good mopping, but she'd felt less motivated lately.

She waved her friends over, and they followed her to the small kitchenette which featured a granite counter and sink, a small timber table with padded chairs, and a small sofa by a large bay window with a drawn lace curtain. "Let's have a coffee, girls." Daniela rushed inside like a tornado while Blanca ambled into the room.

Kim prepared three mugs with coffee, sugar and milk while Daniela and Blanca sat on the chairs.

"Great session, Kim. As always," said Daniela. "It keeps me sane and fit for my dance school."

Kim turned to her briefly and resumed her task of pouring water into the mugs. "Thanks, but I feel burnt out with this. Little return for intense work." She handed two cups to her friends and picked up her own, sitting between them.

Blanca stared at her strangely. "Are you still having second thoughts about the business?"

She shrugged, clasping her hands around the steaming cup and feeling their eyes on her. "I am struggling to keep up with the rent on this building. Business has gone down with this economy, and I cannot keep up with the changing business laws."

"I hear you, girl," said Daniela. "I'm the same with the dance school, but I still love it." She frowned. "It is doing well after all that publicity with my dad. Maybe that's what you need, Kim. I can get Rafael to do an article about the centre. What do you think?"

Blanca shoved Daniela on the shoulder. "Hey, what am I? Chopped liver? I can do an article about her business, too."

Kim laughed. "Daniela is in love and wants her man to do it. If only I had the same kind of love you both have. But I am doomed to have a failing business, no love life, and my mother and father micromanaging my life. It's all hopeless." Daniela and Blanca turned to each other briefly then gave her reassuring smiles. "I know I am all doom and gloom, but I do not know what to do." She sipped her coffee and flinched as it burned her bottom lip. Nothing was going her way, and she wondered where to start repairing her life.

Daniela took her hand and held it gently. "Now you listen to me, girl. All these things are fixable, and we can help."

"But I don't know what else I can do, other than yoga and meditation," said Kim. She was twenty-seven years old and felt she stood at a crossroad.

Daniela sighed and pulled tighter on her ponytail, soft wispy strands nicely framing her face. "It's just a matter of finding your passion and working towards it." She thrust out her chest. "What about the youth work qualification you finished a few years back? Is that an option?"

Kim frowned. "I might have completed the training, but I've never worked in the industry. What experience do I have?"

Daniela pressed her lips together, playing with the gold bangles around her right wrist. "Your nurturing nature, life experience, time with a junkie, spirituality, and wisdom. That counts for a lot, girl."

"Exactly," said Blanca. "What about your sprinting skills?"

Kim appreciated her friends' input, and how much they had recovered from their past ordeals. Poor Daniela had dealt with a madman playing risky games with her, and Blanca had experienced trauma and exploitation. Bouncing back from those challenges only proved they could cope with anything. "Right. I might be a fast runner and won a few awards back in high school athletics, but I don't plan to do that professionally."

Blanca shrugged. "Remember Daniela's financial issues after losing dance clients not that long ago?" Kim nodded. "She found a way out and so can you. You might need time off. Time away to relax and get perspective. Right now you're not thinking straight because of burnout and negative thoughts. Give yourself a chance to take a trip somewhere. Maybe all you need is a change of scenery."

Kim felt grateful for her friends' support and admired the success they were having. Blanca's journalism career had given her the opportunity to work overseas for six months, where she had met the love of her life. She and Carlos planned to get engaged. Kim couldn't wait to celebrate the happy occasion. She was tired of focusing on her own problems and needed an event to bring her out of her pessimistic attitude. "I am sorry. I will figure it all out, but for now I need to vent. I appreciate the advice, and perhaps I will take that vacation." She took a breath. "What is new with both of you? Please distract me."

Blanca replied first after drinking down her coffee. "Well, Rafael and I are writing about a drug trafficking case with the South American cartel around Madrid. So many local gang members under the age of eighteen, it's scary."

Kim flinched, not wanting to think about her ex-boyfriend, Manuel Perez, who had been a drug dealer five years earlier. She had been notified when he had been released from prison three months ago, and luckily she hadn't heard from him. Was he keeping out of trouble, or did he get back into the drug business? "That is scary. Imagine the parents who are stuck and have no way out for them. Particularly when their lives are in danger. They probably can't get out even if they wanted to."

Daniela nodded. "Exactly right, but the Civil Guard and police seem to be taking down a lot of these cartels. It's all a matter of time." She rubbed her hands. "I shudder to think what could have happened to Blanca when she was little."

Blanca swallowed. "Thank God we got a huge chunk of that organisation into prison."

Daniela faced Blanca then turned to Kim. "We have to tell you something."

Kim angled her head. "What is it?"

Daniela touched the base of her throat. "It's about Manuel."

Kim's body ached and trembled. Despite hating the guy, a part of her would always love him.

Chapter 3

A DECISION

Kim dug her nails into her knuckles as she clenched her hands. For five years she had managed to live her life without her gangster boyfriend, and had not heard from him since before he had been released from prison. She couldn't imagine what her friends had to say, so she braced herself for the worst.

Blanca straightened her back. "He came to the house, looking for you. He must have done his research and learned where we lived. He asked to see you and said he didn't want to spook you by coming to your home, so wanted our advice."

Kim's face drained of all blood. "When was this?"

"A few days ago," said Blanca.

She exhaled. "You are telling me this now? Why not then?" She got up and carried the empty mugs to the sink. She turned her back to her friends, pretending to wipe the counter so they couldn't see how her hands shook. She couldn't go back to the chaos, the lies, and the criminal charges.

Blanca replied. "I am sorry, Kim, but we debated whether to tell you at all after the stress he caused you. But in the end, we knew you had a right to know."

Turning back around, Kim nodded. "I never understood why they reduced his prison sentence. Did he tell you anything about that?"

Daniela shook her head. "No, he didn't, but I was surprised by that, too. All he said was that he needed to tell you something important and wanted to make amends. He did seem genuine about it. Maybe he's changed."

Blanca got up and dragged her back down to the chair. "I think he has changed. He seemed different. Prison must have changed him."

Kim sat again, leaning forward. "How did you leave it with him? What did you say?"

"We said we would speak to you and let you decide if you wanted to get in touch," Daniela replied. "He gave us his phone number. Think about it, but don't take too long. I got the sense he has something important to tell you."

Kim scoffed. "The only issue important to him would be his next drug fix. He fooled me before, lied and cheated. It is what drug dealers and addicts do. They lie and pretend they have changed, but he is the same, I am sure."

"Why don't you hear him out and make up your mind then? You haven't seen Manuel for five years. Listen to what he has to say," said Blanca.

Kim rose again. "Would you girls like another coffee or a glass of water?" They both shook their heads. "I need a drink of water." She headed back to the sink and poured a glass. Drinking it down soothed her parched throat and distracted her from thinking about the trauma of the past. "I loved Manuel so much, but he hurt me time and time again. I don't know if I can go through that pain again. He will draw me back into his life and I will be charmed by his looks, his words, his lies."

Daniela intervened. "I hear you, girl. You went through a lot with him, and it's your call. We thought we'd relay the news, but in the end, it's your decision."

"We'll support you all the way, Kim. Whatever decision you make," said Blanca. "Only focus on things you can control right now. We've got your back."

She sat down and squeezed Blanca's hand then patted Daniela's shoulder. "Thank you both. I will think about it."

Daniela handed her a sticky note. "Here's his number if you decide to call."

Kim took it and stared at the number and name. His scrawl hadn't changed over the years, but had he personally changed? Or was it an act?

Daniela got up. "I've got a class now, Kim. I'll talk to you during the week."

Blanca rose too. "Yeah, me too. Sofia and Eva are coming to our drinks night on Friday. You are coming, right?"

Kim nodded. "I would not miss a night out with Eva or Sofia. After what they have been through, they deserve a fun night out." She loved Daniela's sister, Eva, like her own. Sofia, Daniela's friend and fellow dance teacher had endured a lot, too.

She wrapped her arms around her friends and walked them to the exit. Locking the door behind them, Kim proceeded to tidy up the studio. After she finally locked up, she drove home, and decided to sleep on it before making a decision.

Chapter 4

SOUR TASTE

Ricardo Perez played with his beard and moustache as he hiked the trails up to Patones de Arriba. Crossing a footbridge over a stream, he took in the fresh, natural scents on the warm breeze that feathered his red cheeks. The fresh scents of mountainous terrain and greenery gave him perspective and a calm mind, which was what he needed after spending five years in the Madrid police force. At thirty years of age, he had lived a life filled with trauma, death, and all manner of degrading, criminal behaviour as a police officer, and briefly as a detective, but now his life was better and stress-free.

He eventually passed the *Hermitage of the Virgen de la Oliva Church*, which dated back to the eighteenth century. The cobblestone streets were quiet, with only a few passers-by, and the intense smells of fernery, dampness, and dust made him wrinkle his nose.

Walking alongside the *Dehesa de la Oliva* archaeological site, he stared at what was left of a pre-Romanesque fort. He loved the history of the lower and upper parts of Patones, and knew he had made the right decision moving here from the centre of Madrid. He savoured the medieval town, northeast of the country with its historical-looking restaurants, olive groves, craft gift shops, and small hotels. The steep streets contained a history rich in interesting legends.

Ricardo worked in this part of town but he lived in Patones de Abjo, which was the lower part of the region, because it had more amenities than upper Patones. Still, the upper part was more tranquil and helped him forget his troubles.

As he made his way back down to his residence he spotted a group approaching. Several members of the Civil Guard approached in their green baseball caps, polo shirts and cargo pants. His friend, Angel, was the captain of the team and nodded in his direction.

"Hi Angel. What are you guys doing here?" He took a step down the incline to stay level with his friend.

Angel's crew cut enhanced his square jaw. His green eyes roamed. "Ricardo. Have you seen anyone wearing a grey t-shirt and blue ripped jeans around here?"

"No, why?"

He pressed his lips together as the other three team members talked among themselves. "There is a person of interest we are locating. Our sources say he is not far from the stream, but so far no luck. Are you keeping well, my friend?"

Ricardo nodded. He missed spending time with Angel, who had been busy lately, chasing leads in the drug trafficking trade. "Have you had any luck catching any of those gang members?"

He scoffed. "Those bastards have connections everywhere, but we are determined to find every one of them. They won't get away with polluting our nation and killing our innocent community. I will not stand for it."

"I hear you, man. Anyway, let's catch up for a beer. When are you free?"

Angel grinned. "I will give you a call and make time for you, my friend. You take care of yourself. We have a madman to catch. Take care, Ricardo." He saluted, and his staff joined him, climbing the steep track.

Ricardo kept up the pace as he headed home, his mind flashing back to his brother, Manuel. Angel had mentioned his prison release a few months back, but Ricardo had no interest in reconnecting with a man who had no morals. His poor parents had had to move to

Greece for their own safety, while he could take care of himself.

A few times he had considered getting in touch with Manuel to see whether he had changed in prison, but decided against it. Most likely Manuel was the same. The numerous times he'd lied and the stress he had caused his mother when he became violent whilst under the influence. The time Manuel had bruised his brother when his anger was out of control.

No, Ricardo would never be able to forgive Manuel.

Climbing the steps, he bent over to catch his breath before he unlocked his house. It was a spacious, two-storey home with a rustic beauty and history, multiple roofs and multi-coloured brickwork. He was able to get a good deal from the previous owner when he had moved to Patones last year.

He headed for the shower and realised his world was peaceful and content now, knowing that being away from his brother was something he had to do for his own sanity.

Chapter 5

REUNITED

K im bit on her long nails and crossed her legs on the white leather settee as she waited for Manuel to show up. He was fifteen minutes late, and she was starting to regret calling him. But if she didn't meet with him, she might regret it more. She needed closure.

Her eyes scanned her two-bedroom apartment in the suburb of La Latina, not far from the centre of Madrid. She loved the open living room with its matte floorboards and contemporary furniture, including bookshelves filled with books on yoga, meditation, and creative writing. Her one hobby was creative writing, and she hoped to publish her first romance book one day.

The sound of the doorbell broke her out of her reverie. She slowly made her way to the door, her heart beating a mile a minute, her hands sweaty. Why, after all these years, did he still have this effect on her?

She bit her bottom lip and gasped when she opened the door and saw the way he was dressed: a well-pressed ash-black suit, leather shoes, and an open-buttoned shirt that showed his tanned neckline. His towering, lanky build made him look slightly intimidating. He had obviously come up in the world of drugs.

His eyes looked troubled. "Hello, Kim. Great to see you again."

She nodded. "Come in."

Manuel ambled inside and sat beside her on the couch with one leg propped on to the other, which looked ironic, given he was wearing a suit. "Thanks for seeing me."

Kim shifted her body further away from his, ignoring his strong musky cologne. She played with the sleeves of her jacket, wanting to be well dressed for a man she realised she had missed. "Why did you want to see me, Manuel? My friends said you had something important to tell me."

He knit his brows and stared at his hands. "Are you well, Kim?" She nodded, waiting with her arms crossed. "I need you to relay a message to my brother. I'm worried about his safety." He handed her a note with an address on it. "This is where my brother lives, in Patones."

Kim angled her head. "Why can't you talk to him yourself?"

He looked into her eyes as if he was hiding something sinister, then dropped his gaze. "A particular group...they're watching me." He swallowed. "If I go see him they might think I'm turning against them, and I'll lead them straight to him. I know he's kind of protected where he is, and if I don't see him they're likely to leave him alone. I know they have resources to find him, but I cannot give them a reason to find Ricardo if I stay away. Until I..."

Kim shifted on the couch. "Until what?"

"Nothing. Don't worry about it. I trust you implicitly to do this. Please give him this letter."

Kim was curious. "When you say 'they', who are you talking about? The drug dealers, your gang? Who?"

He nodded. "Yes, the drug dealers. I am trying to get out of it, but they're making it damn difficult for me. For now, they said I need to do a few more jobs, then they'll potentially let me go, but who knows. It could all be one fat lie. I have no choice but to obey."

"Why don't you work with the police and live a normal life? Or are you lying about everything, about the fact you want to get out of it? Has prison really changed you, Manuel?"

He swallowed. "It has, and I mean it, Kim. I want my life back. I want to be able to see my parents, my brother, and my cousins. But if I see them, their lives might be in danger. I have to get away from the scene."

She scoffed. "Is my life in danger now that you have come to see me?"

"No, because I made sure I wasn't being followed. My brother can protect you if need be." He leaned forward. "I need to give you these, too." He handed her a chunky locket and two folded pieces of A4 paper. "It's a gift for everything shitty I've done to you. The letters are for you and Ricardo, but read yours later if you choose to. A token of amends. Can you ever forgive me for what I put you through?" His eyes darkened until Kim could not read them. "I need to know we can get closure on this, and maybe in the future..."

Her heart ached. "What, Manuel? A relationship? Is that what you want?" She shook her head. "I do not think so. We are finished and cannot go back to the way things were. Let us part as friends and say goodbye now. It would never work between us. Too much has happened, and I doubt I could ever totally forgive you."

He straightened his body on the couch, hiding the disappointment from his eyes. "Fair enough." He looked over his shoulder. "Now will you go see my brother? Tell him how much I miss him, and that one day in the future, I will be able to see him?" His hands fidgeted as he peered past her. "I need to know he can forgive me. Will you please do that, Kim?"

What was she missing here? "I don't know, Manuel. I still don't understand why I have let you impact my life again when you can ring him yourself. Surely, you can call him?"

"I can't take that risk. He needs to keep his distance until I know it's safe. At least think about it. And that necklace is—" His phone buzzed in his back pocket. He retrieved it and checked the display. "Oh, Christ! I have to go. A friend wants to talk to me. Please seriously consider taking the message to my brother. Like I said, Ricardo can protect you if you need it."

The back of Kim's neck became damp. "Why would he need to protect me, Manuel? What are you not telling me?"

He got up. "I have to go, but you take care of yourself. I hope I can see you again when it's safe." At the door he turned back. "I still love you, Kim. I never stopped." Continuing to stare into her eyes, he added, "You think us gangsters can't be trusted, and I'm sure a few in the police force can't be trusted either. But my brother, Ricardo. He's someone you can trust, and I can never say it enough. He can protect you. Please go see him." Stepping forward, he leaned in and hugged her tightly as if it was their last contact. She ignored the tingle in her stomach, realising she still had feelings for the man.

She pulled away and put up a hand. "Wait. Please tell me what is going on?"

He gave her a reassuring smile. "I have to go. Hopefully we'll meet again."

Kim's chest tightened as she closed the door behind him and rested her back against it. Why did it seem like his leaving was final, or was he truly planning to see her again?

After leaving Kim's apartment Manuel stopped his car in front of the warehouse, short of breath. He wondered what the bastard wanted. He had already shifted the product, so job number one was done. In the next two days, he was required to kill Tomas, or at least make it look real with the help of the police. Wouldn't the boss want to see him then?

Turning off the motor, Manuel thought about Kim, her beautiful, glistening dark brown eyes, full lips, and smooth olive skin which he wanted to run his hands over. If only he could live his life over again. He would definitely not be a drug dealer or hurt people.

But, he told himself, it would all be over soon, and he'd be safe. He might be able to reconnect with Kim once she trusted him again.

He stepped out of the car, opened the heavy timber door and entered the building to see the boss with his cronies, who stared at him with curiosity. What the hell was going on here? "Hey, boss. What's up? I shifted the product and plan to kill Tomas in a couple of days. It should be okay by then. Less heat on us, you know."

The boss approached Manuel. "Right, and who have you been talking to?"

His heart raced. "Excuse me, boss?"

"We noticed you leaving some apartment. Who lives there?"

Oh, no. He was sure he hadn't been followed. "Just an old school acquaintance. Wanted to catch up after my time in prison, but she doesn't want anything to do with me. A bit of a boring person who doesn't want to deal with my criminal record." He chuckled and pointed a finger at his chest. "Who can resist this man?" He spoke with a level of confidence he didn't feel, but he could mask his true feelings.

"Hmm. I see," the boss said, his eyes burning into Manuel's. "You look a little nervous, Manuel."

"No, not nervous. Just tired from all the work you've given me. I guess I need a bit of a break before the hit, you know."

He nodded. "Of course, of course. But anyway, I wanted to talk to you about something, Manuel. Something important." He glared at him and swatted him on the shoulder.

Manuel swallowed, heat permeating his face. "What is it, boss?"

"We managed to track Tomas, but don't worry about it. You have been absolved of your duty to kill him. I have other men on him. It should be happening as we speak."

What the hell was going on? This couldn't be good. "Right. But I was happy to do it. Why have I been unassigned?" Bile rose in his throat, and uneasiness settled in his stomach.

He laughed. "You know, I'm not enjoying you questioning my orders. I am curious about you, Manuel. Curious about why you've been communicating with the fuckin' police. Have you?"

Manuel lost his breath. "What? No, of course not. They just questioned me, thought I was still dealing." His voice shook. "I had to set them straight. That was all. I didn't say anything about the business, boss. Promise."

"Can you promise on the life of your brother, your parents, or your ex-girlfriend, Kim?"

"What?" His face paled and he could no longer form words. They had better leave his family alone or he would kill the lot of them.

"Let's take a walk to the back of the warehouse, Manuel." The boss pushed him towards the other end while his two male companions pointed their guns at him.

He turned in their direction. "Please, you have to believe me, boss. I didn't do or say anything to implicate you. Your business is safe. I am loyal to the business. Hell, I'd been in the business for years before prison. You know a leopard can't change his spots. Please, man."

"No worries, Manuel. Just stand over by those drums, would you. I might take a picture of you first. Send a clear message to your friends." He pulled out his mobile phone and clicked his picture. "They should know better than to mess with us." Turning to his cronies, he uttered his orders. "Shoot the prick."

Manuel gasped, his body shaking as he put up his hand. "No, please. No, I'm innocent. Please, no." He would no longer be able to make amends with his family, but the image of Kim flashed before his mind's eye. Her heart, her beauty, and her wisdom. He would carry her with him into his next life.

His final thought was of the searing pain of the bullets tearing into his chest.

Chapter 6

REFLECTIONS

La Latina café featured an angled timber counter with sharp edges, a potted plant alongside it. Peach walls displayed round mirrors, and dangly bronze lights hung low.

Kim, Blanca, and Daniela walked across the mint-coloured tiled flooring, past multi-coloured rectangular tables with steel-backed chairs as they made their way to the others.

Kim leaned forward and wrapped her arms around Eva and Sofia. Although both women were connected to Daniela, they had become fast friends with Kim and Blanca, too. She hadn't known Sofia for long, but the single parent had endured hardship in her life; not so long ago Daniela had been terrorised by a madman, and Sofia had been involved.

Sofia wore a high-buttoned shirt with a white puffer jacket and ripped jeans. As a dance teacher and former dancer, she had a quiet grace about her. "Hi Kim. Great to see you again."

She beamed. "Same here. How's your daughter?"

Sofia sighed. "Growing up way too fast if you ask me." She wrapped her arms around Daniela and Blanca. "Starting to answer me back as she's approaching her teenage years. I better brace myself."

"Good luck with that," said Kim. "I do not envy you one bit." Sofia nodded.

Eva had a spring in her step. She wore a bright orange jumper with tight black pants. Her dark hair was long and glossy, and her blue eyes sparkled in the artificial light of the café. "I would love to have kids, Sofia. Any time you would like me to babysit, let me know." She had endured Daniela's pain and even more, and had a glass eye to prove it.

Sofia chuckled. "You've got a deal there." The friends ordered dinner and drinks as Kim rested against the chair, her mind going back to Manuel. She wondered whether he might be working with the police. And why did he give her that locket? He had been about to tell her something before getting that phone call.

Reminders of him would make it even more difficult to let him go. She couldn't go back to the past and reconnect with Manuel, despite still having strong feelings for him.

"Penny for your thoughts," said Blanca. "Are they about Manuel? You didn't tell us how your meeting went."

Kim brought Eva and Sofia up to speed then recounted her meeting with Manuel. "It sounded like he is trying to leave the drug world. But I got the feeling he was hiding something."

Daniela rested on her elbows. "Do you think he's in trouble? With the gangs or the police?"

Kim shrugged. "I don't know, but wanting me to visit his brother an hour away means that something is not quite right. He wants to make amends with his family, but he doesn't believe it's safe yet."

"Jesus," said Sofia. "If I've learned anything, it's that I can't take so many things at face value. He might be in trouble with the gangs. I assume once you're in the group, you can't easily get out of it. You can become a liability."

Hearing that, Kim felt her heart race. Her hands went cold and clammy. *A liability?* Sofia reached for her hand. "I'm sorry. Me and my stupid mouth. I didn't mean it that way, but maybe you need to speak to him again."

"It's fine, Sofia. I believe it is better to keep my distance. I can't get back into that world again. He hurt me so much the last time."

Eva shifted multiple times in her seat as if she had something on her mind. "That's understandable, Kim. You need to do what's right for you." Her eyes shifted to a spot on the wall. "Why don't we move on to more positive topics." She faced Kim. "How is your writing going?"

Kim appreciated Eva's light-hearted, positive approach to life. "I have been lazy with my first book, but I plan to get back to writing soon."

"I'm sure we can easily find you a publisher who'd be interested," said Blanca. Kim waved her away. "Do you think you'll get it self-published or go the traditional route?"

"I would like to approach a traditional publisher, but I wonder if my work will be up to their standard. It's only a first draft, but I cannot see it ever being good enough for a publisher. I can at least write it for myself. I don't need to publish it."

"Oh come on, Kim. Believe in yourself, girl. I do," said Daniela.

"What's the story about?" asked Sofia.

Kim leaned in. "It's a romance between a quiet, introverted girl and a boisterous, bad boy...how the obstacles in the family and his illegal activities stop them from being together."

Sofia knit her brows. "Wasn't that your life?"

Kim nodded. "Partly, but names have been changed and I give the couple a happy ending, unlike my own story."

Eva clasped her hands together as the waiter brought her steak to her. "I for one love it, and will be the first to read it. I adore romances with happy endings. My favourite kind. I need to live vicariously through your story."

"Thanks, Eva. If I ever get to finish it." Their meals arrived, and Kim dug into her paella dish.

After a comfortable silence, Daniela looked back up at Kim. "I know, Eva, you wanted positive topics, but I just had a thought." She paused as her eyes roamed around the table. "What if Manuel is working with the police? Like a confidential informant, but he couldn't tell you about it. It is possible that that's his way out. Getting the bad guys."

Kim's chest constricted. "If that's the case, he's taking a lot of risks. I don't like it. Why can't the police find other ways to get their information? It is hardly fair to put Manuel in that kind of dangerous situation."

Blanca gave her a reassuring smile. "Oh, Kim. Manuel will be fine. He knows how they think, and I am sure the police are protecting him. I have worked with informants before and they know the risks, but they also have some protection."

Kim shook her head. "But your informants weren't part of the drug trade, which has to be the worst kind. I hope you are right, Blanca. I pray for Manuel." As she forked the remainder of her rice dish, she found herself short of breath. It was such a mess. She hoped and prayed that Manuel was safe. She knew they could never be together again, but she wished for him to be well and content in his life.

Chapter 7

YOUTH CLUB

Ricardo anchored a small team of teenagers pulling their end of a rope, all heaving as hard as they could against several youths pulling the other end. After twenty seconds the other group fell hard on their backs with a mixture of laughter and groans, ending the tug-of-war.

"Yes, we won. We won." His chest inflated with joy as he felt again how meaningful it was to volunteer with young people in this club in Torrelaguna, focusing on teamwork, leadership, and generosity.

He gave them all high-fives as he walked to a table for a bottle of water. He handed some to a few others in his team. "Great work, guys. Luciana and Alejandro, we did it. Finally, we beat the other team. We should celebrate." The two young teenagers were thirteen-year-old twins who had slowly settled in with the other youths.

Luciana stood by the table, drinking down the water as she pushed her long black fringe out of her eyes. "We can't. Papa is expecting us to make dinner tonight. It's one night he'll be home."

Alejandro threaded his hands through his short, messy brown waves. "Yeah, Papa's never home. But the one night he is home, we have to make dinner."

Ricardo wondered about their father, as he had never met him. The twins had only been with the club for the past month. "What about other nights? Does your mother cook for you?"

Alejandro shook his head. "Our Mama is dead." His eyes darkened. "She got sick."

His heart went out to the poor twins. He was fortunate to have two loving parents, even though it was now challenging to see them since they had moved away from Spain. One day, he planned to visit them in Greece. "I am sorry, guys. That must be hard. Maybe we can celebrate another night."

Luciana's eyes misted. "Okay. That would be nice."

Ricardo approached and put a hand on her shoulder. "What's wrong?"

She shrugged. "Our Papa hates us going out. We can't go to friends' houses or to parties. We're always stuck at home. He acts like a crazy person sometimes."

He was beginning to wonder about their father, and whether he was good for their growth and mental health, but it wasn't his business. As long as he gave them fun, education, and laughter in the club, it could make all the difference.

Ricardo and the twins went to the art studio for painting class. The art teacher had already commenced the lesson, but pointed the twins to empty canvasses and brought them brushes and paint. Ricardo sat in the corner and observed the lesson, waiting for his two favourite teenagers to finish their masterpieces. Luciana displayed a natural ability to draw as her brush strokes created details in the figures on her canvas. Alejandro had no artistic flair as he outlined several stick figures with a lack of detail.

At the end of the lesson, Ricardo approached Luciana. "Amazing work." He turned to Alejandro who stood beside her. "You, too. Good work."

"You're lying, Ricardo. My work's shit," said Alejandro.

"Hey, watch your language, mister."

"Sorry, but it is."

Ricardo regarded Luciana's drawings of three people and wondered how she could create so much detail in her characters. "I love your outlines and the light and shade. Who did you draw here?"

She shrugged. "Just friends of my Papa. They come sometimes, but don't talk much. They give him a lot of money, but I don't know what he does for them."

Ricardo's spine chilled. Something illegal, no doubt. "What does your father do?"

"He's an accountant," said Alejandro.

Ricardo wondered if their father didn't want them going out because of his illegal activities. Was it possible that word would get around if they knew exactly who his children were? But no, he thought. He was being ridiculous and letting his imagination get away from him. He had to stop being a detective.

Chapter 8

GRIEF-STRICKEN

Kim turned on her blender. It purred loudly as she gazed at the assorted ingredients mixing into her gazpacho: tomatoes, green bell pepper, red onion, cucumber, and a selection of seasonings. When the mixture was smooth, she poured it into a bowl and added a slice of bread on top, watching it moisten as it sank in the dish.

As her mouth began to water in anticipation, the doorbell rang. She wasn't expecting anyone. Was it Manuel wanting to convince her to reconnect? No, it was too soon if he didn't believe it was safe yet. Was she holding on to hope that they could reconnect? No, definitely not.

Feet heavy on her carpet, she walked to the front door. Her heart pounded when she opened it. Two police officers stared at her with dark expressions on their faces. She didn't want to speculate about their presence and pushed away negative thoughts. Surely this wasn't about Manuel. "Can I help you?" she asked with a shaky voice, her limbs unsteady.

"Yes, hello. Are you Ms Kim Mai?"

She nodded. "That would be me. What is this about, officers?"

One of the officers was burly and tall while the other one was solid and of average height. "This is Officer Garcia, and I am Officer Rodriguez. Can we come inside?"

No, you can't. "Of course." She directed them to the kitchen and the three of them sat down at the table. Her hands shook and her mind ran rampant. What if this was about her parents or friends? This couldn't be about Manuel. He was fine.

Officer Rodriguez, the burly one, spoke, "We understand that you and Manuel Perez were in a relationship over five years ago. Is that correct?"

Manuel? "Yes, why?"

Officer Rodriguez intervened. "Why don't you get yourself a glass of water."

Not what I expected. "I am fine. Unless either of you officers would like a drink."

The officers turned to each other, knitting their brows. "We are sorry to inform you that we strongly suspect that Mr Manuel Perez has been killed."

Kim's head spun and the world appeared surreal for a moment. Her body froze as she blinked several times. "What?"

Officer Garcia continued. "We believe that Mr Perez was murdered yesterday morning. We have attempted to notify his next of kin, but we could not reach them."

Kim clenched her hands, her chest aching. This had to be a dream. Manuel couldn't be dead. She had only spoken to him a few days ago. He had assured her he would make amends with his family once it was safe. That was pointless now. The burning sensation in her stomach made her want to sleep until it was over. Speaking in an unsteady voice with chills permeating her body, her vision blurred. "What do you mean, *you believe*?"

"There is no body, ma'am," said Officer Garcia. "Do you have any way to reach his parents? Were you close with them?"

A lone tear fell down her cheek, turning away and pushing past the deep sting in her chest. No, she hadn't heard right. *No body?* This had to be a mistake. "No, I never met his brother, and the last time I saw his parents was over five years ago. They are living in Greece now."

Officer Garcia nodded. "We must inform you that Manuel was our informant, and we believe that members of the drug gang discovered what he was doing. Did he ever speak to you about anyone in the gang?"

Kim shook her head, her body shaking. "No." She rubbed her palms. "He came to see me a few days ago. He got a phone call from someone while he was here. He...he wanted to see him." She put a hand over her mouth and started crying. "No, that must have been the day they killed him. It had to have been this person who called him that did this. Oh, no. Please find out who did this. Please."

"We will do our best, Ms Mai," said Officer Garcia. "We would like you to recount everything he said to you. It could be important. Anything trivial might help."

Kim nodded, her cheeks damp and her head aching. "Of course." She remembered the locket, but for some strange reason, she couldn't bring herself to tell them about it. It was the only thing she could keep that was a reminder of him, and she didn't want that taken away. She could not make amends for the cold way she had treated him on his visit. Her bottom lip quivered and she pushed a finger hard against her temple to fight a searing migraine. *Not Manuel! It had to be a mistake.*

Even the letters were personal, but what if handing them in was a mistake? Manuel mentioned he couldn't trust everybody. "How did he die?"

Officer Rodriguez hesitated. "We believe he was shot and his body disposed of in a chemical barrel. His clothes and a photo rested on top. It was a clear message. The killer wanted us to know what happened. I am truly sorry for your loss."

Kim blacked out.

Ricardo sat inside the room, talking to his friend and Lieutenant of the Civil Guard, Angel. He watched as his friend fumbled inside his pocket and fidgeted. "What is wrong with you, Angel? Why was I summoned, man?"

"I honestly do not know how to give you this grave news, but I have no other way to say it, Ricardo. Please know that I am here to support you and will find out who did this."

Ricardo's stomach somersaulted, an uneasy prickle pouring down his spine. "What? Is it my parents?"

Angel played with a file of papers in his hand and placed them into the in-tray. His desk was cluttered with stacks of case files, a computer, and a phone. Sticky notes lined the edges. Bravery and commendation awards hanging on the wall behind Angel showed his long line of achievements in the Civil Guard. "My friend, it is about your brother."

Ricardo angled his head and swallowed, steeling himself for what he knew would be bad news. "I am sorry, but Manuel is dead."

He jerked. "What did you say?" Ricardo surely didn't hear right. His body shook and he couldn't see straight. His head ached like never before and Angel's figure appeared surreal. Words coming out of Angel's mouth didn't make sense.

"Manuel was murdered two days ago. I am deeply sorry for your loss."

His younger brother was dead. Dead. He never got to make amends with him. He never got to tell him how much he loved him, despite his criminal affiliations. He swallowed and ignored the chill in his back and the pain in his chest. Why couldn't he have made more of an effort with him? Now it was too late. "How?"

"His photo and a set of clothes with bullet holes lay on top of a barrel, indicating the drug cartel had sent us a message. We believe his body was dissolved in a mix of chemicals in the barrel. We found two bullet casings at the crime scene, so most likely he had been shot beforehand." He looked away. "It appeared that his body was dumped into a barrel of chemicals. He was reported as missing for about a day while assisting the police as a confidential informant. He stopped by the local petrol station and the service attendant remembered him. He was wearing the same clothes found at the scene. The police traced his movements, but the warehouse is now obviously empty."

Ricardo shook his head, unable to breathe. "Jesus, Angel." He banged hard on the desk. "What the hell! How could this happen? They should have looked out for him, protected him." His chest was on fire and he could barely breathe as he pushed back his tears and closed his eyes, his throat and whole body aching.

Angel got up, walked around to his side, and put his arms around him. "Let it out, my friend. Let it out." After holding his friend, he returned to his seat, his expression dark. "The police in Madrid did everything they could possibly do, but sometimes these situations happen. We cannot foresee every possible scenario when so much is out of our control, Ricardo."

He glared. "That's total bullshit, Angel, and a cop-out. I want answers and I want them now."

Angel nodded. "Then I shall get them for you. Leave it with me, my friend."

Ricardo walked out of there with a heavy heart, vowing to get vengeance on the death of his brother. Whoever did this to his brother would now have to deal with him.

Chapter 9

A LETTER

K im stared at the letter in her hands, her fingers playing with the corners of the page, and her eyes staring past Daniela who sat beside her on the couch. Blanca sat on her other side with an arm around her. The quiet was both soothing and disturbing as she pondered what the letter might say. "I can't read this." She had explained to her friends that someone in the police force couldn't be trusted, according to Manuel, so she had kept the letters and the locket to herself.

Daniela gave her a reassuring smile. "Listen, Kim. I know it's been hard since you found out about Manuel, but the letter might help. It'll give you closure."

Blanca nodded. "I agree. Maybe read it when you're ready. Don't feel pressured by either of us."

Goosebumps covered her arms as she swallowed and debated whether to read Manuel's letter. She wasn't sure she was ready, but what if he mentioned something important? What if it was related to his death? Did he predict he would die in the most gruesome way possible?

She got up and opened the living room curtains to peer into the front garden, as if Manuel would suddenly reappear at the gate. She now missed him and realised that he had wanted to change. He was helping the police, and that showed courage and personal growth.

Turning to her friends, she gripped the letter tight. "I never thought he would ever be a confidential informant. Why would he risk his life in such a way? How could he have been so stupid to make an enemy of his gang?" She wiped away her tears, dropping the letter on the floor. Her heart ached and her legs felt heavy under her.

Daniela wrapped her arms around her from the back. "Oh, girl. He wanted to do the right thing and make a life for himself. I think what he did was damn courageous and ballsy. Don't you think so, Blanca?"

Blanca seemed to be in her own world, most likely thinking about her own ordeal of childhood trauma and corruption. After a pause, she said, "It was very courageous, Kim, and it sounded like he wanted to be with you again. He still loved you." She sighed. "Right now, you need to grieve, and process what's happened. But also decide what you are going to do."

Kim frowned as Daniela pulled away from her. She picked up the letter and shifted on the couch, leaning back. "What are you talking about, Blanca?"

She motioned forward. "Seeing his brother in Patones. It might be good for you to get away and support his family. Talk to him about your last moments with Manuel. It can give his brother closure and be a comfort to him."

She shrugged. "I don't know if I'm up to it. The police would have notified him by now, and I'm sure he doesn't need me disrupting his life."

Daniela sighed, shaking her head. "Why do you always put yourself down, girl? You being in someone's life is not disruptive. Anyone would be blessed to have you in their world, Kim."

She swallowed. "I don't know, Daniela. Everything is too hard, and I have the yoga centre. I have responsibilities here."

Daniela's eyes darkened. "You have a responsibility to yourself and your grief. Close the yoga centre for a while. I'll help you out financially." She knit her brows. "Besides, Manuel wanted you to see his brother. It was his last wish."

Blanca intervened. "I will help, too. Whatever you need, we are in."

Kim shook her head. "I cannot let you do that. You have your own expenses, and I am not a charity case. I have savings, so I will manage."

She fumbled with the letter in her hands and slowly unfolded it. Taking a deep breath, she started reading.

Dearest Kim,

I wish I could have been the man you deserved and could stay with. If only I didn't need to learn the hard way by going to prison, but I am hoping it is not too late to say I am sorry. More than you can ever know.

I am working as a confidential informant with the police, and I am hoping that justice will be served. A part of me believes that someone in the Madrid police force is corrupt, connected to the South American cartel. I know Ricardo can get to the truth. All I do know is that by being an informant, I can compensate for all the bad stuff I've done. I can make things right again.

I remember the great times we had when I took you to the Retiro Park for a picnic and how we laughed after making crazy social media videos and posts. We were happy then.

I'm reminded of the time we swam at the beach, throwing you up in the air, or when I held your hand as we watched the sunrise. If only I had enough belief in myself to not resort to the gang lifestyle. The gangs were like my family, and at the time, I couldn't let them go. Now I realise that no gang can

ever be your family when they can turn against you so easily.
I am deeply sorry, and I love you more than words can say.
I never stopped loving you, Kim. Please forgive me.

I want you to go see my brother, Ricardo and tell him how
much I love and admire him. I need him to forgive me, too.
I know that once this is all over, I will hopefully be able to
reconnect with him. He is ex-police and you can trust him
implicitly, so if you are ever in trouble, please know that he
will have your back.

With so much love,
Manuel.

Kim kept the letter on her lap, bowed down and cried
when her friends hugged her for the longest time. A life
wasted after he had finally changed.

Chapter 10

A DECISION

Kim walked around La Latina a few days later, stepping along the cracked, uneven concrete on the narrow streets as the cool winter breeze feathered the back of her neck. She needed time to herself after reading Manuel's letter, and walking these streets usually calmed her mind.

Passing the tapas bars, restaurants and church, she made her way toward La Plaza de la Paja, ordered a strong coffee and sat under a colossal tree. A hint of sunlight filtered through the leaves as she waited for her hot drink. Umbrellas in the distance surrounded another café, and swarms of people passed by Plaza de la Paja, which meant "straw square," and was the oldest plaza in Madrid.

Sitting with her elbows on the table, Kim realised she had to meet Manuel's brother, Ricardo, to honour his memory. It wouldn't sit right with her if she couldn't talk to Ricardo about what Manuel had said to her, and how he wanted to make amends. She had to give him his letter, too. Ricardo would need closure. She knew it was the appropriate action to take. As much as a part of her didn't want to travel out of the Madrid region, she had no real choice.

What if Manuel's ideas about corruption were true? What if Ricardo's life was in danger and she sat back and did nothing about it? She would never forgive herself if she didn't at least attempt to get him justice. Ricardo had been in law enforcement, and he might have the resources to find out who had killed Manuel so viciously and cruelly.

The stocky male waiter brought over her coffee. "Enjoy."

As she sipped on her drink, two police officers ambled around the plaza and made conversation with passers-by. She wondered whether these officers were corrupt, or did they follow the law? If only Manuel hadn't got involved in such a way. He might have been safer staying in prison instead of turning informant to get a reduced sentence, which had only got him killed.

Kim finished her coffee and entered the bustling Mercado de la Cebado. Her eyes scanned the displays of food as she clutched her shoulder bag and rummaged for her wallet.

A young male server smiled. "What can I get you?"

"Five hundred grams of ham, please." She also ordered a quarter of a kilo of Manchego cheese and two pieces of whiting fish.

The server smiled as he handed her the food and she passed Euros over the counter. Waiting for the change, she sensed in her peripheral vision a man standing a little too close beside her. She turned, noticing his blonde wavy hair as he stared at her. He was middle-aged, with a slim build, and wore a tan cap, ripped jeans and a black t-shirt. She looked away and put out her hand for the change.

"I am sorry," she said. "Were you meant to go before me?"

The man shook his head. "No, not at all." His stern eyes darkened.

Kim smiled at the man, who instead of smiling back, squinted at her. She wondered what his problem was.

Leaving the market, she walked briskly to the Jardin del Principe Anglona, aware she couldn't stay long as she had to get the fish, cold meat, and cheese into the fridge promptly.

In the garden not far from her apartment, she slid her hands across the green hedges. A fountain in the centre of the garden enriched the tranquil atmosphere. Families and individuals strolled through the contained hedges as she inhaled the scents of pomegranate, almond, and strawberry. Climbing roses, boxwoods, and camelia buds waited for the spring, and other shrubs populated the many corners of this garden. Yellow mahonias with their sharp-edged leaves and blue lilacs contributed to the sweet aroma.

Taking a seat on one of the many stone benches, Kim closed her eyes and took deep breaths, immersing herself in the calm.

Her reverie broke when a loud cough alerted her. Her heart skipped a beat when the blonde man from the market walked by her, staring towards her with curiosity. Something about the way he scrutinised her made her wonder whether he knew her. But he was free to roam the garden as she was. It didn't have to mean anything.

Once he was out of sight, Kim made her way back to the apartment, but glanced over her shoulder to see if the man was close behind. He wasn't. Why did he make her feel uneasy? Surely she was being paranoid after what had happened to Manuel.

Ricardo shouted at one of his maintenance employees at the hotel he managed in Torremocha de Jarama, a five-minute drive from Patones. He flicked his pen across his desk as the man seated opposite him hunched. "Oh come on. How many times do I have to tell you about the guest's complaint? Fix the damn TV before we get the worst review in worldwide history. Now, do your damn job."

The grey-haired handyman stood, cross-armed. "Of course. I apologise, Mr Perez, and will get this arranged right away."

Pushing down his guilt, Ricardo let out an audible sigh and shook his head while clasping a long list of all the items that needed to be repaired. He handed the man the document. "See that you do." The man grabbed it weakly then rushed off with a curt nod.

Ricardo was the manager of *Hotel Belleza,* a quaint old building which featured a range of single and family rooms, with a shared lounge and a tour desk, as well as free Wi-Fi throughout the hotel. Several rooms had their own balconies. His hotel appealed to sporty guests who liked to hike and hire bikes in the area.

It had been a week since he found about his brother's death and the pain was still raw. He couldn't sleep or eat and became short-tempered with his staff. How much longer could he be shouting at staff before his own manager sacked him? He needed this job and could not afford to be rude to everyone in sight. But he didn't know of any other way to deal with his grief. He had too many responsibilities to take a vacation. No one else could replace him at short notice. He didn't have the luxury to let so many people down.

As he walked into the foyer, he saw two young men exchanging wads of cash and an A4 envelope. Not everyone was a drug dealer. He was being paranoid. They could have had a business arrangement.

Shaking his head, he thought about the never-ending reminders of Manuel. The other day he had rushed up to a man who resembled his brother, thinking the police had got it wrong. But it wasn't Manuel. It hadn't been the first occasion. Each time he spotted someone resembling his brother's height and physique, he would gasp and rush over to the person only to realise it wasn't his brother. Manuel was dead. He had to accept it.

If only he had pushed Manuel harder, he could have released him from the drug business. The problem was that if someone didn't want help, no amount of cajoling would make any bit of difference. If only he had told him he loved him. Now, it was too late.

Chapter 11

IMMERSED

Kim's mother, Huifen, set a cup of tea on the table opposite her. Her short, petite stature contrasted with her strong personality. Her father, Hu was of average height with salt-and-pepper hair. He sat at the table, too, with a stern expression on his face.

Her mother's eyes pierced her own as if she was processing what Kim mentioned. "Why are you going to Patones? Does this have something to do with Manuel's death?"

Kim knew if she explained the truth that her parents would push her to stay, and she didn't want conflict over this. It was something she had to do, and so she would give them the partial truth. "I am seeing a friend of a friend."

Her father clenched his hands. "What friend? All your friends live in Madrid, so why would you travel to Patones?"

She sighed. "It is not that distant, Papa. Only an hour away."

"But who is this friend?"

"No one you know."

Her mother shook her head. "How long will you be gone?"

"I don't know at this stage, but I will call you once I get there. I need a break from work, too. It will be healing for me to stay in the country."

Her mother pressed her lips together, staring into her eyes as if she didn't believe her. She had always been astute and Kim knew what was coming. "You're hiding something. I can tell. I understand you are grieving for Manuel, but you should be here with your friends, your family. We can support you." She huffed. "What is going on?"

Kim looked past her mother, picking up her tea and drank. She needed time to come up with something, but she could never lie to her parents. "It is something I need to do. Please understand."

Her father intervened. "We found out from June's daughter that you are not getting many students after the economic crisis. Don't you think you should focus on marketing your business, or look at doing something else? I can get you work in the investment business. No problem."

Kim had no desire to work in the financial or investment field when she had neither the skills nor interest in it. "I am fine. Going away will give me perspective, Dad. I need time to figure out my life."

"But you're not getting any younger, Kim," her mother said. "When are you going to settle down and give us grandchildren? It is time. That business of yours is not a real job. You might as well get married and let your husband work. You cannot rely on the business. You were meant to be a mother and not the owner of a yoga centre that is not going anywhere."

She pushed down her pain and the ache in her chest. "Oh, Mother. I am still young and have no interest in a relationship when my life is not settled. As for children, I will have them someday, I am sure."

Kim finished the tea and placed her cup in the sink. Staring out the window, she got lost in the Japanese-style garden with its square hedging, water fountain, array of flowers, shrubs, and bench space for quiet meditation. Her parents were spiritual, and she understood they only wanted the best for her. But sometimes their overprotection was stifling, given that she was an only child. "I have to go, but I will call you as soon as I arrive."

Her father got up and gently pushed her down in her chair. "No, wait. We want to know what is really going on. After Manuel, we worry about you. Did you see him after he was released from prison?"

Kim swallowed, not wanting to lie but hating to start something she could never finish. They would harass her over having seen him. "Yes, he visited me once before he..." She fought back tears. "He wanted to make amends." Her parents were not often speechless, but it must have been the tears running down her cheeks. She could no longer contain them.

Strong arms wrapped around her until she pulled away, her mother's eyes becoming red with her own tears. "I am sorry for you. But it will get easier with time."

Kim nodded. "It's been about a week, so it has become easier every day. But I will miss him. A lot, Mama."

Her father threaded his hand through his hair. "Oh, Kim. We worry because just the other day, a man called and asked about you. He never gave us his name."

She flinched. "What? A man? What did he say?"

"Only that he was a friend and needed to speak to you. Is this the friend of a friend you were talking about?"

She ignored his question. "What did you tell him?"

Her father turned to her mother briefly then faced her again. "I told him you don't live here, and that we haven't had contact for a long time."

Kim angled her head. "Why would you lie?"

Her mother intervened. "Your father didn't know who this man was. With all the troubles with Manuel, he believed he might have been a friend of Manuel's."

She stared at her father. "Is that true, Dad? Do you think he was someone shady?"

He put out his hand. "I don't know Kim, but when a stranger rings, I don't feel comfortable telling them where you live. It felt right to lie." She breathed a sigh of relief, thankful that her father had lied. She wondered if it was a friend of Manuel or someone else entirely. Why didn't he leave a name? "Are you in trouble? You would tell us, wouldn't you?"

Kim shook her head. "No, no trouble, Dad."

"Then tell us exactly why you are going to Patones," her mother said.

Kim had no choice but to explain how Manuel wanted her to get in contact with Ricardo and how he had been a confidential informant. She hoped they would understand that she needed to give his brother closure through the letter and Manuel's last words to her.

Chapter 12

A LONE JOURNEY

K im gripped the steering wheel tight as she drove her grey sedan on the highway to Patones. She felt good for having left on good terms with her parents. They were naturally worried about her. But the way her mother always managed to put her down made her physically sick in the stomach. No, she would put it aside for now.

When *Berlin*, sung by the popular Aitana, began to play she turned up the volume and immersed herself in the music. Spanish music had a way of lifting her spirits when her scattered mind led to all worst-case scenarios.

What if Ricardo loathed her for coming uninvited? What if he wasn't as loyal as Manuel claimed, given that he hadn't seen him in a long time? What if she was doing the wrong thing and should get on with her life, putting Manuel behind her? But no, she had to do the right thing and give Ricardo closure. The least she could do for

Manuel was to honour his last wish, especially when he had died so brutally.

With the window rolled down half-way, she savoured the views of mountains, valleys, and reservoirs north of Madrid until she saw the exit for Patones de Arriba. She knew that Ricardo lived about a twelve-minute drive from Patones de Abajo, the lower part of the region, while Patones de Arriba was a town with fewer amenities.

Kim passed through varying green and brown shades of the olive groves nestled among the dips of the mountainous terrain. She played with the chain of the locket around her neck, her mind turning to Manuel and why he had given her this gift. Had he wanted to show her he had changed by giving her the locket?

Entering the older part of the region, Patones de Arriba, the air around her smelled like moss, a rocky riverbank, aromatic flowers, and fragrant herbs. The flying dust and debris stung her eyes.

The bumpy cobblestone streets caused her to grip the steering wheel tighter again as she whizzed past black slate houses and hiking trailheads. Pinecones, sticks, and rocks surrounded the space as she finally reached her destination, a captivating, rustic two-storey villa. This was where Ricardo lived?

She parked nearby and breathed in the fresh, clear air. A smaller car was parked in front of the villa, so she assumed Ricardo was home on a Saturday. She swallowed, took a deep breath, and lifted her shoulders in the hopes of conveying confidence she didn't feel. What was she doing here? Was this the right thing to do? She might not get a warm welcome while Ricardo was still grieving.

Shaking away these thoughts, she steeled herself as she walked up a steep, hilly path, feeling the stones underneath her sandals as she took in the view of tall ferns, lower brush, and wildflowers on either side of her. She climbed steps to reach the front door, the sounds of birds and passers-by in the distance giving the place a tranquil feel.

Her heart beat fast as she clenched her right hand and knocked on the old black timber door. She wondered what Ricardo was like and whether he had any physical resemblance to Manuel.

With hands sweating as she waited in trepidation, the mild wind feathered the side of her neck. Fiddling with her bag strap, she cleared her throat and found her heart accelerating as soon as the door swung open. She hadn't anticipated his attractive appearance, with chocolate-coloured eyes, a square jaw, subtle outlines of a moustache and beard, short brown hair with blonde highlights and a fringe flicked to the side. She put aside butterflies in her stomach and focused on her mission.

For a brief moment, their eyes locked and Kim's face flushed.

The man angled his head. "Can I help you?"

Kim nodded. "Hi...hello, my name is Kim Mai." She ignored her dry throat, realising how challenging it was to bring him up. Was she truly doing this? "I knew Manuel, your brother."

Ricardo's eyes darkened as he looked briefly at his hands before tilting his head up again. After a minute, he opened the door wider. "Come inside."

She smiled and stepped into the villa, finding an open foyer which appeared more modern on the inside than the outside. Stone floors, smooth painted walls, and tilt-and-turn windows gave the room a contemporary look. He led her to the living room, which led to the view of glass sliding doors showcasing a patio and a view of the green and brown landscape, and a mahogany table with an umbrella in the centre of it. On one side of the living room was a solid wooden staircase, with a suede sofa, a bookshelf, and a large TV on the other side of a central fireplace.

"Take a seat," said Ricardo.

He joined her as she sat on the sofa.

"This is a beautiful place," she said.

He smiled. "Thank you. I love my peace and quiet, as you can see." He rubbed his hands, then rested them on his tight-fitting jeans which showed off his muscular, toned legs. He wore a skin-tight white t-shirt, and his biceps proved he worked out. His tanned skin and slight lines around his eyes appeared as if he'd often exposed himself to sunlight. "I know you're not here for the peace and quiet."

Kim pushed down her red cotton dress, which sat awkwardly above the knees. "I don't know if you heard from the police..."

He briefly turned away. "Yes, they informed me about Manuel's death." His Adam's apple became more pronounced as he faced her again.

"I am so sorry for your loss."

"Thank you, but I hadn't seen Manuel in about twelve years." He turned away briefly. "It is still hard to process and make sense of it. How did you know Manuel?"

She took a breath. "I was his girlfriend for two years, but we broke up not long before he went to prison for five years." She paused, wondering where to begin. "I came here as it was Manuel's last wish that I see you." She retrieved the letter for Ricardo from her bag. "He wrote you a letter and wanted me to give it to you." She fingered the locket around her neck. "He gave me this locket too, I am assuming as a token of amends."

His eyes glistened as if he was fighting back tears. "Nice locket." He sighed. "A letter, ha? Why didn't you hand this into the police for evidence?" She stared past him. "Why are you actually here, Kim? I sense there is more to your visit than just offering your condolences and giving me this letter, which should have been handed in to law enforcement."

Kim twirled her hands and dug her nails into her skin. "He mentioned you being in trouble because you're a former detective and policeman. Manuel was worried about your safety, particularly because he was a confidential informant. He mentioned not trusting someone in the police force, believing there may have been a traitor. That was the reason why I didn't hand in these letters." She clenched her hands. "He wanted to let you know he loved you and wanted to make amends. He was planning to talk to you once it became safe." Her chest tightened. "When he visited me, I didn't know he was a confidential informant. I found out later, but it was obvious he was working hard to leave the drug business." A stream of tears ran down her cheeks, and her breath shallowed. She wiped the tears away. "When he left my place, he had been summoned by someone. I assume that was the day he got killed. The police seem to think his gang leader killed him because he found out he was working with the police."

Ricardo clenched his hands, staring at the floor. "In the most horrific way possible. There is nothing left of my brother, and I promise you they will pay. Whoever did this will not get away with it."

Kim's body shivered. "I can help you."

He laughed. "How? Are you former police, too?"

"No, but I have a lawyer friend who can help investigate, and another friend who is a journalist. She may have contacts."

He shook his head. "If you don't mind, I don't want you involved. I don't even know if I can trust you. You are a stranger to me, as Manuel had been for all those years."

She leaned forward. "Manuel wrote me a letter, saying that he wondered if there was a traitor inside the Madrid police force. He told me not to trust anyone but you. Someone over there might be working with the traffickers, but he wasn't sure at the time."

Ricardo frowned, running his hands over the fold in the letter. "I can read this later." He stared at it, his eyes becoming hard and cold until they softened again.

"What made you decide to get into law enforcement?"

He sighed, peering past her. "I got inspired by Manuel, who always got in trouble with his friends and school acquaintances. I managed to sort our their issues before they escalated. I also realised I had a knack for dealing with bullies at school."

Kim smiled. "It is an admirable skill to have."

"Thanks, Kim."

Had she done the right thing coming here or had she stirred things up? Not if he planned to get justice.

Chapter 13

HONOURING MANUEL

R icardo put the letter on the coffee table, feeling a
tightness in his stomach. He could understand how
Manuel had loved Kim.

When he first opened the door, he couldn't believe how
beautiful she was, with her smooth olive skin, dark brown,
soulful eyes, dainty hands, and full, rounded lips. The
way her red dress pressed nicely against her slim, toned
figure made his body respond. But how could he let her
get involved? This was his fight, not hers.

"Manuel was a man I could never trust, and now it is
obviously too late to make amends. I hope this letter will
give me answers." He looked past her. "If only he had
visited me here, but I can understand why he didn't when

he was trying to protect me." He rose. "Can I get you a drink, a coffee?"

She nodded. "An instant coffee would be great. Thank you." He walked into his kitchen and filled the electric kettle. While waiting for it to boil, he took from a cupboard two mugs and a silver tray. Adding a sugar bowl and milk jug, he set them on the tray and poured the water onto the coffee granules in the cups. He was surprised at how mesmerized he was with Kim's relaxing, timid nature. He imagined she would have debated long and hard about making the trip to Patones but he knew that Manuel could be convincing. He missed his brother, but all he could do now for him was to find his killer.

As he carried the tray to the living room, he noticed how Kim's dress had risen to show more of her bare leg, and he tingled as he imagined running his hands over her thigh. *Hot damn*! His brother was dead, and here he was, entertaining erotic thoughts about this woman. What was wrong with him? She was Manuel's ex-girlfriend and would be off-limits for a multitude of reasons. The grief was causing him to feel things he wouldn't normally feel. He had to get his head back into the game and focus on Manuel. "Here you go," he said as he set the tray on the table.

She added milk and sugar into her cup. "Thank you," she said.

Sitting back down, he picked up his own coffee, holding the warm cup tight. "Where are you from?"

Kim took a sip then placed her mug on the table. "La Latina in Madrid. I have an apartment over there."

"Right. It is quite a difference to this region of ours here. Do you have any siblings?"

"No, just me. My parents live in Madrid too, and they weren't too keen on me making the trip here. They can be a bit strict, given I am their only child." She frowned. "I heard that your parents are living in Greece. Have you seen them recently?"

He peered past her. "No, but I plan to visit one day soon. Now that I have Manuel's killer to focus on, that trip will have to be delayed. But I have spoken to them and they are aware of Manuel's death."

Kim crossed her legs. "How did they take the news?"

"Horribly. My mother cried for so long, I wondered whether to end the call, and my father was in shock and tried to console my mother. They knew one day he would come to his senses, but unfortunately when he did, it was too late for him." He put down his cup and rested back against the sofa, thinking about whether Kim was in trouble. Given that she was associated with Manuel, would the criminals be targeting her? He had to find out and tread slowly without alarming her. "I need to ask you something, Kim."

She exhaled and put down her cup too. "What is it?"

"Have you noticed anything strange happening since Manuel visited you?"

Kim angled her head. "Like what?"

"Anyone following you or any unusual incidents occurring?"

Kim lifted her eyes up to the ceiling. He thought she looked even more beautiful with that expression. "I don't know if this means anything, but there was a man who seemed to be following me when I went to the market. Later I walked to the gardens, and he suddenly appeared there, too. Also, my father got a phone call from a man asking to speak to me, but he never left a name. He didn't give any further details."

His skin crawled. What if this was the beginning of her troubles? But then again, it might have meant nothing. "And nothing like that has happened to you before seeing Manuel?"

"No, nothing really. When we were involved, I didn't know about his drug involvement until much later in the relationship and not long before we broke up. Over that two-year period we were together, I suspected he was doing something illegal, but I was always too afraid to confront him. When I did, he denied it and I had no way to find out the truth. I loved him with all my heart, but in the end, his mood changed as he started using. He finally told me the truth."

Ricardo's heart seized up as if he was jealous of his brother for loving Kim. He didn't know this strange woman beside him, so he must have been too tired to think straight. "I am sorry you went through that. Manuel had always been a free spirit and liked to experiment with life, but his curiosity took him over the edge. Nothing my parents did could help him, and God knows, I tried to help him countless times. But when someone doesn't want to be helped, it's futile to try."

Ricardo noticed how quickly the time had passed. It was close to dinner time, and he realized that Kim must be hungry. "How about dinner? I can cook roasted meat and vegetables."

Kim shook her head. "No, I don't want you to go to any trouble. Besides, I have to get going. I am sorry for taking up a lot of your time."

He hid his disappointment, not wanting her to leave. "Where are you staying? Will you be here a while?"

She rose. "I haven't booked anywhere, but I noticed a guest house on the way. I am sure they'll have a room. I plan to stay for a week. I need a break from the city and my work."

He waved his hand away. "Y

ou don't need to pay for accommodation. I have a spare bedroom. You can stay here."

"No, that's fine. I don't want to impose." She knit her brows. "Besides; you said you didn't trust me, so I don't expect you to have a stranger living with you."

He had to convince her to stay. What if he needed to protect her? Whoever was following her in Madrid might have followed her here. "I have good instincts and doubt you're a serial killer who'll stab me in my sleep. I have rarely been wrong. Please stay here. I have plenty of room."

Kim shrugged. "I don't know."

He needed to make sure she was safe. He played his last card. "What if your life is in danger after what happened with Manuel? I can protect you here. You can trust me, as Manuel told you."

Kim sighed. "Fine. I will stay. Thank you, but I will pay you board."

"Of course not. You can pay me by doing the cooking and a bit of cleaning. It's all good." Her silence must have meant she was okay with their arrangement. "Now, let me give you the grand tour of the villa."

Chapter 14

ATTRACTION

The back of Kim's neck tingled when Ricardo came up close behind her as they walked up the stairs. Their shoulders brushed as he passed her on the second level.

An open bedroom with a balcony overlooked part of the living room and the mountainous vista outside. The room had a pine wardrobe with sliding doors, a window with white pleated drapes and lace curtains, and a lamp on a bedside table. "This will be your room." She had fetched her overnight bag from her car earlier, and now placed it on the double bed.

Ricardo led her to a library. Sunlight streamed through a large bay window with a view to the vast landscape outside. "If you like reading, the previous owner left a few books in a wide range of genres." She ran her fingers across the spines of books on health and well-being, meditation, and fiction that ranged from thriller and crime to fantasy and science fiction.

Next, he led her to a spacious bathroom, filled with natural light. Then he led her to a second room. "This is my bedroom." She swallowed. "This bedroom comes with a terrace-solarium where I do stretches in the morning to birdsong. I absolutely love it." He faced her squarely. "You are free to come out here whenever you like, even if it is a bit chilly."

Kim nodded. "Thanks. I like to meditate and do yoga."

He squinted. "Wow! I never thought Manuel would date a spiritual woman. He was quite the opposite."

"Opposites do attract." Her words hung in the air as Ricardo's eyes scanned her from her eyes down to her lips.

Before he could turn away, his cheeks reddened. They walked back downstairs to the kitchen, which was so spacious with its dining area next to a wood-fired oven built into a stone wall. "I sometimes cook in this oven. Not only does it keep the house warm in winter, but I use it as a barbecue and grill, so you get that woodfire taste in the food." He placed his fingers against his lips and drew them away. "Delicious." Kim touched the long table and four chairs, noticing the cleanliness of the grey-tiled floor. Three windows opposite the oven brought in a lot of sunlight.

He headed over to a white fridge, pulled out a bowl of marinated meat and placed it on the kitchen counter. "I left this overnight so I could cook it today, but I always make extra just in case I feel like having more than the usual. I am very active, so I can have a huge appetite."

Her eyes darkened, feeling a sense of guilt at taking his food when she had arrived unannounced. "I am sorry. Please do not mind me. I can go out and find somewhere to eat. You enjoy your dinner."

He angled his head. "I haven't been very active today, so I can share this food with you. It's nice to have company." Ricardo placed the chops in the oven. He then took a bag of potatoes from the pantry and started peeling them.

"Can I help you peel those?" she asked.

He nodded. "Sure." He handed her a knife and together, they washed and peeled the potatoes by the sink, the proximity making her body tense. Taking a deep breath, she savoured the quiet openness of the kitchen. "Do you like cooking?"

"I do, actually, but given my crazy hours when I work, it is hard to make many home-cooked meals. I tend to have frozen meals or go into the centre of Madrid. It is quicker and easier. But when I visit my parents, I always get the amazing diversity of Chinese or Spanish food."

He grinned. "What do you do?"

"I own a yoga studio with some daytime hours, but also work a few evenings a week."

"Right. Is there someone managing the place for you now?"

She placed a potato into the bowl of water and grabbed another one. Bumping into his shoulder made her hands shake, and the scent of his cologne immersed her in fruity musk. Why couldn't she breathe properly? "I've closed it as I don't have anyone who can manage it." A noise outside jolted her from the peace and quiet. "What was that?"

Ricardo put down his knife and potato. "I'll go check it out." He strolled out the back door as she remained frozen where she stood and waited.

She remembered to breathe when Ricardo returned. "Nothing outside. Probably a cat. They come around sometimes. Being out in the countryside can make things louder because of the open space. The next house isn't that far away, so sometimes whatever is happening next door can sound closer than it actually is."

Once they placed the potatoes into the oven, they relaxed in front of the TV with glasses of wine. A Spanish soap opera played where a man was kissing a woman until they undressed each other. The woman kneeled against the bed and performed oral sex on the man. Kim's face reddened. She couldn't sit here and watch this with a stranger beside her.

Ricardo cleared his throat. "I will change it. There are other programs." As she rested back against the couch, she wondered what it would be like to live in the countryside. She loved living in the city, but she could certainly adapt to this kind of environment too, particularly if she had the right company to share it with.

He rose, dropping the TV remote on the coffee table. "I know it's chilly, but let's go outside on the terrace. We can watch the view for a few minutes."

Kim hugged her body as she made her way through the sliding doors to the terrace, a gust of wind brushing her cheeks. "What an amazing view, Ricardo."

He smiled as they maneuvered around the table and chairs. "I got this outdoor setting at a great price, considering the tables, chairs and benches are made of teak."

The scents of assorted white and purple flowers, tall ferns and high brush brought her back to nature. She imagined enjoying an early breakfast on a spring morning, peering out over the mountain landscape and a town as unique as Patones de Arriba. The vastness of the undulations and plantations surrounding the vast space gave her a warm feeling, in contrast to the danger she knew was lurking around Manuel's death and Ricardo's need for justice.

Chapter 15

STABBING INCIDENT

In Ricardo's car the next day, Kim wound her window down and smelled the fresh smells of pine and wildflowers as the cool breeze brushed her face. They passed mansions and stately homes, as well as a chapel, its Gothic architecture evidence of the town's history in Torrelaguna.

"Tell me again why you volunteer at this youth club?" Kim asked.

He looked at her briefly. "The regions of Spain can be quite isolated, and these children need something more than broken homes, abuse, and violence. I can get the authorities involved if any of these children face hardship. I develop a rapport with them and eventually they tell me their problems. Going out, talking, and playing games give them that respite from home life." He turned to her. "There have been occasions when we've had to arrest one of their fathers or an uncle." He turned down the volume on the radio and stared straight ahead. "Don't get me wrong. The majority of the kids are fine, but you do get those odd challenges."

Kim nodded. "It is very noble and generous of you. Children need that guidance if there is violence or divorce in the home." She wondered if having a job and volunteering would take Ricardo away from finding justice for Manuel. It might have been a bad idea to stay when he was clearly a busy man who now had to babysit her. Could she help him find justice? She had enough in her life to fix and getting involved in drug enforcement wasn't on her list of priorities. As much as she wanted justice for Manuel, the police had to do their job. Ricardo was no longer in the police force, and as a civilian, she didn't believe the police would appreciate him getting involved.

"I hope to show you around the regions of Spain and keep you occupied. The kids will love you." He briefly turned in her direction as they awkwardly gazed into each other's eyes.

Oh, no. She couldn't fall for those dark eyes. She wouldn't. Clearing her throat, Kim stared through the window. "I am happy to help. I have never been to Torrelaguna, but I have travelled to other parts, like San Sebastian and Bilbao."

"The Basque country is like nothing else." He sighed. "But Torrelaguna is an amazing medieval town. The walls were built in the Middle Ages, and you have the Gothic architecture from Madrid. There's a lot to see that represents history. It's great that it only takes about five or ten minutes to get there." He exhaled. "We are here now."

A large, grey building with a multitude of windows displayed a sign that read *Club Juvenil de Espana*. It appeared to be an old house with small garden beds alongside a stone fence on the side. On a large patch of grass, teenagers kicked around a soccer ball. A winding concrete drive led to the side of the building, where Ricardo parked under the towering trees.

As they exited the car, shouts and laughter resounded in the background. More teenagers stood in another small garden, where they were reciting scripts from a play, holding loose-leaf pages that blew in the soft wind. When Kim turned to watch, one youth stopped and gawked at them.

Ricardo waved. "Hey guys. Don't let us stop you. Carry on." As if by his command, the children waved back and resumed their acting.

She followed him through a heavy door into a narrow walkway. Photographs of children posed at a range of sporting events lined the walls. They paused before a receptionist behind a high counter. She had smiling green eyes and a tight blonde ponytail, and appeared to be in her twenties.

She nodded at Ricardo. "Hey, Ricardo."

"Adella. This is Kim. She will be visiting us for a while, possibly helping out with the kids. She's from Madrid."

Adella stood and put out her hand, which Kim shook. "Great to meet you, Kim. Ricardo here is so popular, you might never get to see him."

She chuckled. "Nice to meet you too, Adella. I look forward to helping out."

After Adella resumed her post, Ricardo led her to a kitchenette where young children and teenagers sat at large tables, eating snacks. Some of them did schoolwork. He touched the small of her back and led her to a corner table. She ignored the tingle in her legs. "Everyone, this is Kim, and she'll be visiting with us today." Waving hands and grinning faces warmed her heart as she responded.

"Great to meet you all." She blushed and sat down beside Ricardo, who beamed at two young teenagers. She was hyperaware of his leg brushing against hers but stayed focused on her companions.

A little blonde girl of about nine smiled in Kim's direction. She was standing by the sink, drinking a glass of water. Her hair looked greasy and her green eyes tired. "Hello," she said. "I'm Sara."

Kim beamed back. "Hi Sara. Great to meet you. That is a lot of water you're drinking. You must be thirsty."

Sara nodded. "Sometimes I don't get time to drink at home when I help my dad." She looked away, wistful.

Ricardo turned to Sarah. "I will talk to you later about your father. It sounds like he works you too hard."

She shrugged. "It's fine, Ricardo. See you." She walked off and sat near a group of others at a table.

Ricardo faced Kim. "This is Luciana and her brother, Alejandro. They usually come here twice a week to get help with their schoolwork and do other activities." Nodding in greeting, they remained silent as if they were nervous to meet a stranger.

"Hello. It is great to be here. Please. Keep eating. Don't mind me." She watched the young girl with the bluest eyes she'd seen play with her long black hair, then bite into a sandwich. Her brother was a contrast with his dishevelled messy brown waves and dark eyes.

"Thank you," said Luciana.

Ricardo rubbed his hands. "What's on the agenda after your schoolwork?"

Alejandro replied while wiping his mouth with the back of his hand, finishing the last of his empanada. "We're practising a play, but Maria over there hates me for having the part her boyfriend wanted."

Kim spotted a girl of about fourteen glaring in their direction. While the two siblings got up to wash their plates, she whispered. "Who is that girl staring behind us? Is that Maria?"

Ricardo's eyes shifted. "It is. She only started here last week, but apparently she has issues at home, and has been giving Alejandro a hard time. The boy next to her is her boyfriend. They joined the club together."

Before Kim could say anything more, a tall, lanky man with a beard slapped Ricardo hard on the shoulder. "Ricardo, my man. Good to see you again." He scoured her from head to toe. "And who is this beautiful young lady here?"

Ricardo chuckled. "This is Kim, a friend of mine who has come from the city of Madrid. She is here to visit." He faced her. "This is Hugo, a close friend of mine. He's the

Senior Youth Worker who works the odd Sundays. He's ex-military and ex-police. We worked together when I was a policeman back in the day."

"Hello, Hugo," said Kim. "Impressive background."

He leaned forward and took her hand in his. "The pleasure is all mine." His hands were cold and she slowly drew her hand away from his. *Friendly guy.*

Hugo pulled over a chair by Ricardo and whispered something to him, but she couldn't make it out. He then turned to Kim. "What brings you to this lovely part of town?"

Kim didn't know how to respond so made her reply general in nature. "I was interested in seeing the sights around Patones and thought I would take a vacation from work."

"And how do you and Ricardo know each other?"

Kim swallowed, wondering how to respond. Alejandro and Luciana stared in curiosity as if enjoying the show.

Ricardo beat her to it. "She is an old friend of my brother, Hugo." He rose. "How about we go to the gymnasium and practise the play?"

Hugo nodded, his eyes poring over her as if he was attempting to figure her out. "Of course. Kim, you will be impressed by the talent of these young teenagers. Some of them will no doubt go on to be professional artists."

Luciana laughed and threw her head back. "Who paid you to say that, Hugo?"

He waved her away. "It is true, and sweetie, you are one of them." He nodded to her brother. "Alejandro, too. You both have a natural talent for acting."

Luciana stood by the table, drinking down the water as she pushed her long black fringe out of her eyes. "We can't do the performance today. Papa is expecting us to make dinner again tonight."

Alejandro threaded his hands through his short, messy brown waves. "Yeah, Papa's never home. It is nice when we are together without his friends around." He looked at Maria at the other table who continued to glare at him.

Ricardo put up his hand. "I will ring your father. This shouldn't take too long, guys. Have fun." The teenagers nodded.

Hugo rose, directing his eyes around the room. "Okay, everyone. Let's head on over to the gymnasium and begin rehearsals." Everyone abruptly got up and shuffled out of the room.

Kim turned to Ricardo. "Lead the way."

In the cool, drafty gymnasium she stood against the wall near Ricardo, inhaling a waft of his cologne again. She could hear his breathing as his arm touched hers.

Hugo shouted directions to the children, who spread out along the upper stage. Several fumbled with the scripts that Hugo handed out. "Maria, I want you to stand here and pretend to hate Alejandro. Remember, your relationship will be a slow burn."

Maria huffed as she made her way across the stage, her eyes turning to her boyfriend. She stood near Alejandro with crossed arms but remained silent for a moment. She played with the hem of her top as if she was uncomfortable, her body shaking slightly. Again, she focused on her boyfriend who squinted and glared in her direction. Was it a secret language? "I hate you, Alejandro. So much." A slap resounded in the room, shocking Kim until she realised it was part of the script. *Great acting.*

Alejandro touched the side of his face. "I am sorry. You must know how much I love you. I didn't mean to cheat on you, but I was drinking, and...one thing led to another. It will not happen again."

She scoffed. "I don't believe you." Looking at the boyfriend again, she lifted her jumper. "I hate you so much that I have to do this to you." With her right hand holding the script, her left hand came out of her jumper, and Kim saw the shiny glint of a blade protruding. Before Kim could shout, "Knife, knife," Maria swung her arm and stabbed Alejandro straight into the stomach. Blood spurted and he fell to the floor, holding his arm across his belly. She was about to stab him again, but Hugo lunged forward and knocked the knife out of her hand. He wrestled her to the ground as she writhed.

"Get away from me. Get away!"

Ricardo ran to Alejandro and placed a firm hand over the blood streaming from his stomach. "Call the ambulance. Now!"

Kim grabbed a cloth that lay on the side of the stage, rushed over to Alejandro and pressed it firmly against his wound, her hand quaking. Why would Maria do this?

Chapter 16

HOSPITAL VISIT

Ricardo stood against the wall, his heart racing as he leaned back against the wall at the hospital with Kim and Hugo. His fingers tapped against his right palm while Hugo whispered something to Kim, who was sitting beside him in the waiting room.

Poor Alejandro was fighting for his life. That wretched girl, Maria, had been charged. But even if Alejandro survived, his emotional scars would likely never heal.

If only he hadn't convinced the poor guy to do the play. He could have gone home as his father had wanted. Even Luciana wasn't keen to practise the play, but Ricardo was too stubborn to let them go and be with their father. If only he could turn back the clock.

Luciana had refused to come to the hospital and had been picked up by her father. She was too distraught to see him and had an aversion to hospitals.

He wondered what possessed Maria to stab a young innocent boy when he had nothing to do with the decision to take over her boyfriend's assumed role. It had to have been planned by the boyfriend.

At least they were at the station answering a range of questions. Their parents had accompanied them to the police station, but he doubted she'd be punished as she deserved. One thing was for sure: she would not be returning to the club. Her name would be tarnished around the local community, too.

A stout doctor with a stethoscope around his neck approached them. "Are you Alejandro's father?"

Ricardo shook his head. "No, his father may arrive later. I am a good friend of his." Hugo and Kim got up and joined him.

"How is he, doctor?" asked Hugo while Kim's eyes darkened.

"He is out of surgery, which went well. Alejandro is a very lucky boy. Luckily the knife missed vital blood vessels and organs. Otherwise, he might not have lived. He is expected to make a full recovery. You can go see him, but only one or two at a time. He needs his rest." He paused. "Has this been reported to the police?"

Hugo nodded. "Yes, of course." The doctor walked away. "You and Ricardo go first. I will ring his father and give him the heads-up."

Ricardo prodded Kim forward, brushing her hand as he gave her a reassuring smile. He felt bad that she had to deal with something like this on her first day at the club. No doubt, she'd be heading back to Madrid after this kind of event.

He brushed off the thought when they entered the ward, the pale and gaunt complexion on Alejandro's face making him look fragile. Bandages wrapped his stomach, and his eyes were partially closed. No doubt he was drowsy from the anaesthesia.

"How do you feel, little man?" asked Ricardo.

He shrugged. "Like I've been stabbed."

Kim frowned. "I am sorry this happened to you, Alejandro. Luciana wanted to be here, but..."

He nodded. "Yeah, I know. She hates hospitals, so I won't take it personal. As for my father, well...."

Ricardo knew all too well about his father, who was rarely home, and barely spent time with his children. He had often called the children when he knew their father was working, which was most nights. "Listen. You can stay at my place while you're recovering. I know your father will need to work."

He waved his hand away. "Nah, no need. I can look after myself. Luciana's there and she can help when my father's not around. Even when he's home, he's too busy with guys coming around."

Ricardo angled his head, curious. "What guys?" Before Alejandro could respond, Hugo made his way into the room and Kim slowly walked out.

Hugo slapped him gently on the arm. "How are you feeling, bro?"

He forced a smile. "All good. Can I come back to the club once I recover?"

Hugo knit his brows. "Of course, man. Why wouldn't you? Are you going away or something?"

His eyes turned downcast. "No, but after what happened, maybe it's best if I lay low for a while. Others might think I've made enemies."

Hugo shook his head. "This is not on you, Alejandro. Maria has been charged and she is the one that will not be coming back. She will never come close to you. I promise you that."

Ricardo stood closer to his bedside while Hugo ambled towards the window in deep thought. "When you said that other guys come around to your place. Who are they?"

Alejandro looked dazed as if he was getting sleepy. "Just work friends of my father. I don't know their names, but they talk in his study, and we can't be around when they talk. One time, I ran past the room when the door wasn't fully closed. He bit my head off and punished me by unplugging the TV. I didn't do anything wrong, Ricardo. One of the men stared at me as if he wanted to ask me something, but my dad stopped him." He huffed. "Just because I ran past when he said they needed privacy."

Ricardo drew back. "What do they look like?"

"Some wear suits and others are more casual. Why? What does it matter?"

Ricardo wanted to tell Alejandro to stay away from these men, as he wondered whether his father was into something illegal. But was he reading too much into this? It was possible the men only worked together and had to finish up tasks after hours. Just because Ricardo was ex-police didn't mean that men in suits were a threat. "Nothing. Don't worry about it." If only Alejandro's father were present. "Does your father treat you well or does he often get angry with you?"

Alejandra's eyes were downcast. "He barely talks to us when he is home. I prefer it when he's at work as it makes no difference to me."

His heart went out to Alejandro, who didn't deserve any of this. If only their mother was still alive. At least then

they'd have a semblance of a family who was available to
them.

Chapter 17

A NEW LIFE

T he next day, Kim walked with Ricardo across a footbridge as she eyed the clifftops. The slopes were shaded in green, brown, and crème, with huge boulders around the landscape. Low-hanging brush and bushes dotted the mountainside. Luckily she had brought a pair of sneakers to trek the landscape.

The steep incline made her dizzy, and the cold air reddened her cheeks and nose as she took wide steps to keep up with Ricardo. He was showing her around Patones and its surroundings as they made their way to an ancient structure.

"This is a well-preserved washing trough over a century old. Women would take water from the fountain over there; the one pool to wash and the other pool to rinse out the clothes. It was a social spot for women to gossip and discuss local news."

"Interesting. Everything was more hands-on in the olden days, and now everything is done for us. Yet, people have never been sadder or emptier in their lives."

He nodded. "I totally agree." They strolled along the riverside, the sounds of the rippling water calming her nerves due to feeling things for Ricardo she didn't want to feel. Pushing through her emotions, she focused on the creeks and waterfalls as they walked towards a restaurant. "We can have a nice lunch here. Is that okay?"

"Of course." When they entered, aromas of meat and spice permeated the air. She took in the cosy ambience as waiters bustled past them. Ricardo led her along a row of private dining rooms. Kim wondered how much these private rooms cost.

They entered one of the private rooms that featured a fireplace. Seating herself on a padded beige chair, she smiled at Ricardo who scanned her from her eyes to lips. Blushing, she cleared her throat and waited for service.

The awkward silence broke a few minutes later when a towering elderly waiter with bushy grey hair approached. His eyes were friendly. He slapped Ricardo on the shoulder with a chuckle. "So good to see you, Ricardo. How's life treating you?"

They exchanged small talk. "This is Kim. She's here on vacation." He faced Kim. "This is Miguel. He has worked in this restaurant for longer than I've been alive."

Miguel took her hands in his own. "Well, that is an exaggeration, but I have been here a while, Kim. It is nice to meet you." He grinned. "Here are the menus. In the meantime, what will you guys have to drink?" Kim ordered a sangria and Ricardo ordered a beer. "I will be back shortly with your orders." He rushed off.

"This is a beautiful place, Ricardo. Do you come here often?" He hesitated and she wondered if he'd brought someone special here.

"Not really, as I like my home-cooked meals. But I've been here with Hugo and my other friend, Angel. We do love our meat." Turning to their menus, they decided on their lunch when Miguel returned.

"What will you have, Kim?"

She put aside the menu. "I will order the grilled filet mignon. Thank you," said Kim. He turned to Ricardo.

"I will have the lamb ribs, Miguel," said Ricardo.

The waiter nodded. "It will be a pleasure to serve your stomachs. It shouldn't be too long." He beamed at Ricardo.

An awkward silence filled the room again until Kim broke it. "You never mentioned what happened to Maria from the club."

He scoffed. "I spoke to my police friend, Angel, who said they had to let her go because of her age. At thirteen years old, she's not considered to be criminally liable. But if she were fourteen, she would've been punished. Can you believe that? She stabbed someone with the intention of killing him, and she's not punished in any way. Only sent back to her foster carer."

"That is madness, Ricardo. I don't agree with that law, either. Let's hope she stays away from Alejandro, or at least the boyfriend will hopefully stay away."

He nodded. "Angel mentioned how the foster parents will likely face a civil compensation claim due to Maria's actions. Apparently, she'll be assessed by a psychologist, too. But I get the sense there's more to this story. Angel mentioned she hangs out with the wrong crowd and might be dabbling in drugs."

"Crazy to think that young children of that age have that kind of anger in them to commit such acts. Do you believe her boyfriend forced her to stab Alejandro?"

He put down his beer. "I have no doubt. He's older than Maria and he appears to have a lot of influence over her."

"And you believe it wasn't over a stupid play?" said Kim.

Ricardo shook his head. "I don't know, Kim. Something about this doesn't feel right. My gut tells me there is more to this. I mentioned it to Angel, but his hands are tied."

Miguel interrupted and set their plates of food in front of them. The smells of lemon and ginger deepened her hunger. "Enjoy, and let me know if you need anything else. Great to see you again, Ricardo."

Ricardo waved. "Thanks, man. We'll let you know." He walked off, but not without a strange gleam in his eye. Were they silently communicating something? Was it about her? "Are you still planning to leave after a week?" Ricardo asked.

"I don't know. My initial plan was to give you closure and fulfil Manuel's wishes, but now, a part of me wants justice for him. I would like to know who killed him. Have you heard anything from the police in Madrid?"

He shook his head. "No, nothing. I doubt they'll consider this a priority. Manuel was just a means to an end. They used him as a CI, a criminal informant, and now that he's dead they'll use someone else, and not much care whether the person lives or dies. So long as they're seen to be doing something, they have no interest in whether they catch the bastard or not."

Kim's chill spread throughout her body. "I wonder if it is too overwhelming a task for the police. In any case, I might leave tomorrow. I have a few challenges to work through at home and I cannot do that here."

Ricardo stared as if curious. "Do you mind me asking what kinds of challenges?" He brought the rib to his mouth and chewed on it, the sauce dripping over his chin. She couldn't help the flutter in her stomach at the way his tongue wrapped around the meat.

"Oh, it is nothing you need to worry about. I will get it sorted," Kim said. She didn't need to burden him with her problems. Cutting into her tender filet mignon, she tasted the juicy texture, hitting her in the right spot to appease her hunger. Washing it down with sangria, she watched Ricardo turn reflective.

Licking his lips, he rested back against his chair. "I understand you need to get back, and it is probably for the best."

"For the best?"

"I won't stop until I get justice for Manuel. The letter he wrote me and the fact that he was helping the police, suggested he wanted to get out of that life. I can see how he wanted to change and get his life back on track, but I still have my regrets. If only I could have done more to get him out of that world."

Kim's heart broke. "Oh, come on, Ricardo. I tried too, but it was his choice to live that life. He wasn't ready before prison." Looking past him through the door to the private room, she jolted in her seat when spotting a familiar-looking man. Her blood boiled and her heart almost stopped. *No, no!*

Ricardo leaned forward. "What's wrong?"

Kim waited until he had passed their door. Luckily, he hadn't seen them. "The man outside. I could have sworn he was the same stranger I saw back in La Latina. The one who followed me to the gardens."

Ricardo looked at her with a grim expression. Was he wondering what she was wondering? Did she have a stalker who was from Manuel's old life?

Chapter 18

SUSPECTED DANGER

Ricardo had lost his appetite. Was what she said true? Did a man from Madrid follow Kim to Patones because of Manuel? Was her life in danger? Would it be his fault again?

Watching her cower with shaky hands triggered his protective instinct. She had come here for Manuel, to give them closure and offer him comfort when she could have gone on with her life and stayed home. He wondered if her life was more in danger having come to Patones, or if her life would still be in danger if she had stayed in Madrid. He had to fix this. "You can't leave."

Kim squinted as she put down her fork. "What? I have to go. I have a life back in Madrid. I have issues to sort out."

His eyes pierced into hers. He felt more mesmerised by her each day. He had only known her for two days, but it felt longer than that. He must have been delusional if he was thinking of her in romantic terms when he couldn't offer her anything. He had loved and he had lost, and he wasn't about to attach to a beautiful woman who would leave him. "I understand that Kim, but don't you see? What if someone in Manuel's world is watching you, possibly thinking he might have told you a big secret about their business?"

"But that is exactly what you plan to do, isn't it? Find his killer?"

Ricardo shrugged. "I don't know. Maybe we should lay low until we find out what we're dealing with. It could all be a coincidence," he lied. It wasn't the best idea to make her anxious, but he still had to convince her to stay until they found out who this man was. He could speak to Angel and have him checked out.

Her eyes darkened. "I can see you are lying, Ricardo. I saw this man twice in Madrid and now he is in Patones. It cannot be a coincidence."

Ricardo looked back. "Are you sure it was him? Sometimes, anxiety can get the better of you."

She nodded. "I am certain it was the same man. You need to believe me."

He wanted to wrap his arms around her and make her feel safe. Ricardo yearned to brush away that strand of glossy hair and brush his fingers over her lips. What was he doing? He couldn't get involved when their lives might be in danger. As much as he loved Manuel, he was furious with him for getting them into his mess. But what choice had he had but to join forces with the police?

"Let me do some digging. I will get Angel to check out this guy's background. They can do a composite sketch of him, based on your description. We can then decide from there."

"Okay. Fine. I will wait until you get your information."

"We can go visit Angel after our lunch if you like. The sooner the better." She nodded and he finished his meat and beer.

Kim stared at Angel's hands as he spoke, the enormity of them reflecting his power as Captain in the Civil Guard. He placed one of them underneath his chin, in deep thought as he jotted in his notepad. "Can you find out who this man is, Captain?"

"We can have a sketch artist meet with you. See what comes of that. But in all honesty, this man has not committed a crime that we know of." He looked past her, as if pondering what to say next. "I am sorry for your loss, Kim. Grief is a powerful thing, and I hope you understand that Manuel tried to do the right thing by you and his family. He died an honourable man."

Kim swallowed, pushing back tears. "Thank you, Captain. That means a lot, given he died in horrific circumstances. Do you know if the Madrid police are investigating his death?"

His eyes scrutinised her as if she had asked a stupid question. "Of course. They are using every resource available to them."

Ricardo intervened. "I think what she means is whether they will make his case a priority, Angel."

"Hmm. That is a good question." He pressed a finger against his chin. "You must understand that first and foremost they will be investigating those whose lives are in danger, then focus on perpetrators of the deed. But have faith in the system, and hopefully they will find the man and put him behind bars." He picked up his phone. "Let me contact someone who can do the composite sketch. We might have someone available today."

"Thank you. It is very much appreciated." She turned to Ricardo who gave her a reassuring smile, his hand brushing over hers briefly. Clearing her throat, she faced Angel and ignored the heat in her loins. It was madness to be having erotic thoughts when her life could be in danger.

Angel mumbled a few words then put the phone down. "Someone is available right now to take your description. What will follow afterwards is submitting the picture to our database and potentially enlisting the help of the media if he is a danger to the community. It may also be a coincidence, Ms Mai, and you will have nothing to worry about." He turned to Ricardo. "How about you and I have a coffee around the corner while Kim is doing her work?"

Ricardo stood. "Sure. It has been a while since we got together."

Angel steered Kim outside his office as they headed to another room nearby.

Chapter 19

FRIENDLY SUPPORT

Later that day, Kim peered at her laptop screen, calling Blanca and Daniela through Skype. She sat on her bed in the guest room of Ricardo's villa and waited for a response. She wasn't looking forward to explaining what had happened so far, and that she'd decided to stay a little longer than she initially planned.

The screen lit up with Blanca and Daniela's faces. "Hi, Blanca. Daniela. It is so good to see your faces."

Daniela spoke first. "Us too. Now, tell us the goss, girl, and when you're coming back to us."

Blanca interrupted. "You don't look well. Is everything okay?"

Kim gripped the edges of her laptop and propped it against the bedhead while lying on her stomach. Chills spread up her spine as she explained how a man seemingly followed her to Patones and how Ricardo wanted justice for Manuel. "He doesn't want me coming back until we find out who this man is. He believes I'm not safe and might be a target." She sighed. "It is a mess, so I have to stay here a little longer. Indefinitely." She shifted on the bed. "I have emailed my yoga clients and subscribers, and explained how the centre will be closed indefinitely. I feel bad for those who support the business, but I need to see this through."

"That's crazy, Kim. Why make yourself a target if you are in danger? Come home," Blanca said. "This man. Do you honestly think he is part of the drug world or is it purely a coincidence?"

Kim swallowed, hoping it was a coincidence, but her intuition told her otherwise. "The police are investigating his background as we speak, so I have no idea at this point. I might be reading too much into this."

"Where's Ricardo now?"

"He's meeting with his friend, Hugo, to discuss an incident that happened with two young teenagers at a club. Ricardo volunteers there."

Daniela's eyes dilated. "What incident? Oh, girl, if it's not safe over there, you should come back home."

Kim shook her head. "It did not involve me. A young girl stabbed a boy because she wanted her boyfriend to be in his place in a play."

"Oh my goodness," said Blanca. "Are you okay? How's the boy?"

Kim nodded, putting up her hand. "I am fine, and so is Alejandro, the boy who was stabbed. It was terrifying to see, but thankfully, this girl won't be returning to the club." Daniela and Blanca stared at each other before turning back to the screen.

"If there is anything you need, girl, let us know. We would be happy to put up a sign on the window of your building to say it's closed indefinitely. But you need to be extra careful," Daniela said.

Kim grinned at the support she always had from her friends. "I would appreciate that, Daniela. Thank you. I will be careful, but I have to find out what happened to Manuel. I also need a bit of time away from work, and this is the perfect place to do it. I miss you both."

"We miss you too," said Blanca.

"Oh, and one other thing, girl. Why do you blush every time you mention Ricardo's name?" said Daniela.

Kim's heart raced. "That is not true. I do not blush." Her fingers trembled as she felt her face warm up. She hoped it didn't show.

Before they could respond, Ricardo came up behind her, settling on the side of the bed. The musky scents and feel of his warm body caused her heart to race. "Hello ladies. I'm Ricardo, and you must be Kim's friends." Why had she left her bedroom door open like an open invitation? If she had known he would return, she would have closed the door.

Daniela was the first to respond. "Hi, Ricardo. I'm Daniela and this is Blanca. We are sorry for your loss."

Ricardo turned briefly to Kim as if he was comforting her with his eyes. "Thank you. It is a messy situation, but we will both get through it."

"We are leaving Kim in your capable hands," said Daniela.

He nodded. "I will take care great care of her." He squeezed Kim's shoulder. "I will leave you to it. Nice to meet you both." They responded in kind, and he walked away.

Daniela whispered. "Wow! Oh, wow! What a beautiful specimen. He is hot, Kim. So hot! If I were you, I'd jump his bones right now."

Kim swallowed, shaking her head. Her friend didn't mince words, and no doubt, if she had met Ricardo before meeting the love of her life, Rafael, she would have already seduced the man. "Daniela, please. We are both still grieving right now. How can you say that?"

Daniela's eyes darkened. "I am sorry. You're right."

Blanca shoved her gently on the shoulder. "You need to think before talking, Daniela. It got you in trouble with Rafael in the beginning, didn't it?"

Kim intervened. "It is fine. I have to go now, but I will stay in touch and let you know how this case proceeds."

She ended the call, flashing back to Ricardo's closeness earlier. How could she think of Ricardo in that way when they had enough to worry about—namely, her assumed stalker and the person who had killed Manuel?

Chapter 20

A PHYSICAL THREAT

Ricardo's mind flashed back to the way he had stood close to Kim, the brush of her arm against his hand, making his body react. The soft feel of her glossy hair against his body as he leaned in to talk to her friends. It was crazy. He shouldn't be having erotic thoughts about a woman he barely knew, and who had been his brother's ex-girlfriend. What would Manuel say in the afterlife about him having designs on Kim?

He had gone to work at the hotel after Kim insisted she would be doing her own work on her laptop; something about virtual yoga videos for her newsletter subscribers. It might be a good idea to have space after being together for the last few days. He had to get his head on straight, and couldn't do it with her beauty near him.

Sitting back against the ergonomic chair in his office, he clicked on his computer and paid an invoice to one of his suppliers. The cost of linen had risen, but luckily the budget allowed for the increase when the hotel catered to overseas tourists and locals from the city.

Picking up his phone sitting beside his computer, he called his maintenance staff member. "Listen, Enrico. I need you to come in today. The others are doing other jobs. There's a problem with room six. It's the TV. The guest, Marco Borbon, mentioned that one of the cables has frayed. It needs to be fixed pronto."

"Just finishing up on a paint job and I can have it repaired within the hour."

"Great, Enrico. Thanks." He hung up and breathed a sigh of relief. That was another problem solved after a never-ending day of one problem after another. But when the front desk clerk stormed in with a grimace, he knew something wasn't right. "Mariana, what's wrong?"

The young woman threaded her hands through her brown wavy curls. "It's room six. The guest in the room next door complained about a loud noise. Sounded like a fight. She was worried that the guest, Marco Borbon, was hurt, and now it's dead quiet."

He shifted his posture and rose. "I take it you didn't check it out?"

She shook her head. "I have this uneasy feeling, boss. I would prefer to go inside with you if that's okay. Can you have a look?"

He nodded. "Of course, but I'll go alone. You go back to the front desk. I'll deal with it." He rummaged in a drawer for the ring of key cards and pulled out the one labelled Room Six. He locked his drawer and scurried out of his office, his heart beating a mile a minute. This kind of thing rarely happened, but his mind took him back to a heated argument between husband and wife a few years back. The husband had given her a bruise across the cheek and had had to be charged. He wondered whether they were still together.

He held his breath as he rode up the elevator. Hopefully it was nothing. He didn't want anything happening while Kim was still here. He felt protective over her and wanted to keep her safe, so he had given the word to local police to patrol the area in front of his villa. If Kim knew about this situation, she most likely wouldn't be too happy about it.

When the elevator doors opened, Ricardo strode down the quiet corridor towards room six. He hurried, listening for any noise, but there was none. He used his card to open the door to the room. Where was the guest?

His eyes roamed the room with its large bay window, double bed, and a table in the corner. With the curtains drawn, the room was dark. He could see loose-leaf pages scattered on the floor.

He bent down and peered under the bed, doubting that anyone would hide there, but he had to make sure. It was empty. As he straightened up, strong arms grabbed him in a headlock. He could barely breathe as he elbowed the assailant in the chest, hearing a groan. It gave him enough time to turn around and lunge towards a man in a mask. He kicked him in the groin, and the man bowed down, but recovered and punched Ricardo in the face.

He fell back against the bedside table, a sharp pain penetrating down his spine. The man winded him with a punch to the chest, but Ricardo pushed down his discomfort and swiped at his cheek, pounding into his face again and again. The man dug into his back pocket and retrieved a knife, swinging his arm back and striking at him, but Ricardo dodged, grabbed the lamp, pulling it out of its socket and swinging it at his assailant. The man was too fast, ducking and scraping the knife across his arm.

Ricardo ignored the searing pain as the man said, "This is what I did. It's what happens if you don't stay out of cartel business." Quickly, he opened the door and rushed out. Ricardo ran after him, but the man must have been a sprinter and disappeared around the corner and down the stairs. Ricardo ran to the elevator, hoping it would be quicker. Panting and flushed in the face, he slowed down his breathing and stared at the numbers changing. The bell *ting*ed and the doors opened. He jumped out, his eyes scanning left and right.

Ricardo ran to Mariana at the reception desk. "Did you see a man coming down here? He would have been in a rush, possibly wearing a mask. Most likely he would have taken it off, not wanting to look suspicious."

She frowned. "I saw a few people coming down, Ricardo. What did he look like?"

"He was average height, slim build, and middle-aged."

"What happened?" He explained his fight. "I didn't see anyone rushing out of here. Was that the guest from room six?"

A sudden thought occurred to him. The man had said *this is what happens*, but what was he talking about? "I doubt it. Contact the police. I'm going back to room six."

Mariana leaned forward in her seat. "I wonder if Marco Borbon was fighting with this man, but where is he now?" he asked.

"I haven't seen him come down, boss." She stared at him. "Your arm. Let me disinfect it for you."

"I'm fine. There are priorities here." Ricardo moved to the side, his heart racing and a cold sweat on the back of his neck. "I'll be back."

Mariana picked up the phone. "I'll call the police now."

Ricardo ran as quickly as he could up the stairs to the room. He hadn't thought to check on the guest when the madman ran out of the room. He had been so close to capturing the guy, but for a middle-aged man, he was fast.

In room six, he went straight to the bathroom, the only place he hadn't had the chance to check. A prickle of unease ran down his spine as he swung the ajar door wider. A tangy smell filled the space and he tried not to think the worst.

As the door opened wider, the smell of blood became stronger. Not only the smell, but the sight of a pool of blood on the tiled floor. A body lay as still as a ragdoll on the ground, blood flowing from its neck, a slit gaping from ear to ear. His legs bent at a weird angle, his head tilted to the side, with prominent bruising on his slim biceps. His white t-shirt was drenched red with his blood and his grey pants were ripped at the seams.

Ricardo's vision blurred. He stumbled to the toilet just in time to retch and vomit, almost blacking out from the sight and smell.

This was the warning!

Chapter 21

ENTRAPMENT

Ricardo tapped his phone's screen on Kim's number. He had to make sure she was all right. What if this killer had something to do with Manuel and she wasn't safe?

"Kim, it's Ricardo. I want you to go to the policeman outside and tell him you might not be safe."

"What? Why is a policeman outside your home?"

He didn't want to mention the murder over the phone. "I had to make sure you were protected. At least until we find out about this man who followed you. I should be hearing from Angel soon about his background."

"Fine, Ricardo. I will do as you say."

"Thanks, Kim." He ended the call and walked through the door outside into the fresh air, the wind brushing his flushed face. He was waiting on forensics to finish scouring the room for any fingerprints or evidence, but this looked like a professional assassination. He knew the masked man would have left no traces. He could only hope the assassin wasn't the same man who had followed Kim.

Would Kim be better off going back to Madrid if he was targeted here? Surely, whoever was behind this wouldn't see Kim as any kind of threat. But he didn't want to take that chance without having her in his sights.

One thing was for certain; he would find the bastard who had killed his guest, Marco Borbon, as well as the one who had killed Manuel.

The stout police officer jotted down his notes about the hotel intruder. The man no doubt was long gone by now, and there wasn't enough of a description to get a BOLO, a Be On the Look-Out for him. Being male, five foot six inches with blonde hair described a lot of the population.

"We will check CCTV. Some of our men are questioning the nearby guests and the victim's family," said the officer.

Ricardo gazed behind him, wondering if the man was walking around in plain sight. The mask made it impossible to know where to start locating him, but if it was the same man that had followed Kim they had his sketch. "Angel from the Civil Guard got a sketch artist to check a possible suspect, so you need to crosscheck my description with that one."

The police officer nodded. "If we have further questions, we will let you know, sir." He walked off when Angel approached.

His eyes darkened. "How are you, Ricardo?"

He shrugged. "Pissed off that this man felt he had the right to try to knife me and kill one of my guests. Find this son of a bitch. It might be the man Kim saw." He blew out an audible breath, cross-armed. "Do you have any more information about the guy? It's been far too long in my book."

Angel put up a hand. "I apologise for that. We've had another recent murder case we need to investigate." With a grim expression, he pulled out his phone but then put it aside. "You need to promise me that you will let us do the investigating, Ricardo. You are no longer in law enforcement, and as a civilian, I shouldn't be telling you anything."

Ricardo sighed, realising he had the experience and know-how to help the civil guard. He understood he was a civilian, but he had to keep Kim and himself safe. "This might be relevant to what happened at my place of work, Angel."

Angel nodded. "Fine." He hugged his friend. "I can give you the information now, as you mentioned; it may be pertinent to this incident." He took a breath. "Kim's mystery man has priors from three years ago. Murder, assault and battery. He has been in the system but never incarcerated. The police did suspect him of being involved in the South American cartel, but nothing ever stuck. This man has had a few aliases, but currently he's going by the name, Alvaro Escarra. He is smart, cunning, and transient, so it will be a challenge to find him. He has evaded the police for the last few years, but since Manuel's death, he has returned." He pointed to his chest. "I do not believe in coincidences, my friend."

"Why is this creep after Kim, and why would he get involved in my hotel instead of targeting me at home?"

Angel grimaced. "He wanted to prove he could get to you anywhere, even your place of business. Perhaps he believes you are working with the police. Let us deal with this and don't get involved."

Ricardo sighed, sometimes regretting having left the police force. But he wanted a different life for himself. "What happens now?" Ricardo asked.

Angel pursed his lips, glancing over his shoulder to respond to one of the police officers. "Put out a BOLO on this man." He retrieved his phone and showed it to the officer who nodded and rushed off. He turned back to Ricardo. "Forensics is sweeping the room and we will see how that pans out." He cleared his throat. "You should get that cut checked out, even if it appears to be a graze."

"My arm is fine. I'll go home and patch it up. I've managed tougher fights than this. You know that, Angel. Now how about I check out that CCTV footage."

Angel put up his hand with a shake of the head. "You will do no such thing. As I explained before, you are no longer in law enforcement, Ricardo. Leave it to us. Whatever we find in the room we will divulge, but until then, we need to find this man."

He nodded, pretending to agree with him when he had his own ideas. "Fine, Angel. But you need to canvas the other rooms on the floor, talk to other guests who might have seen or heard anything."

Angel sighed. "Please do not tell us how to do our job, my friend. I think, first and foremost, as the boss you should give yourself the rest of the day off. I am sure they can hold the fort here at the hotel."

"Possibly. I have a few things to sort out in my office then I'll head home. Thanks for your help, Angel."

"Great to hear." He gave him a reassuring smile then walked away into the throng of policemen and the Civil Guard.

Ricardo had somewhere he needed to be.

Kim stared at her laptop screen as she thought about Ricardo's phone call. She got the sense from his voice that more was going on. She would question him later, especially about wasting resources for her. He was no longer a detective.

She walked over to the window and peered through it. The police officer stood outside the front door, intermittently turning his head to look over his shoulder. She doubted the attacker would be stupid enough to come to Ricardo's home when the police were searching for him. Was Kim's presence something the gang didn't want, maybe thinking that she wanted justice for Manuel? The fact that she was visiting an ex-police officer might have made them think they would work together on this case. It was obvious that her visit to Patones had put Ricardo in danger, but Manuel had insisted, and she needed to give his brother closure. Surely Ricardo would want to get involved, but would the police let him?

She wondered if the man believed she had intel from Manuel. Kim wanted justice, but would they ever find Manuel's killer?

She opened the front door and greeted the policeman. He had a round, flushed face and green eyes that scrutinised her, his build a weightlifter's. "Hi, I'm Kim Mai. Who are you?"

"I'm Officer Fuentes, Ms Mai. Good to meet you, but you should get back inside. I got a call from Ricardo who insisted I watch you more closely today."

She frowned. "Why? Did something happen?"

He sighed. "I cannot divulge what happened. Mr. Perez will inform you shortly. Now please go inside." The man peered over his shoulder again, appearing nervous.

Kim nodded, walked back to her laptop and made notes about sequences of a yoga move, which would allow her to add captions to her videos. The mountain pose, tree pose, and chair pose, starting off with simple moves to more complex ones as her followers watched her amateur video. Should she get a professional videographer? No, she couldn't afford it, and this was one way she could supplement her income even if the centre were open.

While jotting down steps: *Follow your in-breath, maintain a straight posture, tuck in your stomach*— she wondered if she could teach Ricardo these moves. Her coming here had added stress to his life. Yoga and meditation could help him stay focused and centred.

As she was typing in a last step as part of the chair pose, a scuffle resounded in the background. The slamming of a door and footsteps. Putting aside her laptop, she opened the front door. Where was Officer Fuentes, who had been standing outside the villa twenty minutes ago? His police car was still here, but he had vanished.

Making her way to the kitchen, she stared through the window but saw nothing. Opening the back door, Kim's body shook as she looked over her shoulder. Climbing down the steps, she steeled herself as she scanned the surroundings, trees blowing in the wind and birds flying overhead. A prickle of unease spread down the base of her spine as she walked around the bushes. She made her way past bushes, rocks, debris, and small trees. Where was that police officer? Did something happen to him? Surely the man who had followed her wouldn't be that stupid to come here with police presence.

In the corner of her eye, a tall figure headed towards her. *Christ!*

Chapter 22

RESEARCH

After Mariana had cleaned his knife wound with disinfectant and dressed it with gauze, Ricardo returned to the second floor.

Scanning the corridor as he stepped out of the elevator, two uniformed police officers stood outside the poor man's room while the forensics team did their work. The scene had been secured with yellow tape outside the door.

He approached a burly police officer standing cross-armed in the hall. "Do you have any leads on the killer yet?"

"Not as yet," said the officer.

"Okay. Thanks." He walked off, deciding to look into his guest's background.

Fighting the urge to scratch under the gauze on his arm, he gazed at his surroundings. Several guests walked down the corridor in the opposite direction. He had a knife of his own in his pocket and wouldn't hesitate to use it if he was threatened again.

Ricardo went back to his office before returning home to be with Kim. He knew she'd be safe with Officer Fuentes so could take his time doing research. He thought about what the attacker had said, a chill permeating his spine. What if investigating Manuel's death risked their lives exponentially? He wasn't worried about his own life, but he was worried about Kim.

If he didn't do his research, he wouldn't know who or what they were dealing with. He would find out what he could, then leave the heavier lifting to the Civil Guard and police.

He typed "Marco Borbon" into a search engine and skipped past listings that were obvious dead ends, stopping on a news item. A Marco Borbon had planned to testify against his daughter's boyfriend and killer, a twenty-five-year-old man. Her murder had been sadistic, preceded by torture, rape, and executed with multiple stab wounds to the chest and abdomen. Her father found the carnage in their home. That poor man! To witness his daughter's brutal death.

The article mentioned that the boyfriend was a drug dealer, part of a mysterious cartel. The police had asked the father, Marco Borbon, to testify against his daughter's boyfriend and alleged killer, based on evidence left at the scene. It sounded like a planned kill with Marco, given he was about to testify against the boyfriend. The man who appeared to have killed Marco was definitely middle-aged, not a twenty-five-year-old. It couldn't be the boyfriend who killed Marco, but possibly someone connected to the boyfriend and cartel.

Ricardo opened a related article and found something strange. The young boyfriend who had supposedly killed Marco's daughter had died in a car crash two days ago, so he couldn't have killed Ricardo's guest. The cartel might have been tying up loose ends.

A cold settled in his chest as Ricardo realised that the cartel must have killed this young boy for knowing too much. It was better to kill one of their own than risk him talking to the police if he was amenable to change. It was the cartel's style to tie up loose ends and not have anyone be a risk to their money-making business. He wondered whether it was the boyfriend who had killed the girlfriend, or the man who had killed Marco. It could have easily been a straight hit of the girl by the cartel, and they could have easily framed the boyfriend.

He called Angel. "Listen, man. The guest who was killed had connections to the cartel. He was planning to testify against his daughter's alleged killer. You need to find this guy."

"What the hell are you doing?" said Angel. "I will tell you again; you are no longer a detective, Ricardo. Anything you do should not be a solo action."

Ricardo's gut clenched at the idea that when his ex-fiancée had died, he hadn't done his best research and had trusted the wrong man. Today, he was much better prepared, without being burdened with overtime hours and little sleep. In his relaxed position, he could help ensure Kim's safety. "I am not getting involved, just doing a bit of harmless research on my guest. That's all."

The silence at the other end was unnerving. What was his friend thinking? "Listen. Seeing as we don't want you going all lone ranger on this, would you be open to the possibility of working as a consultant on this case?"

Did Ricardo want the responsibility on an official basis? He gripped the phone hard, taking deep breaths, pondering.

But if they didn't make it official he might never find out what happened to Manuel, and he might never be able to keep them safe and carry a gun. But would it mean risking their lives even more? No, surely not, if they caught this man he'd be protected by law enforcement, and if there was corruption involved he could investigate that, too. He had good instincts and skills, and not everyone would know about his involvement.

If he only stood by and did nothing, how could they rid the world of evil if people were running scared? He knew now that if he kept his emotions out of it, he could focus on his mission and not get Kim hurt. He refused to fall for her when it could get her killed.

It was the only way for him to work on the case, by being an official investigator again. He had no choice in the matter when he needed to get closure for Manuel too. "Okay. I'm happy to do that, Angel. It will make the situation easier and I won't have you on my back telling me to stay out of it all the time."

The man chuckled. "I will get the paperwork started. I could potentially use your training and skill in strategising in the interview when we find and question this man. We do have a few leads and might know where this man is located. He's become a bit sloppy in his middle age. Hang tight."

Chapter 23

CURIOUS VISIT

Kim slowly turned, ready to face her attacker. As she shuffled on the spot, the voice beside her sounded familiar. "Hugo? What are you doing here?"

He knit his brows. "I was coming to check in on Ricardo. I rang the doorbell but it wasn't working. I banged on the door but there was no answer. Then I spotted your car so assumed you'd be here."

"Officer Fuentes was meant to be guarding out front. Have you not seen him nearby?"

He angled his head. "I saw a police officer further down the road, having a cigarette and chatting up a beautiful woman. I'm not sure if that was Officer Fuentes, though. What do you need with a police officer?"

Kim shook her head, wondering why he would leave her alone when Ricardo explicitly stated that he watch over her. Maybe it wasn't him having a cigarette. She explained how she believed she was being followed by someone, and eventually told him the whole story from the beginning. "Ricardo's not back yet and I'm worried. That police officer obviously forgot his place and got distracted."

Hugo chuckled. "He must have been taking a break, but Ricardo would hate that."

She nodded. "Have you not heard from Ricardo today?"

"No, nothing at all. I thought he'd be home. I wanted to give him an update about the club, but it can wait. No worries. I'll wait here with you, at least until that crappy police officer returns." He came closer to her. "Who would be following you, and why?"

"I don't know," said Kim who walked back around the front with Hugo in tow as she climbed up the steps and headed back inside. They sat side by side on the couch, and she was curious about his visit. "What brings you by?"

Hugo's eyes looked past her as if debating whether to tell her. "It's about Alejandro and Luciana. The Civil Guard arrested the father for possession and dealing of drugs. They're not sure on the father's level of involvement or whether he was threatened, but for now, Alejandro and Luciana are staying with me. At least until an aunt of theirs returns from vacation. But it won't be for a couple of weeks. She has two children of her own, so I'm not sure if she can take them permanently."

Kim's heart broke at the news. "Those poor children. I need to see them. Where are they now?"

"They're at school, and my wife's home if I can't get there by the time school's out." He fidgeted with his hands and uncrossed his legs. His phone vibrated in his back pocket. He checked the display. "Sorry. I have to take this." He walked to the stairs and held the phone to his ear. "Are you kidding me?" His body appeared rigid as he stood with his back facing Kim. She wondered who was on the phone. Did it have something to do with those two poor children? "*Get it fuckin done, man.*" He ended the call and walked back to Kim. "Sorry about that. It's just work."

Kim noticed his eye twitching as he avoided her eyes. He was lying, but why? "No problem. Would you like a coffee while we wait for Ricardo or the police officer?"

He nodded. "That would be great." Scrutinising her for a moment, Kim's spine chilled. *Crazy!* What did she think the man was hiding? She had to stop her paranoia. Hugo was Ricardo's friend.

Kim prepared two mugs of coffee with shaky hands. The space felt cold around her and she didn't think it was the mild climate. Carrying the two mugs to the living room, she found Hugo looking through the large bay window, appearing to be in his own world. "Hugo." He didn't respond, still staring out the window. "Hugo."

He jolted in his spot and turned around. "Oh, sorry." He returned to the couch and took his coffee. "This will definitely hit the spot." He sat and she moved to the end of the couch. They made small talk until the front door opened and Ricardo walked in. He looked at Kim from head to toe, which made her heart flutter, then turned to his friend.

"Hugo? What are you doing here?"

He hesitated. "I wanted to give you some news." Hugo repeated the story about Luciana and Alejandro.

"What happened to your arm?" asked Kim.

Ricardo sat on the armchair and shook his head. "I'll explain later." He faced Hugo. "Those poor kids. I had this strange feeling their father was part of the drug cartel."

Hugo clasped his hands together after setting his coffee on the table. "The police don't know how deep he's into that, or whether he's part of the South American cartel. They're still investigating."

"I need to talk to him," said Ricardo. "He might know something about Manuel."

"Doubtful," said Hugo. "This guy might just be a small-time drug dealer. It doesn't mean he's part of any cartel."

"You never know. It doesn't hurt to ask, does it? I work at the club too, and I have to make sure the kids are safe from their family."

Hugo nodded. "I hear you, man. What about your brother? Any news about his killer?"

Ricardo shook his head. "Not yet, but Angelo is making me an official consultant, so I can help out with the case and anything that might be connected. He will have the ability to let me in on the action. I am not going to stop until I find out who killed Manuel."

Hugo's eyes darkened as he fleetingly faced Kim then turned back to Ricardo. "Let it go, man. You'll be solving nothing by investigating Manuel's murder. These people are evil if you try to get into their business, buddy. For once, don't be reckless. Let it go."

Ricardo rested one leg over another as he briefly gazed at Kim. "If your brother had died, would you be able to let it go, Hugo? Would you? You were part of law enforcement. We can't shake that out of our system so easily."

He cleared his throat. "I understand that, man. But it's too dangerous. These people have a way of not necessarily killing you but going after your family. Do you want to put your loved ones at risk?" Hugo glanced at Kim as if she were one of his loved ones, but that was ridiculous. She was sure that Ricardo had no designs on her and had more important things on his mind.

"Are you speaking from experience, Hugo?"

Hugo blushed. "What? No. What the hell are you talking about?"

Ricardo rose, leaned forward and patted his friend on the shoulder. "Just kidding, friend. But seriously, this is my business, and I won't stop until the police do their job with me. Together, we can do even more with the case."

"Whatever," said Hugo. He picked up his coffee and downed the remainder of his drink. He rose. "If you want to come visit the children, they'll be at my place for the next couple of weeks."

"Sure. I'll do that. See you at the club on Sunday." Once Hugo left, Ricardo's and Kim's eyes locked. Something in his eyes made her gasp for breath. Was he as attracted to her as she was to him? Seeing his arm bandaged broke her heart. She was curious about what had happened. What if this situation got worse before it got better?

Chapter 24

CONFLICTED

Kim watched Ricardo chewing on a piece of rump steak later that evening, the barbecue sauce dripping down his bottom lip. He licked it clean then wiped his mouth with a napkin. The heat in her chest made her turn away and focus on her own food, cutting into the tender meat with its delicate flavour of herbs and spices. He was such a great cook and she wondered if there was anything he couldn't do.

A part of her ached to touch those thick lips and graze her hand over his stubble and around his piercing eyes. Why couldn't she get him out of her mind? They had only known each other for a few days and she was having erotic thoughts and dreams about him.

How could she indulge in such thoughts when Ricardo was Manuel's brother? It was not appropriate to move on to another part of the family. What would Manuel's parents and her own family think? It was not right to fall for another man who would make her feel insecure again. She had to distract herself. But he'd be out of sight, out of mind once she returned to Madrid.

"Penny for your thoughts, Kim."

She came out of her reverie, faced him and finished chewing the tasty meat. "Sorry. I have a lot on my mind, particularly with the news Angel gave you about this man following me. Do you believe he could be related to Manuel's death?"

He shrugged. "I wish I knew for certain, but he's starting to look good for it. Just because he wasn't imprisoned doesn't mean he's not guilty. He's been able to evade the police for the last three years."

She forked a piece of pumpkin and devoured it, savouring the herb flavour. "When he started following me back in Madrid, how did this man know I would be arriving in Patones? I did speak to Manuel, but why does the cartel see me as a threat?"

Ricardo put down his fork, sipped his beer then gripped it tight in thought. "It is possible they may be thinking Manuel's given you important information."

"But he didn't. It wasn't as if he knew the gang was planning to kill him. He didn't even explain that he was a confidential informant. I found out later."

Ricardo nodded. "He wanted to keep you safe and didn't want to involve you. He would have known the risks as an informant. He might have thought if something happened to him, then at least he got to see you one last time. I know you told me about Manuel visiting you, but I want to hear it again. Step by step, word for word, if you can remember. Any little detail might give us a clue."

Kim described Manuel's visit, but she did not remember that he provided her with any crucial details. She flashed back to one of her better memories of their time together and described part of it to Ricardo.

Kim bobbed in the cold, salty water, her body shivering until Manuel wrapped his arms around her. His strong arms held her tight as he flicked her hair out of her eyes and kissed her hard. She tasted the salt on his lips after he ducked his head in the water. Despite the warm air, the chill of the water made her lips tremble.

"I love you so much, Kim. More than I can ever show," said Manuel. His eyes darkened as their faces remained inches from one another's.

"I love you, too." She squinted as they stood in the water. "What's wrong?"

He shrugged, forcing a smile that didn't reach his eyes. "Nothing. Can't I tell my beautiful lady how much I love her? Is that a crime now?" He chuckled as if forcing it.

"Of course you can, but I am freezing and need to warm myself up in the sun. Do you mind if I lie on the towel?" He remained silent as Kim frowned, her body shaking even more as she pushed her way forward and lay on the towel. Manuel joined her.

He sat on his own towel beside her, taking her hand. "Listen Kim." He swallowed. "I just want to say that if anything ever happens to me, know that I will make sure you're taken care of. I will make sure you get all the information you need to stay safe."

Kim turned to him. "What are you talking about? Are you a spy or a part of Spanish Intelligence, fighting against organised crime?" She laughed to herself.

"Of course not, but things happen in life, and you never know." He lay on his back and closed his eyes while Kim wondered if there was more to his statement.

Back in the present, Kim eyed Ricardo who looked pensive. "This was before prison, but I didn't know what he was involved in at the time. At least not until a few months later." She looked inward. "I wonder what he meant by that. How would I be taken care of?"

"I don't know," said Ricardo, "but I plan to find out. I have a few contacts in the police force and I've certainly earned some favours."

She exhaled, wondering if she wanted him involved. Was it a mistake coming to Patones? "Isn't it dangerous to get involved in this, Ricardo? I mean, shouldn't we let the police search for Manuel's killer rather than having you as a consultant? Isn't that too risky?"

He scoffed. "I don't want you involved in this, Kim. I need to help the police, and I can do it discreetly. I know they'll be investigating all leads, and eventually get to these bigger fish in the drug trade. But that could take years."

Kim wiped her mouth with the napkin and rose to put her plate into the sink. She didn't know what more to say until Ricardo came up behind her and put his own dish down. His breath tingled on her skin and his chest brushed against her back. She waited until he moved back to the table to turn around. "Do you honestly believe that Manuel would want you risking your life like this? Let the police handle it."

He tilted his head. "Why do you care what Manuel thinks? He's dead."

"You understand what I mean. He would not want you involved." Kim looked past him, wishing she could explain how she wanted him around and didn't want him to die as Manuel had.

"Manuel knew me, and he would understand. But I am curious. Why are you so adamant about this? I thought you wanted his killer to be found."

She turned to clear the table, then proceeded to wash the dishes, the heat of the water warming her hands. "I do, but as I mentioned, the police will eventually find his murderer. Have faith." Why were her hands clammy?

He leaned against the table. "Have faith. Are you serious right now? You have no idea what these people might be capable of. We need to protect ourselves, especially if this man has been following you, and then threatened me. This has become so damn personal, Kim, and I for one am not going to twiddle my thumbs and wait for someone to hurt me. Now, let's drop this."

Kim nodded, her chest tightening. "If I return to Madrid, the threat might be over. This man might think we want to get involved. I can pack tonight. There is nothing keeping me here. I did my due diligence and honoured Manuel's wish by visiting with you, and now it is done." She was unable to read what was in his eyes.

"Nothing at all keeping you here? What about making sure you're safe or that the threat is over? This man was in Madrid and followed you. I would say that you shouldn't be alone right now." He paused. "I don't want anything happening to you, Kim." When he gazed into her eyes, she cleared her throat and looked away.

"But how long must I stay here? I can't put my life on hold indefinitely. I need to get back to my work, my friends, and my family."

"Please, Kim. Give it a bit of time. Let's see what my police friends report, then we can review the situation. In fact, I will ring them right now."

Kim nodded. "Fine." She took a breath. "But before you do, tell me what happened at the hotel the other day. You never explained what happened to your arm."

Ricardo's eyes were unreadable as he pondered. "I am only telling you this so you know how unsafe it is for you to be alone right now."

Her heart burned. "What is it?" She listened as he recounted the details of the brutal murder of his guest. "Jesus! Do you believe it was the man following me?"

He shrugged. "Who knows, but your description and mine seem to match. It could be."

Kim remained silent, not saying anything. After Ricardo left the kitchen she wiped the cutlery, wondering whether she would ever be able to leave Patones. The place and one particular person were growing on her. But would she ever be safe again?

Chapter 25

A CRIMINAL

A week later, Ricardo followed Angel along the cobbled streets of Patones and waited near a police car. "Are you sure this is the big raid that's about to happen?"

Angel put his finger over his lips. "Yes, this is the raid. We have enough officers going inside, so you can wait here for now. I will keep you in the loop once I get back."

Ricardo watched as Angel joined a group of armed policemen, all wearing bulletproof vests, huddled together, heading towards a colossal mansion with a landscaped front garden, and a water fountain with the water flowing out of a cherub's hand beside a row of several cars in the large driveway. They stormed the front yard as Angel yelled, "Civil Guard. Open up."

A part of Ricardo missed the action, the adrenaline rush he would feel when on the verge of that big bust, knowing they had saved many lives by arresting criminals who preyed on the vulnerable and weak. He had worked in drug enforcement, but most of his career had centred on homicide cases. Despite the thrill of the chase, the work had burnt him out. He had craved a quieter lifestyle, where he could stop looking over his shoulder. If only he had been there for Manuel. If only his brother hadn't shut him out, he might still be alive today.

Shoving away those thoughts, he stood by the car, shuffling his feet as he watched the action until the Civil Guard prodded three men, all handcuffed, and pushed them towards the cars. A media van slowed in front of the house. It stopped abruptly and a cameraman and female reporter holding a microphone shoved their way towards the arrested men. Ricardo didn't need to be on the evening news and had to keep a low profile. He slipped into Angel's police car so he wouldn't be seen when Angel put up a hand to avoid the reporter and headed towards him. His friend got into the car and started the motor but remained quiet.

"Well, don't keep me in suspense. What did they find in the house?"

Angel stepped on the accelerator. "They found a large amount of hash, five lots of weapons and ammunition, not to mention 100,000 Euros in cash, with documentation.

We're hoping they'll tip us off on their ringleaders. It is doubtful when these criminals claim they don't tattle or they'd be targeted. But we have to convince them to talk and can hopefully keep them safe."

Ricardo nodded. "Let me talk to them, man. I'll convince them. They might know something about Manuel's murder, seeing as they're connected from Spain's coast from Malaga to Murcia, as well as Madrid. These criminal networks are all linked and might be responsible for Manuel's death or know something about it."

"We have to investigate, but be prepared that these men may not know anything. They might not be connected at all. They may have never even met their boss."

Ricardo didn't know how to answer. He knew that he would use his professional interviewing skills to get them to talk. He only hoped it worked.

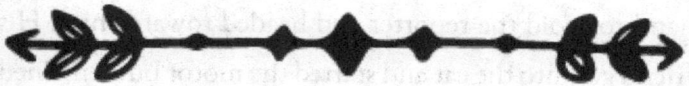

Ricardo stood behind the glass, watching Angel shove his face into the young man's. He had shoulder-length blonde hair, a willowy stature, and appeared to be in his thirties.

"Tell us who your boss is and we can cut you a deal, Lorenzo." He waited, his face still inches from the young man's.

The man shook his head, squinting. "No way. I'm not talking. You have got nothing on me. Nothing."

Ricardo's shoulders slumped. He thought the guy must be terrified. Despite the police claiming to keep him safe, it wasn't always the case when corruption affected a huge part of the police force.

Angel scoffed and sat back down opposite in his seat. He fingered a manila folder, as thick as his arm. "The Civil Guard is slowly dismantling your criminal network, Lorenzo. We have made twenty-one raids in recent months, and do you know what we discovered?" Lorenzo looked down, silent. "We found large shipments of hash, two boats, fourteen large vehicles, five weapons and ammunition, plus plenty of Euros. I would say you are going to prison for life. You'll never see your family again. Now, kindly explain who the ringleader is."

Lorenzo pursed his lips, shaking his head. "I want a lawyer, man. Not saying anything." Angel turned to the glass where Ricardo was standing, shrugging his shoulders. If only he could have a try with this man. He knew a way to make him talk.

Angel pushed a sketch in front of him that appeared to be the picture of the man following Kim. "Do you know this man?"

Lorenzo angled his head, hesitating before responding. "Not a clue." The man was lying.

"Are you sure?" asked Angel.

Lorenzo nodded. "I know nothing."

Angel left the interrogation room, rejoining Ricardo. He put his hands on Ricardo's shoulders, gazing into his eyes "Use your skills and try to get him to talk, Ricardo. But I doubt he will."

Ricardo lifted his shoulders, rubbing his hands. "Okay. Let's go." Sitting opposite the man, he stared at him as if he needed to know exactly what was on his mind. "Lorenzo. Here's the deal." He took a breath. "If you tell us who you're involved with, we can fly you out of here and give you a new life, a new start. I understand you're scared but if you don't work with the police, you'll never see your family again. Is that what you want?" Lorenzo stared at his hands, silent. "No one will know you ratted out your team. We'll make out as if we did the heavy lifting, provided we make out that you're still under arrest. We can keep you in custody until we know it's safe for you to leave. You can go into the witness protection program for you and your family."

The man crossed his arms and glared at Ricardo. "I told you I know nothing."

Ricardo would try for a while longer, but it was possible the other guy in custody would talk.

One thing was prominent in his mind: Kim. He had to at least keep her safe, even if they never discovered who had killed his brother.

Chapter 26

A YOUNG MIND

Kim took a deep breath in as she recited instructions. "Now put your right leg on the inside of your left leg, maintaining your balance. That's it. Good." Her eyes roamed the meeting room as the group of ten teenagers wobbled on one leg, huffing and puffing as if they'd never done any exercise in their lives. They needed to be fitter than this, but then again, what teenager preferred activity to their mobile phones?

Luciana winced in pain. "This is hard. How long do we need to do this, Kim?"

The poor girl's flat expression and stooped posture showed her missing Alejandro, who was still recovering from his stab wound. "You can stop now. We'll take a break and finish with a few more poses outside. Breathe in..." They rushed outside like there was no tomorrow. "...the fresh air," she said to mostly herself and Hugo, who had been watching her. After their meeting at Ricardo's house, he had acted strangely, as if watching her every move. Understandably so, after what she had divulged about Manuel.

Hugo followed Kim to the door. He looked at her reassuringly as if he wanted to give her news. Did he know something about Manuel?

"That was interesting. It is great for the kids to try a well-being activity. Lord knows they need it with some of their backgrounds."

"It is amazing to open their minds and view other horizons. They may not appreciate it today, but they will in the future. Would you care to join us outside?"

Hugo shook his head. "Maybe next time. I'll observe for a few minutes." He rushed ahead of her to the oval, past the teenagers who stared at her. Three potted plants had toppled over each other, dirt and leaves scattered across the ground and the shards of ceramic lining the edge of the grass. Hugo turned towards her, frowning then faced the youths. "Who knocked over these plants?"

Heads shook and a few denied doing it. Luciana crossed her legs on the flat grass and rested her palms over them. She turned to him. "Yesterday they were fine, Hugo. I remember coming out here late."

"Probably the wind," said Hugo. "Never mind. Let's focus on the yoga session."

While Kim demonstrated further poses and recited instructions she had an uneasy feeling in her chest. There had been no wind last night. Perhaps it had been a loose animal running around. That had to be the reason.

Hugo's eyes darkened. "I need to go inside, Kim. You carry on." He scurried away as if he had an urgent errand to run.

She sat in a lotus position. "Take in deep breaths and feel them coming from your belly. Breathe in through the belly. Luciana, you need to take a deeper breath."

After the children closed their eyes in the final meditative pose, she clasped her hands together. Her eyes scanned the grassy area, realising that someone who had been in her session yesterday was not in today. "Does anyone know where Sara is?"

Luciana blushed as she abruptly put down her head and stared into her lap. Pressing her lips together, she looked back up at Kim, then closed her mouth. Again, she opened her mouth as if to speak then closed it.

"What is on your mind, Luciana?" Kim said.

She shrugged. "Nothing, Miss."

Kim frowned and faced the other children who watched the brief exchange. "You can all go now, except for Luciana. Thank you for participating."

Luciana pressed her lips together before speaking. "Are we having another session after school tomorrow again?"

Kim smiled but a few teenagers lingered. "We might have a break for now. I will let you know if we keep doing this, but you can do a few yoga poses at home. Practice makes perfect. How about you all hydrate in the kitchen." She watched as the remaining few rose and made their way back inside, to wait until their parents would pick them up. Kim made her way to Luciana, who shuffled her feet on the ground. "We can speak privately now, Luciana. What is on your mind? I would like to help if you are in trouble."

"No, nothing like that, Miss." She waited. "Sara told me she can't come anymore. Says her father's got a new job and she has to look after her twin brothers."

Kim's heart beat fast, wondering her age. "What? How old is Sara?"

"She's nine, and has to look after her twin brothers, who are only two years old. There's no other family to look after them when she finishes school."

Kim's chest tightened. "Who looks after them during the day?"

"Sometimes her father, but there are times when he has to go to work so he leaves them on their own. He gets called in. I think he is some kind of businessman or something like that, but doesn't work every day. Only when they need him."

"Oh, Luciana. Why didn't you tell us this before? How long has this been going on?"

She swallowed. "A few months, but I only just found out about this a few days ago. I wanted to tell you all, but Sara wanted me to keep it a secret. As her friend, I have to keep my word. Friends help each other."

Kim wondered what kind of business the father was involved in to make him leave his twin sons alone. "Only when it is in their best interests, Luciana. By talking about this to an adult means we can make sure she gets the help she needs. You are not betraying her trust when Sara needs help. She is far too young to be caring for her two-year old brothers. What if something goes wrong and she is not able to manage it?" Kim squeezed her shoulder when she saw the tears falling down her cheeks. "It is okay, Luciana. We will fix this. It is not your fault when you were trying to do right by her. But she does need grown-up help." Taking her hand, Kim led Luciana into the building. "You wait with your friends, and I will speak to Hugo about this." She nodded and walked away.

Kim neared Hugo who angled his head in curiosity. "I have something important to share. Can we go to a private room?"

His head angled. "Of course." He led her to his office then closed the door behind them. "What is it?"

She sat across from him in an ergonomic chair and explained the situation about Sara, not surprised by his reaction.

His eyes widened. "Dear God! We have to stop this. I am going there now and will get it confirmed. I'll need to contact the authorities if it is true. The office manager will close up after the kids leave."

She put up a hand. "Is there anything I can do?" He shook his head and left.

Chapter 27

AN ATTACK

Not long after Hugo left, Kim waved to the receptionist, Adella, as she left the youth centre. As she sat in her car, her phone buzzed in her bag. The display showed an unknown number.

Out of curiosity, she answered the call, thinking it could be Hugo, who might have forgotten something. "Hello." Silence. She ended the call and started the motor when the phone buzzed again. Staring at the display, she answered it again. "Hello? Is anyone there?"

Shaking her head at the possibility of a prankster, she shifted into drive when she heard the back door open and close again. A shiny steel blade glinted in her rear-view mirror as it pressed hard against her neck. "Turn the motor off and get out of the car. Now," said a man's muffled voice. She gasped and clutched her arms, quaking. The cold metal dug into her skin as she turned off the motor, trying to ignore the hand pressing against her scalp. She stepped out of the car and the man moved beside her. He wore a woollen balaclava with slits for eyes. They appeared soulless. "Move to the woods."

Kim swallowed, her heart palpitating and her throat dry. Clawing at her cheeks, she dragged her fingers down and found her skin damp. Was this man going to kill her? "What do you want?" Her voice quivered.

The man shoved her from behind and she almost tripped over twigs and stones, crunching under her feet as he kept pushing her. The setting sun proved ominous with little light, and the milder temperature cut into her skin. In a matter of minutes, the wind sharpened and blew more wildly, thrashing her hair about. She wanted to crawl under a rock as the man stared at her as if she was a piece of rubbish. She knew his glare; it said *I can easily kill you with my bare hands,* but she didn't want to die.

The knife pressed into her back and grazed her. She pushed through the pain and moved ahead towards a large tree with a rope around its trunk. *No!* Was he going to tie her to the tree and leave her in the woods all night? She had to make a run for it and get away. But how could she escape this person who had all the control and could easily stab her in the back?

"Your boyfriend's playing with fire. This will get his damn attention. Now you get to pay the price."

She shook her head as he pulled her by the hair. "No, please. Stop this." He kneed her in the back. She moaned in pain as she fell on her front, narrowly missing the trunk. From the corner of her eye, she saw he had put aside the knife and grabbed the rope around the tree. That split second gave her an opportunity to run and save herself. For all she knew, he had a gun in his back pocket and would shoot her while tied up to the tree. Even leaving her here could mean that no one would ever find her, given they had walked a fair way into the woods.

Kim shifted her body and brought up her arms to support her weight as she picked up the knife and swung it at him. The man shifted back and caught her by the hair again. She drove the blade into his arm. When he retreated, she turned and ran deeper into the woods, dodging trees, boulders, and overhanging bushes for several minutes. He finally caught up to her, his hand swinging hard across her cheeks, the sting of the slap piercing into her skin. "Bitch! You'll die quicker now." He elbowed her in the arm and she dropped the knife. In a quick motion, he retrieved it from the ground.

She pushed back the tightness in her chest and the quiver in her legs, as if she was about to drop. "Please let me go."

His deathly stare gave her chills as he waved the knife in her face while pushing her back to the tree. "Tie that rope around your waist. Now."

Kim wouldn't die without a fight. He planned to leave her here to rot. With a deflated posture, she lifted the rope. As he inched forward, she kneed him in the groin. "Fuck." As he bowed over, she pushed him to the ground and ran for dear life, using her sprinting skills to get out of this place.

Short of breath, she ducked behind a tree and sneaked a peek back, but he had already moved and she couldn't see him anywhere. It was too quiet, so she looked over her shoulder, her hair rising behind her neck. She looked to the side and to the front but couldn't hear any crunching of feet, his breathing, or his voice.

If only she had her phone with her, she could have called Ricardo or the police. How would she get back to her car safely when he knew where she was? If she stayed in the woods overnight and somehow camouflaged herself, maybe she could get help from Hugo or another staff member in the morning.

Staying still behind the tree, she saw the man running around as if he were on a deadline. "Come out, come out wherever you are, Kim. You cannot hide from me." The man reached into his back pocket and pulled out another knife. "We can do this all night, and I am a patient man. You won't get past me to go to your car. You are trapped."

Kim's bottom lip trembled, and the wind chilled her grazed back. Her legs were unsteady beneath her as she blinked a few times, wondering how to get back to Ricardo's house. How did he even know her name? If only she had her phone.

The man headed away from her, pointing the knife in front of him. She waited until he was a few more metres away before creeping out of her hiding spot to another tree to her left. If she could somehow get back to her car without him seeing her. Or she could give him a distraction.

She picked up a rock and threw it in the opposite direction, which made him turn. She had to get him moving away.

When he quickly turned back around, heading in her direction, she stopped breathing. Had he heard the scraping beneath her feet or her choppy breathing that sounded loud to her.

She wondered if he knew where she was staying, and whether it was the same man who had tried to hurt Ricardo at the hotel? Or the same man who had followed her to Patones? She couldn't be sure, but he did appear to be of the same height and build.

The man crept towards her and reached inside his jacket. He pulled out gloves and put them on. Why was he doing that? Did he plan to kill her with his bare hands? No, she wouldn't jump to conclusions.

An hour later, her legs wobbled beneath her. She sat behind a tree, leaning her arms against the trunk. Where was he? How could she get back to her car safely? Would he stay here all night, or would he decide to give up?

When she saw him head away from her, she dashed towards her car, glancing over her shoulder as she ran. The man was nowhere to be found, and each step brought her closer to her car. Ignoring her fatigue and aching body, she pushed on and saw the parking lot. One more look over her shoulder made her shiver as she spotted the man running after her.

Crouching behind a bush, she waited as the man's feet stomped into low brush, stones, and fallen leaves. She was sure it was the same man who had followed her in Madrid. Kim was stuck here for the night, and eventually he would find her.

Tears streamed down her cheeks as she shivered from the cold, her bottom lip dry and sore. Staring up at the man made her sick as he headed closer towards her. What was the point in running if he would eventually catch up to her or shoot her in the back? He had a knife and gloves, and planned to kill her without leaving evidence. If only she had truly lived her life. Now it was too late.

The man chuckled to himself as he tilted his head. He pulled out a gun from his back pocket. "I can see you, young lady. You're not going anywhere." Kim stopped breathing, her mind flashing back to her friends and family as she realised they might never know what happened to her.

Kim knew she was about to die.

Chapter 28

MISSING

Ricardo put his hand over his mouth as his shoulders slumped. He sensed this case with his brother would be more challenging than he had thought at first. It was obvious he'd become too comfortable and complacent about his current lifestyle, and hearing about murders and mayhem again brought him back to the reason he had left the police force; his fiancée's death on his watch. If he hadn't been in a relationship with a woman he was meant to protect from her ex-boyfriend, Isla would still be alive today. If he hadn't threatened the man and been reckless, things would not have escalated with her death. He didn't have his mind focused on his mission, and Isla had paid with her life.

"My friend? Are you with us?" said Angel, who had placed a firm hand on his shoulder. "I know this is a setback, but we will secure other leads."

Ricardo winced, sure as anything that this man, Alvaro who was most likely stalking Kim, had known something about Manuel. They had lost sight of the murderer and now another setback. "How was Lorenzo killed while in custody this morning? The other guy won't even talk. How could you let this happen?"

Angel sighed, his eyes darkening. "I will get to the bottom of this, Ricardo, but we cannot control everything in life."

Ricardo shook his head. "I am sure he knew something about Manuel. My brother was fighting against the South American cartel and Lorenzo was a part of that. He came from Madrid to Patones, as instructed by his group."

Angel leaned forward, nodding in understanding. "We spoke to the officer on duty yesterday, and he was with Lorenzo all night. The next morning, he was dead. It happened before the shift change, but Lorenzo would have been alone for at least thirty minutes. It must have happened in that window of time. We are thinking he might have been poisoned. Forensics is examining his body as we speak, so we will get answers, Ricardo." He placed a stack of papers in an in-tray on his cluttered desk. "We are dealing with a colossal network of ringleaders and multiple henchmen. If one group gets eradicated, another will soon take its place. You know that, my friend. The cartel always likes to tie up loose ends, and Lorenzo was a loose end. They must have thought he was too big a risk and would talk."

"Then we need to get to the top. Start with tracing the money and see where it leads."

Angel frowned. "We are following the money and the documentation we received. It is only a matter of time, but we must be patient."

He scoffed. "What about the man who killed my guest, Marco, and fought with me at the hotel? Any sign of him?"

Angel shook his head, then he rose. "He seems to have disappeared, but we believe he is still in the country. We have notified the airlines and have a BOLO out on this man. We will find him." His phone buzzed. Picking it up from the desk, he got up and shifted beside Ricardo. "Hugo, my friend. Is everything okay?"

Ricardo exhaled deeply, noticing Angel's pallor. When he ended the call, he turned to him. "What's wrong? Bad news?"

Angel sat back down. "I have to leave. Duty calls."

Ricardo left too. "Please tell me what it is, Angel. Maybe I can help."

Angel strapped on his gun. "Hugo mentioned his car broke down. He was meant to check in on one of his club members, Sara, who apparently has been caring for her two-year old twin brothers. He tried calling Kim to make sure she didn't visit Sara, but she's not answering."

Ricardo lost all breath. But he wouldn't jump to conclusions just yet. "That is bad. Those poor children. Where are the parents?"

"That is why I will take a team with me, and we'll check in on them. We may need to contact child services while we are at the house."

He nodded, retrieved his phone, and placed a call to Kim. Her voicemail came on. "I have to find Kim, Angel." He placed a call to the club but no answer there too. "I know she did a yoga session for the children today, but the club is closed. She would have already left." He placed a call to Adella who explained how Kim had left the club before her.

Ricardo gasped. "Kim apparently left before the receptionist at the club, so why isn't she answering?" He wouldn't conjure up the worst-case scenario. He couldn't.

Angel waved a hand. "Not to worry. She may be in the shower or indisposed in some way. There is no need to make assumptions at this stage." He took a breath. "Go home. I am sure you will find her there. I will be in touch."

Ricardo jumped into his car and sped all the way home, refusing to believe something had happened. He would most likely find her in the shower and had nothing to worry about.

Making his way to the kitchen, he scanned the whole house. "Kim, are you here? Kim?" No one was in the kitchen, nor in the living room. He stormed upstairs and checked all the bedrooms, but they were vacant. Where the hell was she? He called again, only to reach her voicemail once more. *No, no, no. Where are you, Kim?*

Making his way to the back of the house, he noticed a few things out of place. A bucket with a mop had been moved. He thought it had been situated next to the window, but he couldn't be sure. He might have been reading into things, being paranoid. Surely, Kim was fine and on her way from the club. She must have stopped somewhere on the way. If she was driving, she would most likely not answer her phone to be safe. He was being ridiculous. Kim was okay. This wasn't about his ex-fiancée. His past clouded his judgement.

He sat on a couch to wait for her. Tightness in his chest made him wince. His throat turned dry, and he shook the worst thoughts out of his head. He was better off finding her on his own if she didn't return.

Ten minutes later, he called Hugo. "Listen, Kim isn't home. I can't reach her by phone. Did you see her leave the club tonight?"

"No. She wanted to stay and clean up, but Adella would have made sure she left before her. Did you hear about Sara?"

"I did. Angel mentioned it earlier." Ricardo's chest squeezed tight. "I can't get in touch with her, man. If she left earlier, then where is she? It has been hours and she should have been back already."

"I am sure she's fine. She might have stopped somewhere on the way. Give it time."

Ricardo gripped the phone tight. "I hope you're right."

He ended the call, not any wiser about Kim's vanishing act. All he could do was wait.

Pacing up and down his living room floor, he switched on the TV and flipped through channels, his mind not on any of them. Kim was most likely shopping and didn't hear her phone. There had to be an explanation. He didn't know who else to call as she didn't know anyone around here. But what if she decided to return to Madrid on impulse, but no, she wouldn't leave without telling him? Running up the stairs, he entered her bedroom and opened the closet. Her clothes were still on their hangers and the suitcase sat under them.

He didn't want to alarm her friends, so waited a little longer. He knew Angel would be busy with Sara. He touched his chest and threaded his hands through his hair as he wore out the floor. He approached the window and drew away the curtain. No one was coming. It was all quiet. He had a thought, and could have hit himself for not thinking about it sooner. The best thing would have been to go to the club and search the surrounding areas. If she wasn't home, she had to be in the vicinity of the club, surely.

Chapter 29

FREE AT LAST

The attacker's steps inching closer towards her, Kim realised she had a choice. She could run and risk him shooting her in the back, or she could wait to die. Taking a deep breath, she made her decision, preferring to take a risk and fight for her life rather than waiting passively to let a man take control of her.

She shook out her legs and shifted into a running stance, ready to run, but the sound of a gunshot stopped her in her tracks. If she had been hit, she didn't feel a thing.

Turning, she saw her pursuer fall to the ground. Had he been shot? If so, who had shot him? Was it the police? She didn't see another soul in sight, so what happened?

Staying behind the tree, Kim scanned the surrounding area, but she didn't see anyone around. She couldn't tell where the shot had come from, but someone had just saved her life.

After waiting for twenty minutes, she stood and made her way to the dead man. His body lay curled with a bloody hole in his head. She couldn't touch the body and knew she had to call the police. Looking over her shoulder, she scurried to her car and rummaged through her bag for her phone. Once she connected with the police, she explained the incident.

"Get out of there. You might not be safe," said the police officer who answered. "Drive home and we will get your statement there. Are you okay to drive, ma'am?"

"Yes, I'll be fine. Thank you." She ended the call. Luckily, the assassin hadn't taken the keys from her car. She floored the car out of there, refusing to look behind her.

She had been lucky this time, but would she be next time?

Ricardo couldn't just sit and do nothing, so he decided to check the nearby streets or possibly go around the club. It was also possible that Kim might have decided to go out for a coffee and hadn't checked her phone. It might have been on silent.

As he grabbed his keys, he heard a car stop outside. When he opened the front door, he flinched at what he saw. Kim stood in front of him, dark, exhausted eyes staring back at him.

Without thought, Ricardo wrapped his arms around her, feeling her whole body shake. He stroked the back of her head, taking in her floral and cinnamon scent. It felt right to hold her in his arms, and he couldn't remember a time he'd been happier to see someone.

Pulling away, he cleared his throat, and took in the pools of despair in her eyes, her dishevelled hair and trembling body. "What happened? Are you hurt?" Kim joined Ricardo on the couch, their bodies close.

She shivered again, and focused on him. "I was attacked, Ricardo. In the woods....after I left the club."

He cringed at hearing how she'd been confronted in the car with a knife pressed against her neck. Why the hell hadn't he been there to protect her? This was all his fault. If he hadn't started snooping around with Angel, this wouldn't have happened. He had to fix this. "Good riddance to evil, Kim. Did you touch the body or take off his balaclava?"

She shook her head. "He was slim, wore baggy jeans and a zipped-up jacket. He might have been middle-aged, but I am mostly certain it was the man following me."

He nodded. "And most likely the man who killed my guest, especially if he wanted to get my attention. I am so sorry, Kim. This was not meant to happen. You were alone and I should have left the club with you."

She leaned forward. "This is not your fault, Ricardo. Let's put the blame on this killer. You deserve justice and this man is now dead. We can at least be sure that we are much safer now."

He inched forward and stroked her cheek, their gazes locking until her eyes became downcast. He was sure her breath had just accelerated. He yearned to kiss her, comfort her, and make her feel safe. "It has to be the same guy who threatened me at the hotel. This is getting way out of control. I don't even know if you're safe here, Kim. I think from now on, you're coming to work with me. I'll get you a room to stay in and hire a security guard to watch over you until we sort this out."

She sighed. "Are you crazy, Ricardo? I cannot let you do that. It is a waste of resources. I can stay here. The man is dead. It should be safe. Please don't worry about me."

"No, you are not staying here alone. We don't know who this goon worked for. If you don't come with me, I will get a guard to watch you here or in a hotel. It's your choice."

She peered past him. "Fine. I can stay here during the day with a police guard out front."

"I'm calling Angel and letting him know what happened to you. I'll also explain how I don't want Fuentes here. Hugo told me he skipped out on you the last time."

She nodded. "Thanks for your support."

He rose. "I'll make you a cup of tea to help you relax and unwind. Don't worry about this. I'll keep you safe, Kim. Do not doubt that. Ever."

Her eyes drifted. "I know. And thank you."

After Kim gave her statement to two police officers about the attack, Angel entered the house, talking on his phone and nodding at Ricardo and Kim.

Did he have good news? The light in Kim's eyes told Ricardo she wondered the same thing. They had a lead. A strong one by the look of Angel.

"Great news, Kim. Ricardo. Not so great for the victim." He put the phone back into the pocket of his jacket. "We have identified the victim near the club. The man who attacked you and killed the hotel guest was the one who was shot. Forensics are analysing his phone, which should give us good intel." Angel rubbed his hands and turned to Kim. "What we know so far is that this man, Alvaro

Escarra, was a Sicario. A hit man for the cartel who tied up loose ends." He touched her gently on the shoulder. "Checking out his background and phone records will bring us much closer to finding the ringleader. Would you mind giving your statement again? Sometimes, having a break can give you more clarity."

She nodded. "Of course." Kim led Angel and Ricardo to the kitchen table. "But what I don't understand is who shot this man, and why? They literally saved my life."

Angel sat opposite her at the table and rubbed his hands. "We don't know yet."

Ricardo focused on Kim. "Most likely the man was a loose end."

Jesus. Was the shooter planning to go after Kim next or did he have another reason to want Alvaro dead? He didn't want to alarm Kim, so stayed quiet.

Kim scoffed. "That bastard would have killed me otherwise, and I am grateful."

"What happened to Sara? I understand you went to visit her?" Ricardo asked.

Angel glanced at him. "Her father has been arrested for negligence, and the children are in the hands of child services."

"How could a father leave his children alone to fend for themselves?" Kim asked.

"That is classified, Kim. I cannot tell you more than that at this stage until it is public knowledge. No doubt it will be in the media." He took out his notepad. "Now I need you to recount step by step, what the man said to you, verbatim."

Ricardo hoped they'd get more leads, but he knew the cartel would always find a replacement killer until the men at the top were caught.

Chapter 30

RESPITE

Kim rubbed the back of her aching neck. Her body felt hot and her breath short the next day. She wore loose-fitted black shorts and a white t-shirt which was drenched with sweat. She bowed over and took deep breaths, until she could stand upright to view the mountains in the distance, with hues of ash black, white, and dark green. The chilly wind feathered her cheeks.

"You have to keep the momentum going, Kim. If you stop for too long, it'll be that much harder to get back into it," Ricardo said from above her on the hilly trail. He still appeared refreshed and full of energy as if they weren't hiking along the paths of La Cabrera.

On the twenty-minute drive from Patones, he had explained how a hike would take their minds off their problems with the cartel. It worked.

She nodded. "Ricardo, I appreciate what you are doing, and I enjoy walks, but this is an entirely new level for me." She struggled up the steep mountain, occasionally admiring the way his tight white shorts hugged his bottom and how his biceps became taut as he hefted a backpack filled with water, food, and snacks.

"There is nothing like a challenging hike to get the adrenaline pumping and the mind clear. This helps me figure things out on a subconscious level, and right now, I crave clarity." He turned back with a wide beam and waved her over. "Now, come on. You're going too slow. If you want to have lunch soon, you'll need to speed up."

"Fine. I am coming." She shook her head and ignored the pain in the back of her legs and lower back. No doubt the exercise would help her sleep tonight; she hadn't been sleeping well lately, plagued by thoughts of Manuel, the cartel, and the attack in the woods. Not to mention her erotic dreams of Ricardo. It would not help her to fantasise about a man she could never have. They were from two different worlds and had different priorities.

Kim heaved and sighed as she pushed herself up, nearly losing her grip on a boulder. Ricardo took her hand, and the tingly sensation made her lose her train of thought as he pulled her up beside him. Their shoulders brushed and he placed his hand on the small of her back as he looked at her. He parted his lips and inched his face forward. She lost her breath and yearned to kiss him. But their moment was lost when two hikers passed, smiling. What was she even thinking to consider kissing the man?

Kim's face warmed as they resumed the hike. Walking down a dirt track, she spotted a stone building in the near distance, the mountainous backdrop making it appear small in comparison. "What is that building, Ricardo?"

He faced her. "That's the Convento de San Antonio. It's a popular place for tourists here in La Cabrera. The convent's about a thousand years old."

Once they reached the building, Kim huffed while ambling up a ramp path that led to granite paving beneath her feet with hedges, conifers, cedars, and maples on both sides. "This is peaceful," said Kim. She savoured the combined scents of musky earth and fresh vanilla as they made their way to a vast garden terrace with a view of the nearby towns and the land of Guadalajara.

Ricardo gazed over the terrace with Kim beside him. "The convent has survived all these years because it was built with rock. They pretty much used any material they had access to nearby. It has been restored but kept into its original form. In January 2020, the convent was declared an 'Asset of Cultural Interest.'"

She turned to him. "Have you been here before?"

Ricardo became silent, his eyes peering past her for a moment. Had she reminded him of something? A memory of Manuel? "I came here once with my...my ex-fiancée," he said eventually.

Kim winced. Ex-fiancée? Where was she now? It must have been a challenging break up. But it was none of her business. "It sounds like you've studied this building. What are the trees I've seen here? I recognise the holm oak, but what about the other ones?"

He exhaled, as if he was grateful she hadn't asked him about his fiancée. "I have read up about this. The trees, I believe are junipers, rockroses, and broom." He rose. "Let's go inside. There's a chapel."

Kim followed him inside the building, careful not to trip on the stones, twigs, and boulders on the way. Several people sat or kneeled in pews under stone arches. A hint of sunlight filtered in from an arched window at the back of the church, illuminating an altar with steps, and statues in the chapel gave it an historical feel. She took a seat on the hard bench, her thigh touching Ricardo's. Her head angled when a familiar-looking man knelt in the front row, his hands clasped in front of him.

"What is it?" Ricardo asked.

She shrugged. "Not sure." She shifted and whispered in his ear. "Isn't that man, your friend, Miguel, the owner of that restaurant? He is over there, kneeling."

"It does look like him. Must be taking a day off work."

She nodded. "He's a friendly guy."

"We'll wait until he turns back, then say hello," said Ricardo.

In silence, they rested against the bench and watched the man as he slowly moved his body back against the bench, staring straight ahead.

The man started to rise and Kim watched him closely. As he walked past, he smiled at them. "Oh, it's not him. A double." Why did she get an uneasy feeling in her chest? Did she believe the cartel would replace her old stalker with a new one? Besides, Miguel was not a threat when he only had a restaurant business and was well-acquainted with Ricardo. She was being paranoid.

"Are you okay?" he asked.

She swallowed, aware of his spicy cologne and was reminded of their near-kiss earlier. Why couldn't she get him out of her mind, particularly when she feared another stalker? Not everyone was out to get her or Ricardo.

As if sensing her discomfort and nerves, Ricardo grasped her hand gently and caressed her palm, staring at it as if it was a new discovery. His thumb trailed her inner and outer hand with precision until his head lifted to meet her eyes. "Kim, I...." He brushed her cheek and she momentarily closed her eyes to savour his touch. When his face neared hers, their lips an inch apart, again she yearned to kiss him as they gazed into each other's eyes in the silence. When she heard muffled voices behind them, Kim pressed her lips together and turned to see a young man and woman holding hands with two young girls as they walked inside.

Kim rubbed her hands and got up. "How about we explore the other side of the convent, and you can explain more of the history."

Ricardo's eyes darkened. "Of course." The cool gust of wind scraped her face as she walked a few metres to the left, viewing a rocky granite area with vegetation behind the convent, listening to the sounds of water running through an old channel. "You've got fig, chestnut and walnut trees, which have been around for a long time."

Kim nodded. "Amazing." The sounds of birds and the wind rustling through made her wistful. She wanted to stay in this space forever and forget the city life.

Ricardo waved his hand around. "The building was used as a church, for quiet study, as a prison, and as a private residence. Now it's an amazing structure for tourists."

After making their way to further spots around the convent, they headed back into the mountains, and Kim's stomach grumbled. "Are you hungry?"

Ricardo nodded. "I am. We can find a space and eat the food I brought. I have cold chicken and savoury pastries in my backpack."

While climbing shallow steps, Kim lost her footing and almost fell back, but Ricardo caught her from behind. The strength of his arms made her feel safe, his hair brushing the back of her neck as she listened to the shallow sounds of his breathing. Once she was upright again, Ricardo inched forward, leaned in, and kissed her, slowly deepening the kiss. Kim got aroused by the way his tongue tantalized her own, the softness of his lips making her desire for more. If they were at his home right now, she wondered whether they'd jump into his bed. But no, this was wrong even if it felt right. Her head got in the way, so she stopped the kiss and put up a hand. "No, Ricardo. What are we doing?"

Ricardo turned away. "You're right. I'm sorry."

Kim led the way as Ricardo followed in an awkward silence.

Chapter 31

A CONNECTION

K im walked beside Ricardo until he stopped at a large tree. They sat under it, and she watched him rummage in his backpack to retrieve a small blanket and lay it on the grassy ground.

She sat on the thin blanket as Ricardo pulled out a container of chicken and two empanadas. His demeanour appeared unusually flat. He hadn't said two words since their kiss. She wondered whether he was thinking about the kiss as much as she was. The awkwardness between them made her second-guess her decision to stay in Patones. It might be time to return to Madrid and be with her friends and family. That was her life. It wasn't here in this remote region of Spain with a man she barely knew, who had been the estranged brother of her now deceased ex-boyfriend. Her presence might have been making it worse for him, given that she had started all this by giving him the news of Manuel. He had already known, so she should never have come here to increase the stakes. But she had had the letter, too.

Ricardo avoided her eyes as he reached for two bottles of water and set them aside. "I think we should talk."

Kim gasped. "About what?" She knew exactly what he wanted to talk about, but was she ready? It might have been best to be truthful from the start. Surely that kiss would now mean she could get him out of her system.

"About what happened back there." Ricardo offered her a piece of chicken, a plastic plate, and a napkin.

Kim rested her plate of chicken on her lap. "There is nothing to talk about, Ricardo. It was a mistake."

"I know. You are right, but I still think we should talk about what's happening between us. Lay it all on the table."

Kim's heart palpitated. "If Manuel were still alive, he would hate you." She pressed her lips together, wanting to tell Ricardo that Manuel was a man she could have loved again if given the chance. She wanted to divulge how Manuel still loved her until his death, but what would be the point of that?

Ricardo played with the ends of his napkin and took a breath. "I know. It won't happen again. We have to focus on the bigger picture and make sure we stay safe. That's the priority right now."

"I agree. We can get past this, Ricardo." She bit into the cold chicken, tasting the tangy flavour and spices.

Ricardo's eyes peered past her as if recalling a memory. "Can you tell me what it was like with Manuel before he went to prison? I hate how we were estranged, but it wasn't like I didn't try. He just wasn't ready to change." He picked at his chicken as if he wasn't hungry.

Kim nodded. "Do not beat yourself up about it, Ricardo. It was why we broke up, but we had good times. We had bad times." She flashed back to the way Manuel would crease his forehead when he was angry, a darkness in his eyes she couldn't change. "Manuel would get enraged easily because of the drugs. I had to calm him down and offered him more constructive coping strategies when life didn't go his way. I insisted he start yoga and meditation, but he couldn't focus at the best of times, so I gave up. For a period of time, he was clean, but he relapsed often. I encouraged him to get help and even my friends intervened, but nothing worked." She pushed back tears. "I think he felt he wasn't worth more than being an addict."

Ricardo reached for her hand but she pulled it away. "Do not put the blame on yourself. No one can help someone who isn't willing to *be* helped. He wasn't ready. You did the best you could at the time."

Kim's heart warmed, but she needed to share good memories, too. "I remember one time he spoke about how you and he would go fishing with your father." She flashed back to the spring in Manuel's step and his broad smile. "How you always managed to catch a bigger fish than him."

Ricardo laughed. "He wanted to throw the fish back into the sea. Felt sorry for them, but he got over that."

Kim gazed into his eyes, dark pools of despair. "He loved you a lot and told me other stories of you growing up together. He explained how you stole one of his girlfriends in high school, and how you two had a fist fight."

He chuckled. "They had broken up. Before they got together, he knew I liked her but I didn't have the courage to ask her out. So he did instead." He scoffed. "It was this competitive streak he had, needing to prove he could have more than me. He got the girl in the beginning and thought he'd won until I stole her back from him."

She shook her head. "That is cruel of you to do that. It was a serious relationship for him." She remembered how upset he'd been, discussing the memory. "He did say she was attracted to you, which was why she broke up with him. He felt bad about it afterwards, knowing he had invaded your territory."

He tilted his head. "I didn't know she broke up with him just to be with me." Kim noticed the hurt in his eyes. "I regret not doing things differently with Manuel. I loved him, but I couldn't help him with his addiction or affiliations. The only thing which helped him change was prison, but by then it was too late."

Kim felt a lone tear stream down her face and she wiped it away. "I know. When I spoke to him that last time, he was a changed man. I could see the potential in him, Ricardo. He wanted to help others, and if he was still alive, he would continue to fight against the drug cartel." She remembered the locket he'd given her, thankful to have a piece of him with her. "He died a changed man. He died as a man who helped his community. The locket he gave me. It's in my room but I chose not to wear it because the pain was still a little raw."

"And now?"

Kim straightened her posture, watching Ricardo finish the last of his chicken. "It still hurts, but it is getting better. I want justice for Manuel. He deserves it." Manuel would continue to be a huge part of their lives. "I know he would want you to be happy. He loved you and wanted to make amends. I know he would have met up with you once he helped the police. He looked up to you and respected you. Take heart in the fact that Manuel was becoming a better person because of his family." Kim took another bite of the chicken then wiped her mouth with the napkin.

Ricardo glanced past her and reached for the bag of empanadas. "I wish I got the chance to tell him I loved him."

Kim wanted to reach out and wrap her arms around him. "He knew you loved him. He told me himself, but he wanted to be worthy of you before contacting you. Have you spoken to your parents recently?" She picked up her bottled water and took a sip.

Ricardo nodded. "I have, and one of these days, I'll be going to Greece to stay with them for a while. But not until we find Manuel's murderer. I want to resolve this and go there with a clear conscience."

Kim's chest constricted, as if a part of her wished to travel to Greece with him. She envisioned them laughing and kissing all the way to the islands on a boat. Where did that image even come from? "Perhaps I should go home. It might make it easier for you, Ricardo. What if me being here is making it worse for you?"

He put up a hand. "No. You need to stay here for your safety. Those guys who killed Manuel are still out there, and we don't know who killed Alvaro or if we're targets."

She nodded. "Okay." Kim couldn't deny that Ricardo made her feel safe.

He tilted his head and chewed the empanada. Kim reached for hers too, tasting the flavours of sausage and vegetables. "Are you sure you don't know anything, Kim? Think back. Manuel might have given you a clue, however small it might be, about who not to trust."

Kim peered into her napkin, pondering. "We have spoken about this. I have told you everything I know. Manuel didn't tell me anything I could use. He didn't even mention being an informant, so why would he tell me anything else?"

He hid his disappointment. "You're right. I was just hoping for something. The police are not having much luck finding his killer. Especially after their last lead got killed in custody. The cartel has a knack for tying up loose ends.

"Killed in their custody?" Kim asked, astounded. "How could that happen?"

"Angel mentioned he was poisoned, so they must have paid someone. Money talks in this town, and who knows who the cartel has in their pocket."

Kim pushed down her nausea, preferring to think of other things.

When they had finished their food and engaged in talk about their families, Ricardo placed the remaining chicken and bags of rubbish back into his backpack while Kim helped pack up. They walked back out into the countryside.

Kim breathed in the fresh oak and vinegar scents as she readied herself for the long walk back to his car. She knew this situation would escalate before it got better.

Chapter 32

SELF-DEFENCE

A few days later, Kim sighed as Ricardo led her into his office again. He gazed into her eyes and shook his head, knowing the only way he could keep her safe after her attack was to have her remain in the hotel with him. Another reason was that he couldn't get that kiss out of his mind, and he missed her when she wasn't around.

He fondly remembered the softness of her lips, her lustful expression and sweet moans, and the way her feminine curves fit nicely with his body. Even her floral and soapy scents aroused him. He wanted and needed more than a kiss. But if he got too close to her, history would repeat. He couldn't have another dead body on his hands. Not again. It was too risky to get involved with Kim when doing so could put her life in more danger. He had to be objective and concentrate on his next move, but so far he had no leads.

"Why do you need to babysit me, Ricardo? I can take care of myself. Besides. I was rescued by someone who shot my stalker. I should be safe now. Unless the shooter is another unknown enemy."

He sat behind his desk and looked at Kim, who had placed her hands on her hips. She wore tight black jeans that displayed all her sensual curves, and a figure-hugging white blouse. "Yes, but it doesn't mean they don't have other goons watching you. I am not taking that risk. I can keep you safe here."

"Truly? You were not safe when that man threatened you here and killed your guest. Who knows who else is part of that man's network. Maybe nowhere is safe, but at least in your home I know my way around."

He squared his shoulders. "I can find you work, or you can relax in one of the guest rooms."

Kim bowed her head, as if considering her options. She looked beautiful with her long, flowing hair draped around her shoulders and her flawless skin. He wondered what it would feel like to dip his mouth towards her upper chest and head down lower. *Stop it!* He had to keep his head in the game and focus on keeping her safe. "Fine. If you want me here, then I will earn my position. I have been mulling this over in my mind for the last few days, and I have prepared notes."

He frowned. "What notes?"

"I considered giving a lecture in one of your rooms. A talk about yoga, meditation, Buddhist philosophy, and general well-being. This will help me make virtual training videos, audio files, and a membership program. I have it set up on my website. I can start a membership program where people will pay a fee to do the work from home."

He shook his head. "Are you mad? Why would you want more attention on you? You should be keeping a low profile, not advertising where you are."

"But that man is dead. What if no one else is after me and whoever shot him saved me. He can no longer hurt me, Ricardo. I need to do this and keep my mind active or I might as well go back to Madrid. You want me to work, and this is me working."

"No, it is too risky."

Kim scoffed. "If someone else follows me, they will realise I am busy focusing on my business rather than Manuel's case. It would paint a picture and they'll leave me alone."

"Or it could make you more vulnerable. I am not sure about this."

She placed her hands on the desk, her eyes boring into his as if she was telling him she was not his puppet. "I will keep it small. This is something I need to do while also finding out what happened to Manuel. If this draws someone else out, then it will be worth it, too."

"I will not have you as bait, Kim."

"I have you in my corner, and the Civil Guard. It will be small. You can control all the variables here. Let me do this. I am going crazy without sharing my work. I love helping people, and I won't let the cartel stop me from doing something that is not relevant to their business."

Ricardo realised he could not change her mind, but at least he could keep an eye on her in the hotel. He could take a break from his work and make sure he stayed by Kim's side while she gave her talk. "If you do this talk, you will follow my conditions." She nodded. "First, you will let me arrange the advertising so it's low-key. Second, I am going to teach you self-defence. Third, we do it in a place of my choosing."

"Fine. Let's do this."

Later that day, Kim stood inside Ricardo's living room. "Is this where we'll be doing self-defence?" She wore a pair of leggings and a tight t-shirt which highlighted her breasts. He had to contain himself and focus on their mission.

Ricardo nodded. "I want you to listen to my instructions and do as I say." He cleared his throat. "We'll go through a few scenarios and I'll explain what to do."

"What if I hurt you?"

He was touched by her concern, and pointed to his chest. "I am made of steel, Kim. Nothing can break me." She chuckled and he loved that sound. "Now, I want you to grab me from behind. Put your arms around me." The sweet scent distracted him for a moment. "I want you to grab my arms and pull yourself in then swing your hips to one side." She did as he explained, and he wondered how he'd manage such close contact. "Now make a fist and hit me in the groin."

Kim stopped, shaking her head. "I'll hurt you, Ricardo. I can't do that."

He sighed. "Do the motion at least." She made a fist and swung close to his groin. "Now turn to me and bring your hands together behind my neck and knee me in the groin upwards. Again, make the motion."

Ricardo's heart palpitated and he ignored his arousal, still feeling the softness of her hands against his skin. This was madness. He had to imagine she was in a real-life situation and was in danger. He couldn't think about her in any other way. "Now let's practise that again a few times, so it sticks."

After practising several more times, she lost her breath and bent down to regain it. "What now?" She licked her lips and he looked away briefly.

"If the attacker lifts you, strike the groin. If you're in a choke hold, lift one arm up. You have to hit the eyes, nose, throat, and groin areas to weaken the attacker. Now, I'll show you the hair grab and what to do. Then we'll do the choke hold." He exhaled. "Get behind me." Kim did as he asked, then they reversed roles.

"Did I hurt you?" said Kim.

"I am fine." After continuing to practise, Ricardo summed up. "You need to be aware of your environment, use your core, strike the groin, and grab the face. If the attacker overpowers you, you need to relax and pretend you've given up. Then you fight when you can, or when the attacker lets his guard down."

By the end of their session, he could tell she appeared to be more confident with her abilities. But he hoped she never had to use these moves. Why did he feel he was digging a grave with his emotions?

Chapter 33

MESMERISED

O ver a week later, Ricardo stood by a tree behind the hotel. The rising sun streamed over his shoulder, lighting up stone beams separating the square concrete ground. Three timber tables and chairs were arranged in a circle. Kim stood at the front, gesturing with her hands as she gave her lecture.

Ricardo figured he could make space in the outdoors by arranging a few tables and chairs outside the back of the hotel, and get sunlight in the session, too.

Three men and six women sat at the tables, some slouching, and others leaning forward as if enraptured by her calm and soothing voice. *Hell, I could listen to her gentleness all day and night.*

"Buddhist philosophy is about living in the present moment, free of thoughts about the past and the future. Yoga and meditation stem from this philosophy; one of mindfulness, existing in the moment and appreciating the now and to free yourself of pain. Let us do a quick exercise to prepare."

As his body responded to the talk, his heart stopped at the way she showed interest in her group, her eyes roaming as if present with her surroundings. Her body glided from one side of the area to another as she gave her full attention to her guests. He realised he hadn't looked closely enough at all the attendees. He had screened them all and hoped that no one nefarious had invaded Kim's seminar. With nine attendees, it was a good turn-out for a last-minute event.

He watched her guide the attendees through a mindfulness meditation exercise while playing classical music in the background, coming from her laptop which rested on a small table beside her.

He flashed back to the way her body had melded with his when he was teaching her self-defence, and at the way she willingly put all her effort into the kicks and strikes. She was a natural without knowing it; having that quiet wisdom that endeared her to him even more. He was confident that Kim would no doubt use her moves if threatened, but would he be around to see it? What if getting involved in the cartel would get him killed, or worse, get her killed? He had to exercise his restraint and not give in to his carnal desires. He could do this. He had to do this. Their lives were at stake.

His reverie broke at her final words.

"I am handing out a list of reading resources on the topics of mindfulness, positive psychology, and Buddhist philosophy." She peered over at him briefly then turned back to the attendees. "If you'd like another session, I will put up a notice for the next one. Remember to practise the art of mindfulness in every menial task you undertake. For instance, when you perform an action such as washing the dishes, you need to be present with the task. When you have a shower, be in the moment rather than thinking about the past or future. Practise will enhance and sharpen your attention to details." She paused. "Any questions?" The group remained quiet. "I will be handing out my business cards, too."

Kim circled the area and handed out her cards. She chatted and laughed with an old man who insisted he could not manage yoga poses in her next session. "Challenge yourself," she said. Kim approached Ricardo, his eyes lingering on the outline of her cleavage in an open-necked blouse. "How was it?"

"Amazing. You have a way with words. You can hypnotise a room, Kim." He watched the guests rise and make their way out of the outdoor area and back inside the hotel. "I imagine your yoga centre in Madrid brings in a lot of people."

She nodded. "It does, but I am reconsidering my future. I have started writing a romance novel and plan to start a non-fiction book about yoga and meditation. I am even exploring how to start up on online membership program."

"Sounds interesting." He frowned. "Books about yoga and meditation, ha?"

She nodded. "Books also about general well-being and Buddhist philosophy. I have so many ideas it's scary."

"Hmm. You should do well. I know I wouldn't have the discipline."

She chuckled. "I don't believe that, Ricardo. You seem to be passionate about everything you do."

He yearned to tell her how his passion for her was growing, when his phone buzzed in his back pocket. "Angel. What's up, man?" The silence suggested he was braced for the worst.

"Hugo's been shot." Ricardo's heart pounded and he dropped the phone.

Chapter 34

HOSPITAL VISIT

Two days later, Kim stood by Hugo's bedside with unsteady legs as he lay there like a vegetable. His bruised and battered face, and the humming of the life-support machine was an ominous sign that he might never wake up.

A nurse walked in and jotted notes on Hugo's chart. Putting it aside, she smiled at Kim. "The doctor will talk to you shortly." She scurried to the next ward while Angel and Ricardo stood by the window in a quiet, intense conversation. No doubt strategising about what to do next.

"What happened to him?" Kim asked.

Angel approached and rested a gentle hand on Kim's shoulder. "That information is classified, and we have further avenues to follow."

Kim's heart palpitated. "Who could have done this?"

Angel clasped his hands, turning briefly to Ricardo. "We don't know yet. What we can only hope for now is that Hugo wakes up as we have questions for him."

Ricardo knit his brows. "We have to catch whoever did this, Angel."

A towering man with a stethoscope, hair greying on the sides, entered the room. "Are any of you related to Hugo?"

"No, we are friends of his," Ricardo answered. "His family's on the way."

He nodded. "I am Doctor De Leon." He paused. "Hugo sustained a gunshot wound to the head, which could have been much worse. We managed to reduce the swelling in the brain, and luckily there wasn't significant damage to the tissue. It is now a matter of waiting to see if Hugo is able to wake up on his own. The body needs to heal itself, and his unconscious state will allow him to do that. He will need time to recover." He toyed with his stethoscope. "We are hoping he will wake up soon, and it does help to talk to him and encourage him. I will check in with him later in the day."

"Will he make a full recovery, doctor?" asked Ricardo.

The doctor nodded. "I believe so, but it was touch and go there for a while during surgery. He is a lucky man. But it is up to him now."

"Thank you, doctor," said Kim. The doctor walked out with a curt nod.

Kim remembered how Hugo meant to visit Sara's family several days earlier, when his car had broken down. Was that orchestrated to get him into a vulnerable position? But why would someone shoot him?

Ricardo answered his phone. "Hey, Alejandro." His eyes lit up, obviously showing his love towards the boy. "What's going on?" He nodded, then ended the call. "He wants help with a school assignment. Apparently, he's doing an article about law enforcement. He wants to write about the life of a police officer." He turned to Kim. "I feel bad about leaving."

Kim gave him a reassuring smile. "There is nothing you can do now, Ricardo. Help Alejandro."

He nodded. "How about you stay with Angel and I'll go and meet Alejandro at the local café, then see you back at the house later."

Angel squeezed Kim's shoulder. "I'll take her back to the house and stay with her until you get back. Not to worry, my friend."

"Thanks," said Kim. Her heart warmed at the idea of protection, but she didn't need babysitting. She could take care of herself. But what good would it do to argue with

Ricardo as he would not shift his position on wanting to protect her?

Ricardo glanced at Hugo. "Let me know if he wakes up anytime soon." He waved at them and rushed out of the ward.

Ricardo spotted Alejandro inside the crowded café after school. Customers waited to order at the counter, while a waiter bustled about to clear tables. Aromas of coffee and sweet pastries made his stomach rumble, but he wasn't here to eat or drink.

Staring at his phone, Alejandro didn't notice Ricardo until he stood beside the table. When he looked up, his serious expression turned into a beaming smile. "Hey, Ricardo." His hands quaked as he gripped the phone.

"Where's your pen and notepad? I thought you wanted to work on your assignment."

Alejandro leaned forward, his eyes roaming the café as new patrons entered in groups. What was he looking for? "I...I have to talk to you, Ricardo. It's important."

Ricardo tilted his head and took a deep breath, not liking the terror filling in his eyes. He was afraid of something, but what? "What's going on? You look worried."

Alejandro cleared his throat as he turned back to look at the entrance of the café until no new customers were coming in. "I did something stupid, man. I'm sorry."

Ricardo's heart ached at the idea that this poor teenager possibly did something with harmful consequences. "Start from the beginning, Alejandro. I've got your back. Always."

"I never meant to do this, but I needed money to buy Luciana a birthday present. When I asked my dad, he said that I was old enough to earn my own money. He said that if I want to make money, he knew people who would give me a job straight away." Ricardo didn't like where this was going, considering his father was involved in drugs.

"What did you do?"

Alejandro's eyes teared up and he pressed his lips together. "I was only going to do this once, and the men said I didn't need to do more jobs, but then..."

Ricardo scoffed. "Spit it out, man. Please tell me what you did."

He whispered. "I...I was supposed to sell a few small bags of drugs to people at school and then hand in the money, but... I mean, I sold two of them, but this guy bashed me up because of the price. I told him I didn't make the prices but he bashed me real good. I got half of what I asked for, and had to put in my own money to make up the other half. If my dad finds out I stole from him, he'll have my head. Anyway, I got so spooked after that guy beat me up that I was too scared to sell the rest of it. I flushed the rest of the drugs down the sink and decided to get a real job to make up for it. But I haven't been able to get work, Ricardo. What do I do now?"

Ricardo stared at his hands, a chilling fear penetrating him over what this poor boy had signed up for. "How in hell could you do something so stupid, Alejandro? What possessed you to take such a risk? Are you crazy?"

"But my father was released. He might not go to prison."

"They might not have enough evidence yet, but they will get it. And you and Luciana will be alone. Do you have other family you can stay with?"

He nodded. "My aunt."

Ricardo took a breath. "Okay. First of all, you will not go back home for any reason. I'll buy you whatever you need. Now does anyone know about your aunt?"

"I think my boss knows."

"Okay. Hang tight." He placed a call to Angel and waited for his answer. "Angel, I need your help. Alejandro's in trouble."

"What happened?" Ricardo explained the situation. "Bring him over to his aunt's place and I'll arrange a police guard right now until it's sorted out. If you wouldn't mind, stay there with him until we get police presence."

"Of course I will, Angel."

"It sounds like a small-time issue, and he should be fine. But because we do not know what we're dealing with, it's best if he stays there until we tell him otherwise."

"Thanks, man." He ended the call, then faced Alejandro. "You are staying at your aunt's house, but there are ground rules. Follow them. If you don't, I'll beat you myself." He explained the rules. "For no reason are you to leave your aunt's house without permission from me or the police. No talking to any of your friends. Got it?" Alejandro nodded. "But you will need to give us names, particularly that of your boss."

He nodded. "I will tell you what I know. I will. Thanks." He stared at him. "Your friend, Miguel, is friends with my boss, but I don't know my boss's name."

Ricardo's spine chilled. "What?" *Christ, no!* He trusted the man. "Are you sure?"

"Yeah. I saw them patting each other on the back and exchanging envelopes when my dad took us to Miguel's restaurant."

Ricardo had someone he needed to talk to, but he prayed that this situation could be rectified. He couldn't believe Miguel was involved. They had to have been threatening him, giving him no choice but to comply with their rules. That had to be it.

Chapter 35

A LIFE TAKEN TOO SOON

Ricardo shifted in Miguel's office, his back pressing against the steel-backed chair. He was waiting for Miguel to finish up with a group who had a large order. He had to make this right. If Miguel knew things, he would need to bring him in to the police station.

He had dropped off Alejandro at his aunt's house and left once a police officer stood guard outside the home. Hopefully he'd stick to the rules he set out.

"Sorry to keep you, but the group couldn't make up their mind about the order. Luckily my waiter showed up, even if it was ten minutes later." Miguel sat across from him and played with a stack of tattered papers in the centre of his desk. "What can I do for you?"

"Are you working for the cartel? Laundering money into the business?"

Miguel's bushy eyebrows turned inward then his eye twitched. "That's crazy, Ricardo. You know me."

He knew Miguel was lying. "Hmm. Tell me the truth. If they're pressuring you, we can protect you. Tell us everything you know, man. Please."

The restaurateur's eyes became a shade darker, and his body shrank, appearing smaller and weaker. "I had no choice. When I refused, they threatened to kill my family. I had no choice," he repeated. He appeared broken and haggard, his shoulders deflated, his eyes downcast.

Ricardo rubbed his hands so hard that his bones clicked. He couldn't believe a man he had trusted for years would get involved. Why hadn't he come to him or Angel? "What do you exactly do for the cartel? I need specifics and no bullshitting, man. Now, spill."

The man looked broken with his quaking bottom lip and distant gaze. "They transfer drug money into my account and I overestimate my expenses and report to them every month. Sometimes. I mean...if someone is suspected of cheating the cartel, I get intel by being friendly and gaining their trust. I hate doing it, but they keep threatening my family. I have no other option."

His blood ran cold. "Jesus, Miguel. How many people have died because of what you did? Because of the intel you got if they were cheating the cartel?"

The man shrugged, his shoulders deflating. "I can't say."

"How long?"

"Since before your brother's death." His face paled. "Specifically with the laundering, each month they deposit an instalment of funds and I play with the supply records, listing them as more expensive than they should be. They had an accountant arrange the payments, and I don't even touch the books anymore. Alejandro's father works for them on their books, but they got someone else after he was arrested." He exhaled. "Once when I checked them over, they realised I was online and paid me a visit." He pointed to a scar above his right eye. "They cut me as a warning. If I did more than that, they said they'd gut me. Of course, I believe them."

"I am sorry, Miguel. But you need to come forward with this." His spine chilled. "Tell me how it all started."

Ricardo listened as Miguel explained how he'd been approached as a popular and well-established business. "I can go to the Civil Guard as I know they've been investigating the cartels for years. But I need protection for my family. I don't care about me, as long as my family is safe."

Ricardo had to make this work. "Only speak to me, and I will relay things to Angel and the rest of the Civil Guard. We have to be extra careful of any moles in the police force. Manuel believed that the Madrid police couldn't be trusted. With links to the Patones police force, there's corruption everywhere."

"I know, and I am happy to help. But first, I want assurances about my family. Please."

Ricardo took a breath. "Who first approached you?"

"Alvaro. The man who died recently. He wasn't only a hitman. He did other things for the cartel, like setting up meetings and vetting potential workers."

Ricardo nodded. "I'll talk to Angel, and we'll get your family to safety. We can arrange a hush-hush witness protection program. I know someone who's had success with this." His phone buzzed, and it displayed an unknown number. "Hello."

"Hello, is this Ricardo?"

"Yes, who's this?"

"I'm Valeria, Alejandro's aunt. He speaks about you constantly, and had your number in his contacts. But I'm worried. Alejandro's left."

His spine turned cold. "What do you mean, left?"

"He mentioned getting a message from his friend, Arturo, and said he had to help him with an assignment.

They were going to meet at his house. I told him he couldn't go and that he was only safe here. He agreed until I turned my back, and he jumped through the bedroom window. I couldn't get to him. He left his phone behind in his hurry."

"Do you know this Arturo guy?"

"No, first I've heard of him."

"Okay, I'll check his house first and I'll contact the police. They'll do a search. Hang tight, Valeria. Thanks for letting me know."

"Please find him," Valeria begged.

Ricardo ended the call then rang the police, giving them details about Alejandro. He looked at Miguel, whose face had turned pale again "What's wrong?"

Miguel's hand shivered. "If it's the same Arturo, he is a bad man. He came over last time when the new accountant checked over the books. If Alejandro spoke to him, that can't be good. He is impulsive, unstable, and a risk-taker."

"Oh, Christ," said Ricardo. "I have to go, but don't talk to anyone until I tell you to." He rushed out of there, hoping that Alejandro would be okay.

***

Ricardo parked by the kerb. He noticed the dying carnations and blossoms, the wilting low brush, and the cracked concrete path leading up to a scratched heavyset timber door. Two potted plants sat on either side of the front door, but one of them had been knocked over. Probably a stray cat in the area.

He was about to ring the doorbell when he noticed the slight gap in the door. Why would the door be open? He didn't want to presume anything suspicious, yet.

Swinging it wider, he entered the quiet home with its narrow passage, crooked landscape painting displays on the wall, and a dead silence. "Alejandro, are you here?" Silence. A prickle of unease tingled up his spine as his eyes roamed the living room that featured strewn magazines, a jacket across the couch, pillows lying on the carpeted flooring, and an overturned vase of flowers spilling water behind the coffee table. He didn't touch anything, but didn't want to make assumptions, either. His mind couldn't go there yet. Alejandro might have accidentally knocked the vase down, possibly angered about something. He was known to have spurts of anger when it came to his frustrations with schoolwork. That was all this was. He was jumping to conclusions. It was possible that Arturo had another load of drugs to sell, that was all.

"Alejandro. Are you here?" He crept towards the nearby kitchen and spotted nothing unusual there. Two glasses lay in the sink, as well as a small plate filled with crumbs. Nothing strange about that.

Walking towards the bedrooms, he glanced at the master bedroom where Alejandro's parents slept, which was empty. Wandering to Luciana's bedroom, he steeled himself for the unexpected, but it was empty, too. A pile of clothing lay across a chair, schoolbooks on a desk. Aches in his back slowed him down when he made his way to Alejandro's bedroom, not wanting to think the worst.

As he stepped inside the bedroom, a tangy smell penetrated his nose. He swallowed and slowed. His body jerked and his breathing stopped when he saw a sole running shoe protruding from the far side of the bed. He recognised the shoe as Alejandro's. He ran to the teenager, despite knowing he was too late.

Blood pooled under Alejandro's head. One hand lay across his chest while the other one was at an awkward angle behind his back. Ricardo pressed his thumb against the teenager's wrist to check for a pulse. Nothing. No pulse. No breathing. Dead.

Ricardo's body sagged as he stared at Alejandro for what felt like hours even though it was only a few minutes. A single tear flowed down his cheek as he bowed his head, dropped his phone and shifted to a chair beside the window. His shoulders sagged as his eyes turned downcast. More tears fell down his cheeks.

If only he had got here earlier. If only he had bypassed those trucks ahead of him. If only he had known earlier about what was really going on with Alejandro. He could have prevented this.

After taking time to grieve his huge loss, Ricardo took a few deep breaths, then clenched his fists. He gritted his teeth in sudden fury. "I'll get those damn bastards. I'll get them, Alejandro. Justice will be served." Bending down again, he wiped his face and shook his head, vowing to kill the villains who did this.

He called the police.

Chapter 36

SAD NEWS

Ricardo stood in a daze as he watched a forensics team stream back and forth from their van to Alejandro's house. Angel shouted instructions.

The captain approached Ricardo, who was feeling that the surroundings, the police tape across the door, the police vehicles, the forensics team, had all become surreal. This had to be a dream. Surely, Alejandro wasn't really dead. He hadn't just witnessed his body, had he? A young life taken way too soon. "My friend. I am sorry to do this, but I need your statement," Angel said.

Ricardo pointed. "I already gave it to that officer over there."

Angel nodded. "I understand, but I will need it again to ensure you have remembered every detail. Now that you have had time to let it slowly process, your mind will be clearer."

He scoffed. "Process? I will never have time to process this nightmare. Never, Angel. That poor boy didn't deserve this. Why would this happen?"

Angel's eyes darkened as he wrapped his arms around his friend. "We have to be on the lookout for Arturo, who is the most likely culprit. Not to mention finding that kilo of heroin washed down the drain. The bit he told you about."

Ricardo nodded. "I wished he wasn't telling the truth about the drugs."

Angel ushered him towards his car. "Let's sit in my car." Ricardo took the passenger seat. "I do not want to presume anything until we investigate further, but it appears that Alejandro had been in communications with a leader who had instructed him to sell the drugs to interested buyers at his school. One of the buyers was Maria from the club. We believe she stabbed him as a warning after he initially refused the job. We checked his phone. This started a few months ago. I am assuming that is how long he has been involved."

"Jesus, Angel. I never thought he could get mixed up in that world. Have you traced who he's been in communications with?"

He shook his head. "Only Arturo. No one else."

After giving his statement to Angel, Ricardo had a new thought. "Why would Alejandro not come to us earlier?

Instead, he gets cold feet and decides he can no longer sell the heroin, so dumps it down the sink. He would have known it was a huge risk."

Angel glanced past Ricardo. "You need to go home and take time to grieve. No doubt you will need to support his sister, Luciana, and his parents."

He hadn't seen any of Alejandro's family, and desperately needed to speak to Luciana and offer his support. "Where's the family?"

"They've been notified and are on their way to his aunt's house. They will need all the support they can get, my friend." He took a breath. "Go home and let Kim know. I left her at your house before I got the news. She is unaware of what happened."

Ricardo had forgotten about Kim in his grieving state. "Oh, Christ. Of course. I will go now. Please keep me up to date with the investigation."

Angel nodded. "Of course. Now leave!"

Ricardo rushed to his car and raced home, thinking of Kim and how she would cope with the news. She had been close to Alejandro and would no doubt want to see his family.

His heart racing, he stepped into his home and stopped at the door as he saw Kim on the couch, typing on her laptop. She looked up with curiosity.

"Kim. I am so sorry."

Her body stilled. "What's going on, Ricardo?"

Ricardo took a few deep breaths and clenched his hands. He gritted his teeth in sudden fury. "I'll get those damn bastards. I'll get them." She waited for more. "Alejandro's dead. Gunned down by a thug in his own house."

Kim's face turned pale. "What?

"He's gone."

Tears streamed down her face. "Are you sure?" He nodded. She rose, approaching him with hesitant steps. Wiping her cheeks with the back of her hand, she put a hand on his shoulder and squeezed. "I am so sorry, Ricardo. So very sorry."

Ricardo pulled her into his arms and stroked the back of her hair. He was comforted by the sweet smell of roses and soap, momentarily forgetting about the death of that sweet boy. First, he'd been stabbed, and now shot to death. A poor young boy with no future. No life. No longer existing.

He looked past her. "I have to go see Luciana and her parents."

Her bottom lip quivered. "Can I come with you?"

"Please," said Ricardo.

Arriving at the aunt's house, Ricardo slowly walked into the large home with a front garden filled with varying shapes of hedges, towering ferns, and gardens filled with colourful flowers.

Kim squeezed his free hand as he rang the doorbell. "Thank you for coming with me," he said. "Luciana needs all the support she can get."

She gave him a reassuring smile. "I am glad to be here, Ricardo."

An older woman answered the door. She looked grief-stricken, and her eyes were bloodshot. Her blonde hair looked as if she had threaded her hands through it multiple times. "Can I help you?"

Ricardo swallowed. "Hi, Valeria. I'm Ricardo, a friend of Alejandro. We spoke earlier today. This is Kim."

"Oh yes, Ricardo. Sorry to meet both of you under these circumstances. Please come inside. Luciana will be happy to see you." They followed her into the house. "We are very sorry for your loss," said Ricardo.

The woman teared up, then straightened her posture. "Thank you. Luciana is in her bedroom. Her parents are in their rooms and don't wish to speak to anyone for now. They're too distraught, as you would understand."

"Of course," said Ricardo.

They followed Valeria through a narrow foyer to the living room, smelling of fresh lavender. An eerie silence filled the darkness of the house.

Valeria led them into a bedroom and stepped away. Luciana lay on her bed with her eyes partially closed, holding a framed photo of Alejandro to her chest. Her body stilled and her bottom lip quivered. A small television rested on top of a large cabinet with a cast iron bookshelf on the side. A set of tables nestled opposite the bed.

When Luciana saw Ricardo and Kim, she rushed into his waiting arms, crying as Kim looked on. "He's dead. My brother's dead, Ricardo."

He stroked the back of her head and frowned in Kim's direction. "I am so sorry, sweetie. So sorry." He pulled away from her. "This is a shock to all of us, Luciana."

She stared over at Kim who pulled into her embrace too. "I am sorry too."

Luciana sniffed and wiped at her eyes then broke apart. "I miss him." She whimpered and fell back down on the bed, staring into space. "Who did this to my brother, Ricardo? Who?"

He joined her on the edge of the bed while Kim looked on. "I wish I knew, but I am sure the police will find out who did this."

Her eyes were red with tears. "Do you think so?" Her chin wobbled and her body shook.

Ricardo nodded. "I know so."

He vowed to get this bastard, even if it was over his own dead body.

Chapter 37

CONDOLENCES

Kim lay in bed that night, watching Blanca and Daniela's wide eyes on her laptop as she explained her perilous situation since her arrival in Patones. It had been a week since Alejandro had died and her chest still ached at his loss. He should have had the opportunity to get married and have children. He should have had a future. If only he had approached Ricardo earlier.

"Kim, you need to come home. It is not safe there," said Blanca.

She shook her head. "I wish I could come home, but I need to see this through. I need Ricardo's help to find out what happened to Manuel. He believes it is not safe for me to leave. That I might still be a target."

"Understandable," said Daniela. "Given he's ex-police, but are you guys any closer to finding out who killed

Manuel? Do you think it's all connected to this poor boy, Alejandro, or your attack?"

Kim shrugged. "I have no doubt, Daniela. But I wish I knew who shot that man who tried to kill me. Was it someone from the drug cartel, or a vigilante?"

"Oh, girl. I hope you guys find out the truth, but you need to be extra careful. Don't go anywhere on your own. Where's Ricardo now?" said Daniela.

"He's in bed, obviously taking it hard after Alejandro died. I'm giving him his space."

Blanca spoke up. "I wonder if whoever killed that man in the park might have been covering his tracks. I know it's hard to hear, Kim, but these groups can be ruthless. If you even stare at them funny, they can hurt you. You need to make sure Ricardo's with you at all times until this is done. Do you hear me?"

She nodded. "Yes. Ricardo is always with me." Looking over her shoulder at the idea that Ricardo might want to talk about his pain, she resigned herself to the fact that he wasn't an emotional kind of guy. He would want to deal with it on his own, and she'd respect that. "I have started teaching meditation and yoga classes at the hotel. If I don't work, I will go crazy thinking about the drug cartel."

"Of course, but I do worry. Please stay safe," said Blanca. "Sofia and Eva say hi and will speak to you soon."

"Wait," said Daniela. "Can I ask you a personal question?"

Kim angled her head. "Of course."

Daniela said, "About Ricardo? How do you feel about him?"

She hesitated, wondering how much to reveal. "Ricardo has been amazing." Her heart warmed at the way he held her tight, and the softness in his eyes when he noticed her tears. She was getting more attached to him each day, and it concerned her.

Daniela grinned. "Ooh, young love. It sounds like you're falling for the guy. Are you?"

Blanca shoved Daniela on the shoulder. "Oh, leave the woman alone. She has enough on her mind without complicating it with romance."

Daniela waved a hand. "I am only curious, Kim. How do you feel about Ricardo?"

Kim cleared her throat, feeling her cheeks redden. "I like him, but we are friends. Nothing more. He has issues, and I cannot possibly get involved with Manuel's brother. It would not be right."

"Love has no rationale to it, Kim," said Daniela.

Kim drew back. "Who said anything about love?" She refused to fall for a man who was over an hour away from where she lived. Long-distance relationships never worked. *Crazy!*

"Have you at least kissed the guy?" asked Daniela.

Kim's spine tingled at the thought of their last kiss. "We might have kissed once."

Daniela leaned forward. "Do tell."

Blanca chuckled. "I think Daniela's more excited than you are. Rafael's in Barcelona on a story at the moment, so she needs to live vicariously through your romance."

"There is no romance, Blanca." Kim started yawning, remembering that Ricardo had plans for tomorrow. "Listen, I need to get some sleep. I will be in touch."

"Keep us in the loop," said Daniela.

"We love you, Kim. If there is anything you need, please let us know," said Blanca.

"Bye. Love you both," said Kim.

Kim put aside her laptop and lay in bed. She stared at the locket on her dressing table, hanging over the jewellery box. A part of her felt guilty for having the locket, given to her by one man when she cared for another. But she couldn't bring herself to get rid of the locket with its shiny gold and intricate patterns over the heart.

Later, she tossed and turned in bed, until a crashing sound made her sit up. She rose and pulled on a dressing gown from the nearby chair.

Ricardo stormed into her room. "Kim, are you all right?"

She nodded. "Yes, but I heard a noise."

"Wait here. I'll go and check in the back. I lined up some old glasses as an alarm if someone was sneaking around at night."

"Good idea. But I am coming with you," said Kim.

"Stay behind me." Kim followed him through the back door and down the steps. "No one's here." He bent down to where the stack of glasses lay unbroken. "The glasses are intact, too, so it could have been an animal."

Walking back inside, he led her to the kitchen. "Care for a glass of water?"

"Okay. Thanks."

Ricardo filled up a glass of water and as she moved closer to him, he turned abruptly, and knocked into her. The water dripped down her open cleavage in her nightgown. "I am so sorry, Kim." He grabbed a tea towel and handed it to her.

"It's fine. It will dry." She turned away to dab her chest. The way he stared at her cleavage was too much to bear, and she wanted to kiss him.

Hot damn! The way her flimsy nightgown barely covered her slim body aroused him like never before. Even his ex-fiancée hadn't spurred such a strong reaction in him. He yearned to take her in the kitchen and make love to her, nice and slow.

The way she moistened her lip with her tongue when she was nervous. The way she blushed in embarrassment, and how her body shivered when he stared at her cleavage. It was too much and damn his mind for thinking this was all wrong. That she would hurt him just like his late fiancée. Why couldn't they share one special night without getting the mind involved? What harm would one night be? They could get it out of their system and that would be that. No harm, no foul. One night of pure bliss without having to follow rules or obligations. Only pure indulgence of the flesh. Nothing more, nothing less.

Kim turned around and refilled her glass. He watched her drink it down until she rinsed out her glass and placed it on the dish rack. "Would you like water?" she asked. He shook his head, mesmerized by her beauty, the reflection of the moonlight outside adding to it. The scent of her floral perfume was heady as he took a step towards her. Their eyes locked and she swallowed, then pressed her lips together.

Ricardo inched forward, drew a lock of hair away from her eyes and kissed her. Gently at first, then with a deep hunger, parting her lips with his tongue. The taste of her was minty and fresh, and he wrapped his arms around her tightly as she reciprocated and caressed his upper back.

He broke away from her and pulled her by the hand, her eyes inviting him to take her into his bedroom. Before laying her gently on the bed, he opened his top drawer and drew out a condom, then lay down beside her and met her lips again, sweeping his tongue in and out of her mouth. He couldn't get enough of her as his lips trailed the side of her neck, her moans arousing him further. Her nails scraped his upper back until reaching lower down and pressing into the top of his buttocks.

He glided his hands through her glossy hair as he delved deeper into her mouth, their bodies pressed closely together and moving in a gentle rhythm until his hands trailed in between her thighs, inserting a finger over her wet panties. He pulled them down as he kissed the centre of her chest, and lifted her nightgown, smoothing his hands over one breast and then the other. He kissed one erect nipple, devoured the other, savouring her moans and writhing. He trailed his lips down to her abdomen then back up to her jawline, his fingers probing her mound while kissing her hungrily again.

He pulled off his own pants and underwear, wrapped the condom around his penis, and guided himself gently inside of her, the heat making his whole body sweat. Her head fell back as he took her breast back into his mouth, their bodies moving in unison as he stroked her back and caressed her inner thighs. Their eyes locked as they voiced their desires while pushing himself further inside her, devouring her slick heat and planting his hands around her back. He captured her face in his hands as she closed her eyes, reciprocating his kiss. "I need you." he said.

Riding her faster, he was close to coming as she writhed even more and met his kiss with even more hunger and need. The strong friction between their naked bodies felt like an electric shock as he shuddered with a climax, followed by Kim's own blissful end.

She pressed close to him, and they fell asleep in each other's arms.

Chapter 38

SEEKING ANSWERS

The next morning, Kim slowly opened her eyes. She remembered her sensual night with Ricardo and turned. His side of the bed was empty. But what did she expect? It wasn't like they were a couple. Simply one night of mistaken abandon without thinking about the consequences. She wasn't surprised he'd left her bed when sex had occurred on impulse. Neither of them had been thinking straight, and despite the way he made her feel, she had to put it out of her mind and focus on the reason for her visit here. Getting justice for Manuel, and now for Alejandro. That had to be their priority. Not their whims or desires.

She stepped into the ensuite shower, the sprinkles of hot water soothing her aching shoulders and pelvis. They had made love several times last night, and in a range of positions that had her wanting more. But it had been nothing more than fun. Despite needing and wanting to experience that feeling again, she knew it was best they stayed apart. Ricardo was still grieving for Alejandro, and no doubt that had factored into reaching for her last night. Her chest tightened at the thought, and she fought against amorous desires.

Slipping on loose pants and a woollen jumper, she left her room to face the man who had fulfilled her desires last night. She heard clanking pots and pans as she approached the kitchen with hesitant steps. Her heart raced, knowing they would both feel awkward this morning, but one look at the man before her made her shoulders slump.

Angel! "What are you doing here? Where is Ricardo?"

He put the frying pan down. "Good morning, Kim. He had an errand to run and called me to watch you. He shouldn't be too long."

She hid her disappointment. "What errand?"

"He mentioned something about collecting some of Alejandro's belongings from the club to give to his family."

Kim nodded, then sat at the table while Angel pushed a plate of bacon and eggs in her direction, with a side of toast. "Thank you, Angel. It smells great."

"Eat up. You will need your energy for all that is happening." He frowned. "Again, I am so sorry about Alejandro. How are you?"

She picked up her fork. "I am fine, but worried about Ricardo. He was angry yesterday and vowed to get justice for Alejandro."

"Understandable." Angel sat opposite her, ate a piece of bacon and sipped orange juice. "What would you like to drink?"

She put up a hand. "It's fine. I will grab a drink later." She looked up at him. "I wanted to ask you about Sara from the club. What happened to her father?"

Angel tilted his head. "He was arrested for abandonment and neglect. The man was involved in other matters, too. Nothing I can share with you, naturally."

Kim bit into her toast, dipped the rest into the eggs and enjoyed the saltiness and warmth of the food. "Ricardo never mentioned why Alejandro was killed. Was he in trouble?"

Angel looked into the distance, his eyes unreadable. "He was selling drugs, but the latest stash he threw down the sink."

She put a hand over her mouth. "No. How could such an innocent boy get involved in drugs? He was only fifteen. Only a monster could get a child involved in that."

"Agreed, but I wanted to ask you about whether you have seen Alejandro talking to any strangers at the club or anyone he might have been close to. It is a matter of their safety."

"I've only been there a few times, but he was always talking to other teenagers." A lightbulb went on. "That girl who stabbed him. Could she have shot him?"

Angel shrugged. "We believe it's someone else, but he's in hiding." He looked away from her for a moment. "We won't give up until we find him."

Kim remembered visiting Hugo a few days earlier when he had finally woken up and was on the mend. "What is the story with Hugo?"

His eyes turned serious. "All I can explain is that the man has been charged with a crime. He will be discharged from the hospital tonight."

Kim's body shook, refusing to believe he would commit any crime. "What did he do?"

"I cannot tell you that, Kim. You know that."

She frowned. "I understand." Her eyes shifted. "What about Manuel's killer? Do you have any leads?"

"We might be making progress and will let you know in due course." His phone buzzed and he answered it. "Right. Okay. I will be there shortly." He looked over at Kim. "Sorry. I need to go, but I will bring you with me. You can wait at the station until Ricardo can pick you up."

"I will be fine here. Please go."

Angel looked confused. "I don't know. Ricardo will hate me for leaving you alone. Come with me."

She put up a hand. "I will be fine. I plan to go to the hotel and teach a yoga class. I won't be far behind you. Now, go and do your job. You need to get to the truth, Angel."

He stood up and placed the dishes in the sink. "Are you sure?"

"Yes. Thank you." Angel smiled before walking out the door. Through the window, she watched him drive off, grabbed her own keys from the hook in the kitchen, picked up her bag and headed out. It was time she started getting answers.

Kim walked into the ward, stopping for a moment to watch Hugo sleeping with his hands cuffed to the bed. *What had he done?* She needed to talk to the man and get to the truth. She had to find out whether he knew anything about Manuel or Alejandro.

Waiting for him to wake up, she sat and scrolled through her phone. A text message from Ricardo popped up. *Will be home in twenty minutes.* She wouldn't be there, as she could no longer sit on the side-lines and do nothing about this situation. The police didn't appear to be getting answers, so she had to do her own work. She couldn't let whoever killed Manuel and Alejandro get away with it.

Kim flashed back to her attack near the club, when she felt sure she would be killed. The memory brought her back to another time, another place.

Knocking on the door of Manuel's apartment, she perked up at the idea of seeing the man she loved. The door swung open and Manuel stared at her with glassy, red eyes, his legs unsteady. "Manuel. Are you okay?" Was he high?

He nodded with a smirk. "Come in."

She hesitated, wondering if it was a good idea. But she had to make sure he was all right and would not hurt himself. It was her duty as his girlfriend to help him refrain from drug use. It had to stop. "I will make you coffee." She closed the door behind her.

Manuel licked his lips, his eyes fixed on her, scanning her from head to toe. Inching towards her, he flicked her hair out of her eyes, touched her roughly on the shoulders and kissed her hard, his tongue flicking in and out of her mouth. She pushed him away, but this seemed to encourage him further. He pushed her against the couch and straddled her, his arms locking her in place.

She gasped, shaking her head, a prickle of unease running down her spine. "No, Manuel, please. Stop this. You are not well."

His glare intensified and he slapped her hard across the face. She cried out in pain and shoved him hard with her hands, but he was too strong. His body pushed against hers as he ripped open her shirt and pushed his hands hard against her breast. "Fuckin bitch. You're mine, and I have needs."

"No, please get off me, Manuel. This is not you. Please." Streams of tears poured down her cheeks. She pushed up her knees but he held her down, his head moving down her chest as he licked the middle of her chest. Lifting her bra, he fingered her nipples. She could barely breathe as he undid his zipper with his free hand.

He was not going to take her by force. She had to do something. Her decision made, she plunged a fingernail into his eye and he winced in pain.

But that angered him further. He placed his hands around her neck and squeezed. Kim gasped for air, watching him in terror as his eyes glazed over, as if he was in another world.

Twisting her body, she brought her right arm around and punched him in the side of the head. His grip loosened for a few seconds, so she pushed him away and kicked him hard in the back. "Bitch!"

She opened the door and ran out without looking back.

Kim brought herself back to the present, her body cold from the memory. After the attempted rape, she'd broken off her relationship with Manuel and refused to accept his apology the next day. He explained how he'd taken methamphetamine and was not himself. He mentioned he would attend a private rehabilitation facility, but he never did.

Not long after that incident, Manuel was arrested for drug possession and received treatment in prison. This hard life had forced him to change and eventually work with the police, culminating in his death.

Despite her calm nature, Kim had a deep fighting spirit which would only be used when needed. Most of the time, she didn't need it. Her rigid upbringing caused her to find inner control even if she didn't have external control. But a part of her always felt unworthy, especially because of her mother's incessant criticisms growing up. Her parents had always judged her in everything she did, saying that not following their rules meant she was dishonouring the family. They did not approve of Manuel, and in that case they were right. She had been on a roller coaster with him, and in the end, love was not enough.

She broke out of her reverie when Hugo opened his eyes. "Kim?"

She brought the chair closer to him. "How are you feeling?"

He sighed. "Better every day." He looked at his cuffs. "I am sure you've heard I've been arrested." He turned away as if ashamed, but was it an act or was he innocent?

"Why were you arrested?"

Hugo shook his head. "I have never sold drugs to anyone, Kim. I might be having financial issues, but I would never resort to illegal activity. I've been set up. It's exactly what I told the police. You have to believe me."

Kim lifted her shoulders. "Do you know who would set you up?"

He shrugged. "Not really."

"What do you mean?"

Hugo shifted in bed and lifted his body higher. He motioned to the jug of water, and Kim poured him a glass and gave it to him. He drank, then handed it back to her. "Sara's father, Andres is one possibility. He is part of the cartel, which is why he'd often go on jobs and leave his kids alone. The day I meant to visit him was the day my car broke down. The only reason I suspect him is that he wasn't happy that I rang him and said that Sara would be removed from his care. He is getting his revenge, and I believe he somehow planted a stash of drugs in my home. Or at least ordered someone to do it. His wife was the one who encouraged Sara to be a part of the club and sports. She is no longer around."

"What happened to his wife?"

His eyes darkened. "She died in a car accident."

"Where does Sara live? Is she still at home?"

Hugo angled his head. "Don't get involved, Kim. This is too dangerous."

She exhaled. "I only want to talk to Sara. Nothing more than that. I can make sure she is doing all right."

Hugo relented. "Her grandmother arrived from San Sebastian. I believe she is planning to take the children back home with her once they've had the court case for her father. It could take weeks, though."

"I need the address, Hugo." She handed him a sticky note and he scrawled an address. Kim sensed that Sara might have picked up on things with her father.

Chapter 39

A YOUNG MIND

Kim parked at the kerb and scrolled past a notification on her phone; another text from Ricardo. He had arrived home and wondered where she was. She texted back, "I had to take care of something. Will explain later. Sorry."

Expelling her breath, she stepped out of the car and cringed at the sight of the dilapidated roof with loose tiles, paint-chipped window frames, and overgrown garden. She walked up the uneven paved pathway to the weathered timber door. She hugged her body against the chilly winter wind and knocked on the door. She rehearsed in her mind what she would say as she waited.

A short, petite woman with a greyish tinge in her light brown hair, tied up in a bun, opened the door. She angled her head. "Can I help you?"

"Yes, hello. My name is Kim and I am from the youth club Sara attends. Is she home?"

The woman's eyes lit up. "Oh, yes. Sara has spoken kindly about you. I'm Martina, Sara's grandmother. Please come inside. You'll catch your death of cold out there."

"Thank you." Kim entered, the dank smell making her wince as she followed Martina into the kitchen and seated herself at a round table scattered with dirty dishes.

Martina picked up the plates and placed them into the sink. "Can I get you a drink, a cup of coffee or tea perhaps?"

"No, thank you. I won't be staying long."

"Sara's in the shower so she'll be here in a moment. The twins are still sleeping for now." Martina knit her brows. "Was there anything in particular you wished to speak to my granddaughter about?"

Kim took a breath, her eyes roaming to the large window covered with a stained lace curtain above the sink, letting through a tad a little sunlight from behind the grey clouds. "I wanted to see how she was doing after what happened with her father. It has been all over the news."

Martina put a hand over her chest, her eyes misting. "My poor Sara had to take care of her twin siblings all on her own because my son-in-law could not do the right thing and get help for them. After my daughter died, he got involved in shady things, and would get calls all through the night asking him to go to work. But what kind of employer doesn't let you have your rest in the night and calls you at midnight or at three in the morning?"

"I am sorry for what Sara has gone through. If only she explained earlier what was happening."

"A matter of pride. She is stoic and doesn't like to rely on anyone, but as soon as I heard that that horrible man was arrested for dealing with drugs, I came straight away. I will stay until the trial then take the children home with me in San Sebastian. It is best that way. It is not safe for them to stay here."

"Why? Has anything happened since his arrest?"

Martina shrugged. "I wouldn't know, but Sara might tell you more. She has chosen to remain quiet, but she respects you and might tell you what has happened."

Kim clasped her hands together, her body filling with unease. If only she had realised what Sara had been going through. But then again, it wasn't as if she had been a part of this world after breaking up with Manuel.

Sara shuffled into the kitchen, baby blue eyes lighting up and a huge grin on her face as she bent down to hug Kim. "Oh, what a surprise." She threaded her hands through her dirty-blonde hair.

"Hello, Sara."

Martina got up. "I will give you two privacy." Kim nodded.

Sara took a glass from the low cupboard beside the sink and filled it from a bottle of orange juice in the refrigerator. Sitting opposite Kim, she sipped her drink and wiped her mouth with the back of her hand.

"How have you been, Sara?"

The girl shrugged, her bottom lip quaking. "I'm okay. Can't say the same about my dad. He is in big trouble and may not come home."

"I am sorry about that. Is there anything I can do?"

She looked past her. "No, my grandma is very nice and helps me. I don't have to look after the twins anymore. That means I get to spend more time on my schoolwork. But I can't come back to the club. I will be leaving soon."

"Your grandmother mentioned that."

"Will you be going back to Madrid or staying here?" said Sara.

Kim smiled. "I will return to Madrid soon, but I will be here for a while." They discussed her schoolwork, her hobbies, and the chilly weather until Sara blurted something that shocked Kim. "What did you say?" she asked.

"My father was scared of his friends. Said they were not nice people. I know he had drugs in the house, and I found them in his backpack one day. I asked him about it, but he said it was a special flour for one of his customers. He worked in a bakery sometimes, but other times, he did different things."

"What other things did he do? Did you see anything unusual, or did he say something?"

She nodded. "I heard him arguing with another man one night outside my bedroom door. It was midnight and they woke me up." She exhaled. "The voices were hard to understand, but I heard the man say something about drug dealers getting punished. That he is the boss of them. My father just said yes, but I could hear in his voice how scared he was, Kim. He didn't like his friends." She rubbed her stream of tears. "I know he didn't want to be doing this kind of work. He loved us."

Kim leaned forward and held her hand, stroking it. "I am sure he will be fine." Sara's eyes darkened as she remained silent. "Was there anything else you heard or saw?"

Sara shook her head. "My Papa tried with us. He didn't mean to leave me with the twins. He was more scared of these men than leaving us alone. He knew I could do it."

Kim's chest tightened at the idea of Sara being exposed to this kind of world. She wondered whether her father had managed Alejandro. "You have been very brave, Sara.

It is amazing that you have your grandmother looking after you. I will miss you when you leave."

Sara got up and wrapped her arms around Kim again. "I will miss you, too. Can you come visit us in San Sebastian one day?"

She nodded as they separated. "Of course. I will get the address from your grandmother. Can you call her?" Sara nodded and walked off, returning with Martina.

"You're leaving?" asked Martina.

Kim smiled. "Yes, but before I go, can I get your address? I would like to visit after you've settled in."

"Of course, dear." Martina dug around a drawer, picked up a notebook and scribbled down the address. "Here you go."

Kim took the note. "Thank you. I had better leave." She faced Sara. "You take care of yourself, Sara. It was nice to meet you, Martina. I will be in touch." She waved goodbye, then walked outside.

As she entered her car, she got the feeling she was being watched. Her eyes roamed in front and behind, but it was deserted. She was being paranoid. No one knew she was here.

Chapter 40

INTIMACY

Ricardo paced the floor and kept looking at his phone. *Where the hell is she?* She knew better than to go anywhere on her own when she might still be a target. He could have killed Angel for leaving her by herself, but then again, she must have convinced him somehow to leave her to her own devices.

If anything happened to Kim, he would never forgive himself. He could not go through all that again. He refused to have history repeat itself.

He moved to the couch, rummaging under the cushions for the remote. TV would distract him until she returned home, but if she didn't answer in another half an hour, he would ring the police.

He flipped past a few channels but before he could settle on a show, the purring of an engine outside got his attention. He stood and faced the door with his arms crossed.

His mind turned to their love-making last night, and a part of him felt guilty for leaving her so early in the morning, but he couldn't face her again so soon. It would have been awkward for them both. Instead of getting her out of his system, he yearned for more.

The way she touched him in all the right places, the immense look of desire on her face, and her sexy moans had aroused him even further. He couldn't get her out of his mind all day and missed her like crazy. But right now, she had to explain herself.

Kim opened the front door and stopped when she saw Ricardo glaring. "Hi."

Ricardo glared. "Where the hell were you? I told you not to go anywhere on your own. You do know how damn dangerous it is right now, don't you?"

Kim huffed. "I went to see Sara. I was worried about her."

He stood inches from her face. "Bullshit. You wanted answers and you figured she'd have them. Did she?" He wouldn't get distracted by her fresh, minty scent or the calming sound of her breath.

"I found out a few things. The police don't seem to be getting any answers."

He scoffed. "Damn it, Kim! You cannot do that again or I'll send you straight back to Madrid. I rang Angel and he said you convinced him to leave. Why would you be so bloody stupid? Do you think this is a game? Do you think you can meditate your way out of this, or perhaps strike a yoga pose to protect yourself? This is the drug cartel we're talking about. It's not a game."

Kim's chest thrust out, her nostrils suddenly flaring. "How dare you make me feel like a helpless victim? Why belittle me and my work? I thought you respected me, but you obviously don't."

"Oh, get over it! I was making a joke, but if you want to be so sensitive about it, then fine. That's your problem, not mine."

Kim took a step back and made her way up the stairs. "I refuse to talk to you when you are this angry. I will let you calm down then we can have a civil, adult conversation."

Ricardo grabbed her firmly by the arm, but Kim used her other arm to push him away. "Oh, no you don't. We are having a conversation and now is as good a time as any. I want to know why you risked your life for the sake of answers. You should have waited for me."

Kim stilled, her eyes meeting his. "What is wrong with you? I can't be here as a prisoner. If I knew this would happen, I would have already been in Madrid. I can take care of myself, so take away your patriarchal attitude and leave me alone."

He shook his head. "Don't you know that if anything ever happened to you, I would never forgive myself. I care...damn it. Just don't do it again."

Kim's eyes softened. "You care about me. Is that it?" She swallowed. "I find that hard to believe when you decided to leave me in bed alone. How do you think that made me feel? I don't sleep with just anyone, Ricardo. I have morals and I thought..." She bowed her head. "Never mind."

He noticed she was fighting back tears, and in that moment, he felt like a jerk, a bastard. What she must have thought when he left her alone. He didn't mean to make her feel cheap. What they did last night was special. "Oh, Kim. I am sorry. I needed time to think and I wondered if it would be awkward between us. But last night was special. You're special, Kim." He squinted. "My fiancée was killed by her ex-boyfriend because I threatened him. Things escalated and he killed her. It was reckless, I know."

"I am sorry, Ricardo. But that wasn't your fault."

As their eyes locked, Ricardo drew a hand across her cheek and caressed it while Kim closed her eyes, savouring his touch. Without thought, he leaned in and mashed his lips against hers. His hands trailed the back of her head as he plunged deeply into her mouth. She tasted so good.

He pushed her back to the couch and she followed his lead as she lay down. He gently lay on top of her, undoing her buttons and nibbling around her ear, then trailing his mouth down to one breast while kneading the other. Undoing her bra, he fingered her erect nipples while she moaned and pressed hard into the small of his back. His hands travelled down to her inner thighs. He needed to undress her, so he unbuttoned her jeans and pulled them down. Next came her lacy underwear, pulling them off easily while kissing between her breasts. Kim caressed his penis gently and he worked hard to not climax until she did. "I want you to come for me, Kim. Let me hear you come."

He stroked her clitoris and watched her eyes close in desire, her head tilted back. He loved the way she licked her lips in arousal and the soft moans that escalated as he quickened his fingers, probing and pushing them inside her, savouring the feel of her wetness. "Oh, you are killing me, Ricardo." She shifted her body, twisting, turning, her hand threaded through her hair. He was so excited, watching her desire.

Eventually climaxing, Kim opened her eyes. Her fingers reached for his jeans and underpants, pulling them off while she wrestled inside his mouth with her tongue, hungering for more as she deepened their kiss.

He wriggled out of his jeans and shirt and dug a thumb into her mouth, which she sucked and licked. She fondled his bare manhood until he grew even more erect, then guided it gently inside her, getting into a slow rhythm while pressing his fingers into her soft buttocks. He moved his body up and down as their bodies lay pressed tightly against one another's until they matched each other's arousal. A few minutes later, they screamed out in climactic bliss. Ricardo knew in that moment, he was totally and deeply in love with her. But would it be enough?

Chapter 41

INSTINCT

K im opened her eyes, wincing at the sight of Ricardo staring at her. "Morning." She couldn't describe her senses, overwhelmed with attraction towards Ricardo. That was all this was. Pure attraction and lust. Nothing more.

"Morning, beautiful." He leaned forward and kissed her tenderly on the lips, his hand feathering one of her breasts.

Kim pulled his hand away. "Don't you think we have had enough for one night? You need to get to work, and I have a yoga class to teach."

He smirked. "You are right. But first things first." He sat up in bed and picked up her hand. "You never told me what happened with Sara yesterday. What did you find out?"

Kim explained her conversation with Sara and Martina. "I wonder if there's a connection to Alejandro."

He pressed his lips together, his eyes staring past her. "Good news. Angel rang earlier this morning. He arrested the people who gave Alejandro the drugs to sell. The ones who worked with Arturo. But they're still searching for him."

"That is progress. Hopefully they can give clues as to his location. How long have you been awake?"

He shrugged. "An hour or so, mainly talking to Angel and watching you sleep. Oh, and I managed to have a shower, but I thought we could have one together before we start the day. It's still early."

Kim chuckled. "Okay. "He put his arms under her and carried her into the bathroom, where he stripped off her nightgown and undressed himself. Turning on the taps, he entered the shower and Kim joined him under the warm water. He soaped her around her breasts and arms, and down to her belly. When he reached between her thighs, she leaned her head back and enjoyed the sensation.

Putting away the soap, Ricardo knelt, his hands reaching for her breasts as he bent down to kiss her abdomen, trailing his tongue around the curve of her hips, brushing his hands over her thighs, and spreading her legs even more. His mouth reached her mound, his tongue probing and pushing hard against her clitoris. She lifted her head back and closed her eyes, moaning in a heated frenzy. The arousal was out of this world.

She lay a gentle hand on his head to prod him further as his tongue kept tantalising her, enjoying her as if she were his last meal. He pushed two fingers inside her, then replaced the fingers with his tongue as his breath aired her mound. He dug his tongue deeper inside her, his hands holding tight around her legs which were unsteady. "Oh, Ricardo." She loved the flick of his tongue penetrating her private part, his muscular hands pressing hard against her legs as his own guttural sounds was music to her ears. Did she love the man? No, she was only in the throes of passion and wasn't thinking sensibly.

Kim was short of breath as she threaded her hands through his hair, motioning him deeper inside her as she climaxed.

Ricardo stood up and kissed her hard; she tasted herself on his lips. Knowing she was wet and ready, Ricardo brushed a hair strand out of her eye. He pushed himself inside her and they fell into a rhythm until they screamed out in bliss. Who would have thought she'd climax a second time in such a short period?

Later that day, Ricardo sat at his desk, thinking about making love with Kim. He couldn't focus on anything else.

She was teaching her yoga class on the grounds outside the hotel while he was failing to work. He couldn't get enough of the beautiful woman and wondered how challenging it would be once she returned to Madrid. They couldn't have a life together when they lived in two parts of Spain, but they could enjoy each other now.

He thought about what Kim had told her about Sara's father, Andres. Could he have had something to do with Alejandro's death? As a father himself, could Andres kill a young teenager in cold blood without thinking about how this would affect his parents? Or was it someone else from his group, such as Arturo?

He turned to his computer to search for information about Andres' arrest. A few articles came up, showing photos of Andres covering his face with his hands to ward off reporters. In the background of one of the photos, he spotted someone familiar. He leaned forward, closer to the screen and realised who it was. The police officer who had guarded them not long after Kim arrived. Officer Fuentes. He would have thought nothing of it, given he might have been one of the arresting officers, but in the photo, he whispered in Andres' ear. What was that about? They appeared almost friendly, as if they knew each other. Were they friends or was it purely Fuentes telling him something trivial, such as *you're in big trouble*.

He retrieved his car keys and walked to the underground car park. Getting into his car, he wondered if researching this police officer might lead to sinister results. It was worth a try. He had to get answers, and if this man was corrupt, he had to bring him down.

But he was not surprised. This happened all the time in law enforcement. Now even Hugo had been arrested while protesting his innocence. Ricardo didn't want to believe his friend was guilty, but he might've been framed by Andres. After what Hugo had said about Sara's situation, it was reasonable to expect Andres would want vengeance on Hugo.

He went to the dilapidated local police station and stopped at the front counter, manned by an elderly officer. "I am here to see Officer Fuentes. Is he in?"

The desk officer nodded. "What is this about, sir?"

Ricardo touched the base of his throat. He didn't want to give anything away, but had to find out whether Fuentes was hiding a secret. His hunch told him it was all connected. "It's a matter I can only discuss with him."

"Take a seat." Ricardo headed over to the waiting area, glancing at the others seated around, some of whom looked back with glazed eyes

Five minutes later, he heard a voice. "Mr Perez?" Officer Fuentes called out. "Come on through."

Ricardo nodded and followed him down a narrow walkway for a few minutes until reaching his open-plan office. Cluttered files stacked on top of one another with strewn newspaper articles and stationery scattered from one corner of the desk to the other. A half-finished cup of coffee and glass of water sat in the middle of the desk. "What brings you by, Mr Perez?" The man fiddled with his collar.

"I know you work closely with Angel. He's been a bit strict with my involvement in all these cases. I thought I could get you to sway him a little so I can get more involved."

Officer Fuentes frowned. "I have minimal power here, Mr Perez. I don't see how I can convince Angel to do anything of the sort."

"Please call me Ricardo." The man toyed with his collar again, and Ricardo assumed he was getting nervous. "Listen, I have the feeling that someone on the inside is involved in this mess. With Alejandro. I know he flushed the drugs down the sink and cost the cartel a huge sum of money. I believe that's why he was killed." He had to test the man to see if he'd react to his next comment. "I think there's a traitor on the inside."

The man averted his eyes, his body stiffening. "I cannot assume anything at this point, and you might be working as a consultant, but you have limitations. If you need answers, please talk to the Captain."

"I understand, and I will. But I just wanted your take on whether you feel there might be a traitor either in the police force or the Civil Guard. Someone who's getting a cut of the money from the drugs. I assume you have an opinion."

The officer stood, shuffling papers around his desk and putting loose documents into an in-tray, lining them up neatly. "I believe we are done here, Mr Perez. I have to ask you to kindly leave the premises. This is above my pay grade, and I can get into a lot of trouble by even giving you my opinion. Please leave."

Ricardo noticed his eye ticking and his face turning a beetroot red. The man was obviously hiding something, and he knew exactly what he had to do. "I apologise if I overstepped, but I will talk to Angel about this, too." The officer stayed silent, and rushed out of the room. Ricardo followed him. "Thanks for your..." But the officer had already stormed away. "...time," he finished.

Ricardo returned to his car and drove a few hundred metres away. He stopped, watching his rear-view mirror. Surely, if the officer was running scared, he'd meet up with someone.

Alert to his surroundings, he quickly scrolled through his phone and checked his mirrors again. Nothing. No one was leaving. But it was too soon. He could tell that Fuentes was getting nervous in the room, and he had to be hiding something. Usually in cases where a problem occurred, a member of the cartel would meet to discuss a solution to the problem. If someone was asking questions, they would want to tie up loose ends. Ricardo would be a loose end in their eyes.

His phone buzzed. "Yes, Mariana. What is it?"

"Sorry to disturb you, and I know you've taken some time off, but I need you to sign off on supplies for a few rooms on the first floor."

He huffed. "It will have to wait. I'm running an errand at the moment and should be in a bit later today. Put it in my in-tray and I will get to it."

"Okay. Thanks, Ricardo." He ended the call and shook his head as he turned around with Fuentes still in the building. *Damn!* Where was this guy? Surely, he'd be meeting with someone. He was definitely lying about something.

Leaning back against the seat, he closed his eyes briefly before checking his mirrors again. An image of Kim flashed in his mind. He became aroused thinking of the slim outline of her body and the softness of her smooth skin. Even remembering how she tasted on his lips, and the sexy moans coming from her mouth as he devoured her body in every way possible. Now he'd had a taste of her body, he wanted more. Needed more. But this was crazy. He was bound to hurt her or get her killed just like his fiancée and he didn't want to risk her life. She was better off without him.

Besides, she lived in Madrid, which was a long way to be commuting for a relationship. Not that they were in an official relationship, but he would have to set her straight and explain how he wasn't thinking when he'd made love to her. She would most likely feel the same. But then again, could he hurt her that way?

Shifting in his seat half an hour later, he was about to start the motor, thinking he didn't have time for this when a flash of movement caught his eye. But his shoulders slumped when he realised it was a pair of officers he didn't recognize, stepping into a police vehicle and driving off. He started the motor and shifted into Drive when Fuentes walked out of the building and looked around. Ricardo slid down in his seat to avoid detection and put the car

in Park again. What was Fuentes doing, standing outside
with his arms crossed? Waiting for someone?

Ricardo raised his body slightly to look behind him. A
black station wagon pulled up to the kerb beside Fuentes,
who quickly got into the back seat. The driver sped off and
Ricardo followed.

Chapter 42

A LEAD

"**S**traighten that posture and take a deep breath in, and out. That's right. Nice and easy." Kim watched the group of six guests, ranging in ages from thirty to sixty, struggle to maintain their balance on top of rectangular blue mats. Not that she blamed them when they hadn't practised yoga before.

The cool breeze brushed her face and the trees waved in the distance as she closed the session with meditation. "Take a lotus position and close your eyes, focusing on your in-breath and outbreath. Good. Nice and deep, getting a sense of your position and comfort. Let it all out, easing tension." She proceeded to close her eyes and continued with her instructions as she inhaled the natural scents of oak and fern around the grounds.

When she ended the session ten minutes later she felt as if her body was floating. "Thank you for coming. I might see you next time." The guests wiped themselves with towels and waved goodbye. She picked up the mats to put them into the supply closet behind reception.

Wiping a brow with her own towel, she picked up her bag from the cupboard and rummaged for her phone. She clicked on a message from Ricardo, telling her he had an errand to run.

She sat on a chair, remembering their love-making last night. The way he made her feel when he trailed kisses around every inch of her body, and how he wanted to please her first and foremost. She loved running her hands over his biceps and feel the dip below his navel as she caressed him in places that aroused him. He wasn't afraid to voice his desire and was sensual with her in every way. What he could do with that mouth was unbelievable.

Shaking her thoughts away with flushed cheeks, Kim placed her bag strap over her shoulder and found Mariana at reception. "I will be leaving now Mariana. Thanks for your help setting this up. It wasn't a bad turn-out."

She grinned. "No worries, darl. I hope to see you back here soon. Take care."

"Thanks." Waving goodbye, she left the hotel and slid inside her car with thoughts of Ricardo floating through her mind.

She started toward Ricardo's house, hoping he would be there when she arrived. They needed to discuss what was going on between them, but how could they work it out? She lived in Madrid and he lived an hour away in the country. Did he even feel about Kim the way she felt about him? Was she falling in love with the man? No, impossible. She shook the thought out of her mind. It could never work out.

Kim unlocked the front door with the key he had given her, and headed to her room. She pulled the drawer of her dresser open a little too harshly, knocking her locket to the floor. She saw it had opened, and a small note stuck out of it. Kim sat on the edge of her bed and unfolded the note.

All it said was *Post - TorP#46*. What did that mean? But then again, why would Manuel insert the note there if it didn't mean anything? Was it even in his handwriting?

Something nagged in the back of her mind. She closed her eyes, flashing back to Manuel's last visit. He had given her this locket and was about to tell her something about it when he got that message from his boss. Too distracted, he had failed to explain more. What if it was a clue? A message he needed to relay about the cartel? She might be reading too much into this, for it could have been the previous owner who had placed the note inside it. But no, it had to be Manuel sending her a message.

Taking a deep breath, she retrieved a casual top from the drawer and changed into tracksuit pants, her mind still on the note. It mentioned the word "post," so could it be a post office box? With the letter, P, it had to be a number at the post office. But she didn't have a key so how was she meant to open the post office box? It was possible that Ricardo knew how to pick a lock in his law enforcement days. She could call him.

Kim could have kicked herself for not finding this note inside the locket sometime over the past few weeks rather than only now. But this entire case had distracted her.

She rose from the bed, picked up her phone and called Ricardo. It went to voicemail. She had to explain her find. But if she handed this over to the police, whom could she trust? What if she was digging a deeper grave when the traitor realised what she'd discovered? She pressed on Ricardo's number twice more, but he still didn't respond.

Pacing, she sighed, knowing she had to work out how to check the post office box without a key. She didn't even know where it was located. Most likely in Madrid at Manuel's local post office, but she couldn't be sure. What should she do? She sat on the floor, her back resting against the bed, and closed her eyes. She always got insights after taking stock of her emotions and thoughts, and now she needed to listen to that inner voice, the wise, knowing voice that never steered her wrong. *How to find the box and open it up.*

Kim focused on her breathing, nice and slow, her legs crossed in a lotus position, letting go of her thoughts and focusing on her anchor, her breath.

Manuel wouldn't give her a post office box without a key, so where could she find it? She opened her eyes, flashing back to his visit before her died. He had hugged her tightly and had wanted to tell her something, but held back. He might have given her a trivial statement she didn't heed, or was it something else? Didn't she wear a jacket on the day of his visit? Was it possible he had slipped the key inside her pocket?

Getting up quickly, she walked to her closet, knowing she had brought that same jacket with her to Patones. Pulling aside coat hangers, she found the jacket and rummaged inside the pockets. Sure enough, there was a key. It had to be for the post office box. But why hadn't he told her about the key?

He must have wanted to protect her and get Kim to find out for herself. He had always labelled her as smart and wise, so he must have had faith that she would figure out his clues.

Grasping her bag from the floor, she wondered about the location. It had to be in Madrid, right? Where Manuel lived? But the clue had the abbreviation, *Tor*. What if it stood for Torrelaguna, not far from where Ricardo lived? He might have been expecting Ricardo to help her out.

Manuel must have visited Torrelaguna recently to open up a post office box. As far as she knew, he had never kept one before. But it was time to visit.

Before long, the doorbell rang.

She wondered who it was. Did someone know about her locket and had come to finish her off? But would they ring the front doorbell if they wanted to hurt her?

As a precaution she got a knife from the kitchen. Gripping it tight, she swallowed, her eyes scanning behind her and in front as she crept to the window and drew open the curtain. She didn't recognise the car outside. The hair on her neck stood on end and her hand shook while holding the knife.

Opening the door a crack, she saw a flash of colour. A man. She couldn't see his face. Her hand sweated against the knife as she opened the door a little more. This man could be her attacker. She raised the knife higher, ready to strike if he was a threat. If she had to defend herself, she wouldn't hesitate to use the knife. The man wore a white jumper, bending over something on the ground. The jingle of keys resounded as he picked them up then stood up straight.

Chapter 43

DOUBTS

The man swiftly put up his hands. "Hugo?"

"Woah. Do not shoot the messenger, Kim. Put that knife down."

Kim took a breath. "I thought they arrested you."

"They let me go on account of not having enough evidence. I am here on Ricardo's orders. As I said before, I believe I was set up, Kim. By Sara's father, Andres. Ricardo thinks the same thing. Now can I please come in?"

Kim nodded and opened the door wider, closing it behind him after checking for any intruders. She somehow believed he was innocent. If Ricardo had faith in him she had to trust his intuition, knowing they had been friends for years. She placed the knife on the coffee table as he followed her to the living room. "Why did he want you to check up on me, Hugo? What is going on?"

He put his hands across his waist, walking slowly as he was still recovering. "He found out that one of the police officers might be working with Sara's father, Andres. Obviously corrupt. Ricardo wants to make sure you're protected and he trusted me enough to check in on you."

"Why can't I reach him? I tried calling but he is not answering."

Hugo stepped nearer. "He followed this police officer and has turned off his phone. In case it rings, he didn't want to make noise while watching him."

"Which police officer?"

"Officer Fuentes."

Kim's body shook. "The man who guarded this house? But he appeared to be caring, making me feel safe before he ran off that one occasion. Do you still believe it was Andres or Fuentes who set you up?"

He nodded. "It's possible." He peered past her. "Why did you raise a knife on me?"

Kim's head pounded as she realised this situation was escalating, and they were all in danger. "Do you believe Fuentes is working with someone else in the police force?"

"I guess we'll find out once Ricardo gets his intel. Let's sit down." Hugo scrutinised her. "Now answer my question."

Kim ushered him to the couch while she stood by him. She lifted her shoulders, realising she needed to confide in someone about the note. Hugo might be able to help. "Wait here." She headed upstairs, picked up the note and started walking downstairs. She stopped short at overhearing his phone conversation.

Hugo had his back to her. "I said to bloody get it done. Watch her. If it is happening, she needs to pay." He exhaled. "I don't care what you do, just do it." He ended the call then paced the floor, reaching the window to gawk outside.

Walking down the stairs, she put on a happy face while her mind ran rampant with thoughts about whether Hugo was involved with the cartel. Who had to be watched? Who needs to pay, and for what? Was it Kim or someone else?

Hugo angled his head as he returned the smile and rubbed the back of his neck as if it ached. "What did you want to show me?"

She swallowed. "Nothing. Would you like a drink?" Kim had to distract him from his former question.

Hugo nodded. "A glass of water's fine."

She made her way to the kitchen and filled up a glass of water. A part of her wasn't sure about Hugo after that phone call. He could have easily played them all. "Here you go," she said as she returned to the living room. He would know how to bypass the system, given his police and military background.

"Thanks." He retrieved the glass, scrutinising her. "What's wrong? You look nervous."

"I'm fine," she said too quickly, hoping he'd finish his drink and leave. The knife was on the coffee table, within easy access if he tried anything.

He set the glass on the table and reached into his pocket for his phone. "I'll try Ricardo again." He placed the call. "He's still not answering, obviously still keeping watch on Fuentes." Peering at his phone, he shifted his stance. Taking a step towards her, his eyes locked on hers, as if wanting to see into her soul. He reached inside his jacket. *No, did he have a gun?* Was he going to shoot her in cold blood?

Her heart raced and her hands fidgeted as she took a step back. Where was Ricardo? Was Hugo truly going to kill her? "Hugo, please."

He pulled out a handkerchief and blew his nose. "What is wrong with you?"

Kim sighed with relief and forced a smile. Her imagination was wild. "Nothing. Only nervous about this entire cartel situation."

He squinted. "I need to go. Something to do. I'm sure Ricardo will call you once he finishes."

"I know, and thanks for checking in," said Kim, as her heart pounded.

Once she locked the door behind her, Kim waited until he drove off, grabbed the key and her bag and headed out the door. She looked over her shoulder to see if she was being watched, but it appeared all clear.

Resting in the driver's seat, she closed her eyes for a few moments. When she started the engine and headed out, the bumps and hilly road brought her back to the present. The drive was quiet, and glancing in the rear-view mirror appeared quiet. She had to make sure she wasn't being followed. But was Hugo the one telling someone to keep watch on her?

Arriving at the Torrelaguna post office, Kim stepped out and dashed to the building, with passers-by surrounding her in all directions. Again, she peered over her shoulder and around the area, but nothing looked suspicious. Her heart raced and light-headedness made her unsteady on her feet. She could do this.

A long queue stood outside the post office, but luckily she didn't need to stand in the line. The post office boxes were well-aligned and all she had to do was locate number 46. Her eyes roamed for a few minutes as she looked over her shoulder, an unease prickling her spine. No one was following her.

She pushed her way forward and around the people, and spotted the number. "There's forty-six," she said to herself.

No one around even noticed what she was doing or didn't care. The queue outside got shorter, the people only staring straight ahead and not at her.

Kim walked outside a moment to get her bearings, her chest palpitating. *Get a hold of yourself. You can do this.*

The breeze scraped her skin, her heart racing and her hands dampening. How long could she stand here without being noticed? Why didn't she unlock that post office box now? *Breathe, Kim. Breathe.* She rushed back inside.

Inserting the key with a sweaty hand, she opened the door to see a large envelope. Before she panicked even further, she snatched it, scurried to her car and drove away, intermittently staring at the light package on the passenger seat.

Finally back at Ricardo's house, Kim ripped open the envelope at the kitchen table. She pulled out several pages filled with numbers. Beside the numbers were the names of businesses in Spain and South America, ranging from nightclubs to hotels, to funeral homes and research facilities. One column appeared to be the amount of profit made by these businesses over the last year on a monthly basis. Another two columns showed the actual profit, then a new amount for a range of supplies with exaggerated costs. *Obviously leading to a much higher profit margin.* These had to be the companies laundering the drug cartel's money, hiding it in so-called legitimate businesses.

Her finger landed on one listing. "This is Miguel's restaurant," she said to herself. She couldn't believe that easy-going, friendly man was involved.

Kim turned to another page which had a message written in Manuel's scrawl. Her blood boiled at the italicised writing:

A traitor in Spanish law enforcement in Madrid. Cross-communication with police members in Patones. Mystery for now.

Kim picked up the document and scanned it further. She had to get this to someone she could trust, but if she went to the police, it might end up in the wrong hands.

It was too risky to take this to a reporter, but she could talk to Ricardo. Wait and see what more he could find out. He was in law enforcement, and he'd know what to do with this information.

She took a breath. But who was this cartel member? Whom could they trust?

Kim's lips quivered as she poured water into the electric kettle and turned it on. Picking up a mug from an overhead cupboard, she added coffee and placed sugar in a bowl.

Staring at a spot on the wall, she winced at the idea that Ricardo might be in trouble. What if they found out what he was doing? But she knew he could take care of himself. He was trained for this. But if she lost him, a part of her would want to die herself. How could she not have realised earlier that she was totally in love with Ricardo. If something happened to him, she would not be able to bear it. She had lost Manuel. If Ricardo died, how could his parents cope with the loss of a second son? No, he would be all right. He could take care of himself. She had to believe in him. Surely he would find out who to trust and who not to trust.

Focusing on the present, Kim poured the boiling water into the cup and stirred. Her phone in her back pocket buzzed. Picking it up, she looked at the display. *Ricardo.*

Chapter 44

CAPTURED

Ricardo bent down low as he stood behind a large oil barrel, peeking on the side as Officer Fuentes approached a tall man who was holding a clipboard. When he turned around, his shoulder-length, dirty-blonde hair swayed. In a corner, steel shelves held rifles, guns, coiled rope, and ammunition.

Ricardo scanned the large warehouse. Boxes stood stacked in a corner, and shelves bearing more boxes lined the walls. Under the shelves were rows of more barrels, and his stomach tightened at the thought that his brother had died in one of them. This was a policeman's dream and he had to notify the civil guard. But first he needed to apprehend and secure these two men.

He secured his grip on his gun, which he carried in the compartment. He had maintained his firearms licence, because he'd made a lot of enemies as a police detective.

Fuentes shouted. "Damn it, Luis. That bastard suspects a mole, and we have to do something about him."

Luis put up a hand and placed his clipboard down. "Hold up. That creep has no information on us, so don't worry."

Fuentes shook his head, peering behind him briefly. "If the boss finds out, we're in trouble. We need to put a stop to him. Why can't you go to his place and put a bullet in his brain, man? We don't need this shit right now, not when we've got this new shipment in a couple of days. Man, we're going to be rich, but not if that loser has anything to do with it."

"Did he give you any details, Fuentes? Does he know about our plans?"

He shrugged. "I don't think so. All he knows is there's a traitor, but what if he thinks it's me? He came by the station and looked at me in a weird way."

Luis scoffed. "Come on. If he thought it was you, he'd be all over it. Ricardo has nothing on us. No information, so he's not a threat yet. Besides, we can't do anything without the boss's approval. You know that. Keep your damn comments to yourself. Now, let's go grab some dinner, then we'll talk strategy about worst case scenarios with Mr Wise Guy."

Fuentes's shoulders relaxed. "Fine. But you're buying. I paid last time, and I'm short on cash, man."

Ricardo stood up slowly, looking through a window behind him to make sure no one else was coming by. Taking a deep breath, he ignored the erect hair on the back of his neck and the cool mist of air surrounding him. He could put an end to this once and for all.

Ricardo moved around the barrel and pointed the gun at Fuentes and Luis. "Hello, gentlemen. Nice to see you guys."

Fuentes nudged Luis, turning to him. "You idiot! I told you we should've put a bullet in his brain."

Luis shook his head. "If you had brains, you would realise that it's too damn late for that." The man swallowed. "If it isn't the man himself. What brings you by?"

Ricardo ignored him. "Fuentes." He gestured with his gun. "Get that rope from the shelf. Tie him up."

Fuentes sneered. "Make me. You won't shoot."

Ricardo knit his brows. "Try me. Now, move." Fuentes crossed his arms and stood still. Ricardo fired, hitting him in the foot. The man cursed.

"Ah, fuck! You damn bastard." He bent low, inspecting the graze, and winced.

"I said tie him up, or I'll shoot your other foot."

Luis spoke up. "You do realise you're no longer a cop. You can't detain us and you can't arrest us."

Ricardo pulled out his phone and hit speed dial. "Hello, police? I'd like to report a stash house." He recited everything he could see in the warehouse. Ending the call, he grinned at his prisoners. "You won't get away with this. Tell me who your boss is."

Fuentes scoffed as he grabbed the rope, then proceeded to tie Luis to a steel post. "What? Are you going to shoot me again if I don't tell you?"

Now, Fuentes. Ricardo put down his gun and secured the rope to the post with his hands behind his back."

"Ssh. Don't say anything," said Luis.

Ricardo shook his head. "I might have to shoot you, Luis. Now tell me who your boss is. You might get off easy if you co-operate with the police and civil guard."

Luis stared at Fuentes a moment as if they had a shared understanding. "Fine. You want to know who our boss is." He hesitated. "It's Hugo. Just because they didn't have any evidence against him, doesn't mean he's innocent. He's had this planned for years, and right under your nose. How long have you two been friends?"

Ricardo chuckled. "You guys set him up. I know Hugo's innocent."

"Is he?" said Fuentes, who pulled at the rope as if he hadn't secured it tightly. "He's playing nice and all, but he wants your girlfriend to lower her guard, then he'll pounce. He's played both of you guys."

Ricardo struggled to breathe. No, he refused to believe them. They were still framing Hugo, surely. But then again, was it wise to get him to check on Kim? Was he truly playing them, or had he been framed? Ricardo realised how many accidents connected to Hugo. The attack on Kim near the youth club. The attack and death of Alejandro. The time Hugo had shown up when Fuentes had disappeared. Had it all been orchestrated, or was he innocent? "I don't believe you." He said it with less conviction than he wanted to. "Is there anyone else in the police involved in this?"

Luis replied. "Don't know." He smirked. "Do you think your girlfriend's safe? You know you can't protect her twenty-four-seven." He chuckled and threw his head back.

Quickly, Ricardo called Kim. "Hey. Is everything okay there?"

"Of course. But I have something to show you. Hugo just left, mentioning he had something to do. Are you all right?"

What did Hugo need to do? "I'm fine. I managed to catch a couple of criminals in the act. I'm waiting on the police to arrive to check in on a drug warehouse. I'll be home soon."

"That is great news."

"What do you need to show me, Kim?"

"It's evidence we can hand in. Get here soon and I'll show you. Focus on your duty at the warehouse."

"Okay. We'll talk soon." He ended the call, realising how much he missed hearing her voice and how excited he was to see her again. He had to find out if Hugo was innocent or not. But first things first.

He snapped a photo of both Fuentes and Luis, as well as parts of the warehouse, in case anything went wrong.

"What do you guys know about Manuel or Alejandro?"

The two men stared at each other, shrugging. "We are not saying anything."

"Where's Arturo? Did he kill Alejandro?" The men remained tight-lipped and looked away. Their silence told him it was Arturo. He couldn't wait to get his hands on the bastard.

Watching over these two criminals, he stood by for another fifteen minutes in silence when the humming of engines and the slamming of doors jolted him. Sirens blared and footsteps resounded as the door opened.

Brandishing their guns, police officers and the Civil Guard swarmed in.

Two officers approached Fuentes and Luis and handcuffed them, reading them their rights as both men resisted, eventually overpowered by the officers.

Fuentes looked over his shoulder, glaring. "You just dug your girlfriend's grave, Ricardo. She'll die because of what you've just done."

Ricardo tried to ignore his constricted chest, walked out of the warehouse and bumped into Angel. "Hey, man."

Seeing Ricardo's gun, Angel's eyes darkened. "Are you all right, my friend?"

He nodded. "I am, but not so much with those losers inside."

"Great work, Ricardo, but I wish you would have called me first. You could have got yourself killed."

Ricardo put up a hand. "I can take care of myself."

Angel chuckled. "No doubt. Listen, I have to process what we find. Also, you might want to make sure you keep your wits about Kim. If you don't, you could get her killed." He paused. "Thanks for your help. Now leave and stay safe."

Ricardo waved goodbye and made his way to his car with a heavy heart. Angel was right. His feelings for Kim could get in the way, and he had to be objective. He needed to find out who had killed his brother. Surely someone would talk if they could make a deal with the police.

Chapter 45

FEAR FOR SAFETY

K im jolted off the sofa at the sound of a car. Ricardo was finally back. Her body tingled and her heart soared, and she thrust her chest out. She wanted to shout "'I love you" from the rooftops—but not if he didn't feel the same way.

When the door opened, their eyes locked as Ricardo took a few steps towards her. But instead of kissing her or wrapping his arms around her, he stood cross-armed and averted his eyes. "What did you have to show me, Kim?"

She swallowed, hiding her disappointment. What kind of greeting was that, and why was he so cold? "Come on through." Her body chilled like his tone. He obviously didn't feel anything towards her. Was it only a fling for him?

Ricardo noticed the documents on the table and picked one up. "Oh, this is gold. We knew they were laundering money through these businesses to make them look legitimate. But these documents confirm it. We can hand these over to Angel later until he figures out if there are any other corrupt organisations. Leave them in your room for now, Kim. Angel's got a few things going on. After these arrests and possible new leads, I'll hand this evidence over to him. The Civil Guard can investigate further."

Kim neared him. "Who did they arrest?"

"Fuentes and another guy named Luis."

She squinted. "Do you believe these men will talk, Ricardo?"

"If we make a deal with them, possibly. I mean, these guys might not be murderers. The police might be able to reason with them. Who knows?" He looked down. "Great work, Kim. I knew my brother had goodness in him and did something to help." His eyes misted, and Kim wanted to reach out and touch him, but refrained.

Kim squeezed Ricardo's shoulder. "Are you all right?"

Ricardo nodded. "I'm fine."

"Are you sure? Is there anything I can do to help?" Kim asked.

"No, nothing more. The bad guys have been caught. I was hoping that Fuentes was the only cop involved, but from Manuel's message here, it's doubtful."

Ricardo looked at Kim, but she couldn't decipher his expression. "Why don't we have dinner? I can grill steaks."

She put up a hand. "No, I will make dinner. You relax and put your feet up." She made her way towards him, yearning to touch him. Stroking his cheek, she inched forward and kissed him hard on the lips. Ricardo reciprocated for a few seconds but then pulled back.

"What's going on, Ricardo? I thought..."

He hardened. "You thought what? That we'd have a happily-ever-after? That you're my woman? Well, think again."

She froze, her heart clenching. "But what about what we shared? Did that not mean anything to you?"

He shrugged, avoiding her eyes. "It was fun, but that's all it was. Nothing more."

Her heart clenched tight. He had to be doing this for her safety. "You don't need to pretend with me, Ricardo. I don't sleep around. I..."

His jaw tightened as he looked at his shoes. What was so interesting down there? "You what?" He scoffed. "Don't tell me you believe in fairy tales? Really? Fantasy? Get a grip on reality, Kim. Life doesn't work that way. I don't work that way. You're my brother's ex-girlfriend, and I don't think you want someone else in the family. You have your life and I have mine. Two parts of Spain. Do not kid yourself and think we have a future together, because we don't. I like to have my sexual release and you gave that to me. It was pure physical pleasure, that was all. I can get that pleasure anywhere."

Chills ran up and down Kim's spine and her throat dried up. "I don't believe you. I know you felt something for me. Why are you doing this? Why? Is this about your ex-fiancée?"

He stared hard at her. "Isla died because of my involvement with her. Her ex-boyfriend killed her just to get back at me, so why should I believe in relationships anymore? They don't work and are not for me. Besides, you and I have nothing to do with that."

Her heart broke and she fought back tears. "You're lying." Her vision blurred. "I am sorry about Isla, Ricardo. But that's a cop-out. You're not responsible for another man's actions."

He sighed. "You know what? I'm suddenly not hungry anymore. I'm going to bed. I suggest you eat something if you're hungry." He walked up the stairs without looking back at her.

Kim rushed into the kitchen, sat on the chair, buried her face into her hands and cried her heart out. She couldn't believe she'd fallen in love with a man whose feelings had turned hot and then cold on her again. Whether he was doing this to protect her or not, she was done with his changing moods.

Ricardo lay in bed, staring at the ceiling, drained of all energy. Chills enveloped his body as he flashed back to the expression on Kim's face. He had stood there and lied to her. Lied about his feelings for her. But it was best this way. He had to protect her, and this was the only way he could. Getting involved with him would only get her killed. It was best to pretend he didn't love her for her own survival. He loved Kim with all his heart, and he didn't know how he'd survive without her once she left for Madrid. When all this was over, it might be safe to love her.

He felt like a prick for hurting her that way, and he wouldn't wish that kind of pain on anyone. But in the big scheme of things, he'd done what was right. Sometimes, sacrifices had to be made for the greater good. He still had to find out who had killed his brother and Alejandro. What if it wasn't Arturo who killed him? Who could be that evil to kill a teenager in the prime of his life?

Footsteps approached. Underneath his door, a flash of light appeared. That meant that Kim had come up and chosen not to have dinner, either. The footsteps stopped in front of his door, and no doubt, Kim stood outside, trying to decide whether to open the door or not. He didn't know if he'd be strong enough to turn her down once he looked at her beautiful, innocent face. He yearned to wrap her in his arms and make sweet love to her again. But at least he could imagine it. He had that small comfort.

The light went out. Kim had obviously decided against opening his door. A part of him was disappointed and wanted her to fight for him. But no, it was best this way.

Chapter 46

HAUNTING DISPLAY

Ricardo sat across from Angel at his desk, his mind on Kim as they discussed the arrests of the day before. He had left his home at the crack of dawn to avoid bumping into Kim, knowing she'd be safe now that these bastards had been arrested. It was only a matter of time before they caught those responsible for the recent deaths.

Angel clasped his hands together, light shining in his eyes. "We secured leads on a few other members of the cartel, and have all the information on a new shipment in two days. Thanks to you, we can stop it. Great work."

Ricardo's spirits rose. "That's great, Angel. What about your investigation on Manuel or Alejandro? Any progress?"

Angel shook his head, shuffling through a stack of papers and piling them in a corner of his desk. He answered a call on his desk phone. "Are you sure?" His eyes darkened after slamming the phone down.

"What's wrong?"

Angel took a breath. "We confiscated their phones, and apparently, the drug shipment has been put forward. That can either be a blessing or a tragedy."

Ricardo knew how bad this was when they had to prepare strategy at the last minute. "How soon?"

"Later this afternoon. Damn it. Damn it!"

Ricardo leaned forward. "Do you think the cartel knows that Fuentes and Luis have been arrested?"

"Doubtful. It's not like they've been keeping tabs on the guys. We managed to keep the media out of it. It could be for any number of reasons." He peered past him. "We will need to cut our meeting short."

Ricardo clenched his fists. "Can I come in on the raid? You guys could use all the help you can get." He paused. "I know Kim's safe now. She is safe, right?"

He nodded. "Of course. Luis was one of the other men watching her. No one else has any reason to hurt Kim. Unless you have new information I don't know about."

Ricardo didn't mention the documents Kim had found, as he didn't want Angel distracted from this drug shipment. He would explain that later. "Anyway, what about my help?"

Angel leaned forward and slapped him roughly on the shoulder. "Fine, Ricardo. But you listen to my every instruction. If I tell you to breathe, you do it. If I tell you to sneeze, you do it."

Ricardo put up his hand. "Fine. Fine. I understand. Thanks, man." He texted Kim about helping in the raid.

Angel got up and placed a call. "I want the team to assemble in the conference room. We need to talk strategy for this afternoon." He ended the call. "Come on, my friend. There is no time to waste."

A knock on the door made Angel look up. "Come in."

The stocky receptionist with buck teeth entered carrying a large box, and rested it on Angel's desk. "This package was sitting on my desk when I returned from the bathroom. It's addressed to you, Angel. It feels a bit heavy."

Angel tilted his head. "Thanks." Once she left, he closed the door and cut through the top of the box with a letter opener. He turned to Ricardo. "It might be a lead. I was expecting files on our deceased criminal, Alvaro."

Ricardo watched Angel as he opened the box, and saw his eyes bug out and his breathing stop. He leaned in and could only whisper "No," as he saw the bloodied head of his old friend, Miguel. A note attached to the scalp read: *Don't lose YOUR head in this investigation.* He ran to the bathroom and retched.

Kim rubbed her eyes as she got out of bed. Her mind flashed back to the brief conversation she had had with Ricardo and pushed back the tears. She had cried herself to sleep last night, knowing he either didn't feel the same way as she did, or had said what he had to protect her. She had her own priorities and would not let it affect her.

She took a deep breath, realising she had to face Ricardo and explain exactly how she deserved better. If he wanted nothing to do with her, she wanted to know he had cared about her. She had to know he hadn't used her for his own need for pleasure. She would give it to him straight.

Coming down the stairs, all she heard was silence. "Ricardo?" Her eyes roamed as she headed to the kitchen, but he wasn't there. She opened the front door to look outside and saw that his car was missing. He must have left early to avoid talking to her. It was still only eight o'clock.

Brushing aside the thoughts, she retrieved an apple from the fridge. Biting into it, she sat at the table, and began scrolling on her phone. She saw a message from Ricardo. "Had to meet Angel for a drug shipment today. Will keep you in the loop."

Kim's shoulders slumped as she realised how cold his text had been. No "hello," no "I am sorry for leaving this early," and no mention about having to talk about last night.

She bowed her head and pushed down her pain. If anything, she had to focus on finding justice for Manuel and Alejandro. They deserved to know who had killed them, so the murderers couldn't hurt anyone else. If it was over her dead body, she would get to the truth, with the help of the police.

She headed back to the bedroom when the sound of a motor alerted her to the window. Drawing the curtain, she spotted a policeman park in front of the house. Rather than walk towards her, he sat in the car and waited. Why was a policeman watching over her? Had something happened? She went out to meet him.

For now, she had to forget about her feelings for Ricardo and focus on priorities.

Chapter 47

DRUG SHIPMENT

Ricardo walked beside Angel. Distant views of undulating greens and browns would have captivated him if they weren't intercepting a shipment of drugs coming by helicopter, or if he hadn't seen poor Miguel's head in a box.

He couldn't get that vision out of his mind. Poor Miguel didn't deserve to suffer that way. Angel had arranged for a policeman to watch over his family and another one to watch over Kim in case they were in danger. But who could have known that Miguel had spoken to him? He hadn't mentioned their discussion to anyone, so who had found out? Had Miguel voiced his concerns to someone he thought he could trust? He had given the man strict instructions to only report to him.

Shaking away his ruminations, he took a breath and concentrated on this raid. They were one step closer to finding out who had done all this. Kim would be safe with the police guard in front of his house.

They reached an isolated flat spot in Torrelaguna, with a group of police officers and Civil Guard making their way towards the landing, the stomping of feet prominent in his mind as they carried weapons and watched the surrounds with sharp eyes. "Are we sure this is the drop-off for the shipment?" asked Ricardo.

Angel nodded. "This is what Fuentes and Luis mentioned. It's still early, so we wait."

Another Civil Guardsman named Marco joined the conversation. "It's costly to fly drugs into Spain and they need experienced pilots to be able to fly at a low altitude to avoid being seen by radar." He patted his gun as if to check it hadn't fallen. He had messy, black wavy hair and stubble across his chin. His huge bulk appeared menacing. "It is then too easy for them to drop off their drugs at a range of spots throughout Spain."

Angel nodded. "A helicopter means these men can cover a wider space. So even if it's more expensive, they are more difficult to intercept, which is why we got lucky with this one."

Ricardo frowned, thinking how creative these cartels were becoming, particularly with the advent of technology. "Not that I have much experience in this world, but even using drones or light aircraft is hard to intercept when you have many using them for good."

Marco touched Ricardo on the shoulder. "Even crop sprayers are being used to transport drugs. Crazy, ha?"

"Crazy, all right," said Ricardo.

They headed back to their cars a few metres away, out of sight behind the cover of a tree in a stranger's driveway. Angel responded to a call on his phone. "They tracked the helicopter as being ten minutes out, so let's get ready to move."

Ricardo reached for his phone in his back pocket to check for messages. He hid his disappointment at not having a return text from Kim. She could have acknowledged his message.

Deciding to send her another text, he typed, *Waiting to track a drug shipment. Call you soon. We need to talk.* He turned to his friend. "How much of the drugs are we looking at? Over six hundred kilograms?"

Angel stared straight ahead. "At least nine hundred kilograms, possibly more. They might have made last-minutes changes."

"Right," said Ricardo.

When ten minutes were up, Angel took out his binoculars and watched a group of men run down the hill, waving over the helicopter which was about to land. "We wait," he said to the other men. "They will need to check on the goods, so we do not want to spook them. Do not move until I give the order."

Once the helicopter landed, Ricardo's heart pounded in his chest as his adrenaline increased. This was pure gold if they could infiltrate one means of transport for drug transportation. These men might also divulge their ringleader. "Shouldn't we move?"

Angel waved to the others. "Let's head out. We have to be swift and undetectable until we are very close."

The men made their way along the field, and climbed a hill which led them to an isolated patch of flat ground. A helicopter sat in the centre, and two men huddled around the pilot's window in deep conversation.

"Freeze," Angel shouted, pointing a gun at the men. Other police officers followed his action. Ricardo holstered his own gun and sprinted after one of the goons who was running away. He got close enough to grab him by his jumper and tackled him to the ground. "Stop, you dirt bag." He had handcuffs in his back pocket and secured the smuggler's wrists, then pulled him back to the helicopter. The man's hair was curly and dishevelled, but he looked anything but intimidating.

"I am sorry. Sorry," the man said.

Ricardo stared at the man. "You will be sorry once we arrest you."

He shook his head. "I had to feed my family, signor."

Angel patted down another towering man while Marco cuffed the third, who cringed. Angel pushed them all towards the waiting cars. "You are all under arrest for the illegal distribution and possession of drugs. You will face many years behind bars."

A group of Civil Guardsmen went into the helicopter, then stepped out with a nod to Angel. They had the drugs.

"Wait for the truck and get the drugs loaded. I want everything to be accounted for in your notebooks," Angel said. "Everything."

A few of the men stayed at the field while Ricardo, Angel, and Marco got into the car to question the men at the station.

Ricardo leaned forward into the car, speaking to one of the criminals. "Are there any other helicopters expected to land today or any time soon?"

The man shrugged. "I do not know. I was paid one thousand Euros to control the shipment. I need to feed my family. I only spoke to the man on the phone."

"You are going to prison for a long time."

He shook his head. "No, please. Help me."

Ricardo knit his brows, thinking this man might have more information than he was willing to admit. "If you speak to us about anything you know, you can avoid arrest."

His eyes glazed over him. "No, they will kill me. My family, too."

"We can put you in witness protection." The man remained silent, thoughtful.

Ricardo realised that all three men must have been paid a hefty amount, but weren't the real criminals. They had obviously been forced into it or were desperate enough to survive. He knew that once the cartels found someone of interest, they would either agree to their terms or they'd put a bullet in their head. If they didn't kill them, they'd make them suffer by targeting their families and loved ones. A never-ending cycle of abuse, threats, and murder.

Chapter 48

FEAR OF THE UNKNOWN

The next morning, Kim tossed and turned in bed. Images flashed before her. It was a man who looked familiar, his hair cut short, with blood dripping from his fingers and mouth. The man's shoulders drooped and he closed his eyes until a large hand slapped him hard, forcing him to awaken. Kim ran towards the tortured man, but a strong gust of wind pushed her back. Reaching out with shaky hands, her body froze. The wind pushed her away, and she lost sight of the man. She was alone in a large, spacious building.

Beads of sweat lined the back of Kim's neck as she suddenly awoke, realising she'd been dreaming. Sighing with relief, she realised that the man in the dream looked like Ricardo, but surely he was all right. It was only a dream.

Stepping out of bed, she pulled on a fluffy pink robe and headed towards his bedroom. The door was ajar, and she peeked inside. The bed was made. Had he already left, or maybe he hadn't come home last night. He might have been late with the drug shipment and decided to stay at Angel's house, but it would have been nice if he'd let her know.

Walking downstairs with a gentle yawn, she rubbed her tired eyes. She had not slept well, and wandered through all the rooms, as well as gawking out the back door. Ricardo was nowhere to be found.

In the kitchen, she turned on her phone and tapped his number. Her call went straight to voicemail. She tried again a few minutes later, but still no reply. She wouldn't think the worst.

After showering and dressing, Kim called him again, but still no response. She contacted the Civil Guard, who put her through to Angel.

"Hello, Kim. This is a nice surprise," Angel said. "How can I help?"

"Is Ricardo with you?"

"No, why? Isn't he home?"

Kim gasped and tried to control her breathing. Surely there had to be an explanation. Ricardo was fine. He had to be. "He didn't come home last night. I don't think his bed has been slept in, and I can't reach him on his phone. Was he working with you yesterday?"

"He was, but he left the station in the late afternoon to go home." He paused. "I will ring around and let you know if I find him. I'm sure he's with Hugo or one of his other friends. I am certain he is fine. Have you contacted Hugo?"

"No, but I will do that now. Thanks, Angel." Kim ended the call and ignored the ache and uneasiness in her chest. There had to be a reason he wasn't home. For all she knew, he could have been avoiding her after their last argument, but he had texted her yesterday saying they needed to talk. Nothing more after that.

Kim called Hugo, but got no response. She shouldn't be getting Hugo involved in this anyway. He had a wife and baby and should stay safe. But then again, a part of her wondered if Hugo could even be trusted. It was most likely for the best that she couldn't reach him.

She opened her laptop and glanced at emails from Sofia and Eva explaining how much they missed her and hoped she'd come home soon. She typed out a quick reply, telling them she'd be home once this was over then closed her laptop. She jolted when her phone rang. "Angel. Have you found Ricardo?"

"Kim. Sorry, no. I have tried my other contacts. Two of my men checked on him at work even though he has taken time off to focus on this case. No one has seen him. Are you still at the house?"

"Yes. Did Ricardo give you the evidence from Manuel?"

"What evidence?" he said in a voice she barely heard. Why was he whispering?

She explained the information. "Ricardo wanted to tell you, but I assume with the drug raid, he forgot about it."

"Listen, Kim. I believe there is a traitor in the office. Do not come here. Stay where you are. I can secure the evidence until I investigate further. I'll leave now."

Kim's heart palpitated, her body frozen. Manuel did mention police members, plural, in Patones involved with the cartel. But then again, who knew how many of them were working with the drug cartels all over the world. It wasn't surprising. "Okay. I will wait here."

Kim opened the front door to see Angel. "I am so glad you are here. Come in."

He smiled, carrying a large briefcase. "A pleasure." His eyes shifted past her. "Where is this evidence, Kim?"

She ushered him to the kitchen and handed him the envelope. "All these companies are involved. We also found something else." She moved to the other side of the table and showed him the accounts of Miguel's restaurant.

Angel nodded, scrutinising the documents. "You did amazing work here. I will make sure this evidence is secured." He straightened the documents and shoved them into his briefcase. With a reassuring smile, he turned to Kim. "We need to get you into a safe house. If someone's kidnapped Ricardo, they'll be after you next due to your connection with him."

Kim's heart broke. "I cannot leave Ricardo. What if he comes back and there is a perfectly reasonable explanation for all this? He may be in hiding, investigating this on his own, and not wanting to endanger others." She didn't believe what she was saying, but the possibility that Ricardo was safe gave her the hope.

She had a life in Madrid to return to, and this indefinite stay in a safe house meant her life would change forever. Would they ever track down those responsible for Manuel's death? She had no choice but to comply with the man. "Fine. When do we leave?"

Angel peered over his shoulder briefly. Approaching the window, he pulled back the curtain and peered through. "I ordered the policeman to leave. Pack your things for the next few days. I'll take you now."

Kim nodded and headed upstairs. She grabbed her overnight bag, the heaviness in her body unbearable as she took a moment to sit on the edge of her bed. Bowing her head, tears streamed down her face. Her neck and head ached and she missed Ricardo so much that she felt that she wanted to die herself. Clenching her hands, she picked herself up and stood while flicking through clothes to pack on their hangers. Ricardo had to be okay.

Kim shivered. Pushing down her fear, she reached for her brush on the dressing table and threw it into the bag. Rubbing on her cold hands, she steeled herself, picked up her bag and made her way downstairs.

Chapter 49

A TARGET

R icardo tasted metal in his mouth, his head lolling with fatigue. His hands were tied behind his back with corded rope. Musty smells of mould and timber made him cringe as his eyes scanned the surrounds. A spacious area. He was in a warehouse.

Large cardboard boxes stacked on top of each other, while other boxes and crates sat on tall steel shelves over a dusty linoleum floor. Mould and mildew visible in the corners of walls and spiderwebs hung from the high ceilings.

His jaw and eyes ached after the goons who brought Ricardo here had played punching bag with him, thinking he knew more than he let on. He refused to tell them about the list of companies involved in money laundering. He last remembered stepping into his car after the drug raid. Angel had driven him back to his car, parked near the police station when someone had hit him over the head with a hard object. The attacker must have carried him here while he was unconscious. What a gutsy move to knock him out near the police station.

If only he had investigated the companies involved in the laundering and had handed the list over to Angel straight away. If he could find out who the top leaders were, then they could wipe out at least a few of the cartels. Now that he was involved, he was risking Kim's life as well as his own. He didn't sign up to be a part of the investigation of cartels, but he had to seek justice. He also needed justice for poor Miguel. No, once he discovered who had killed and ordered those hits, he was no longer getting involved in police business. He was done.

His mind flashed back to Kim and their last argument. If only he could admit he loved her deeply and intensely, but he'd been afraid to hurt her. Afraid to risk her life by being with him. If they knew she held those documents, she would be held captive as he was right now. Hopefully, she would take the evidence to Angel, who would have the Civil Guard investigate those businesses and put a stop to laundering dirty money.

Footsteps approached. His heart pounded and sweat dripped down his neck. He couldn't take any more pain.

His captors had swung a poker into his eye and jaw, and the pain was still acute.

Two men approached him. One of them had used the poker on him while the other one watched. The poker guy had buck teeth, oily wavy black hair down to his shoulders and soulless black eyes. The shorter man had deep, green eyes that seemed to bore into him and appeared to be less intimidating. The shorter one had clenched his hands and turned away when the other man had struck him in the face. Could he sway this green-eyed man? Was it possible this other man had a soul and a tad of empathy?

Poker guy leaned forward, his breath smelling of stale cigarettes and coffee. "We taught Miguel a lesson." He chuckled and threw his head back. "That'll teach the loser to never open up his trap like that again." He turned to the other man. "I'd say he lost his head...but too soon?"

Ricardo's head bowed. The man was a psychopath, mentally deranged. If he got his hands on him, he'd be eating those words. Poor Miguel had been sucked into this game to keep his family safe, without evil intent. "Why did you kill him? He was open to your laundering."

The man slapped him hard across the face and Ricardo winced, the stabbing pain increasing in his jaw. "We were watching him. Didn't trust the guy to keep his trap shut." He scoffed. "It is about loyalty, *cabron*. The lack of honour and betrayal gets you killed. If anyone betrays us, they pay the price." He turned to his colleague. "Isn't that right, Gael?"

Gael nodded. "Too right. They get punished." The man averted his eyes and didn't sound convincing. Ricardo could work with this guy, if only he could get him alone. But would they leave him on his own with Ricardo?

"Why am I here? Why haven't you killed me yet?"

Poker man scoffed. "If it was up to me, I'd put a bullet in your brain, *cabron,* but it's not. When I get the order, I will take pleasure in shutting your trap. You can visit your brother in hell."

Ricardo glared. "What do you know about Manuel? Who killed him?"

The man shrugged. "I'll tell you just before I kill you. How's that?"

"And what about Alejandro? He was just a young boy and didn't deserve to be gunned down like that. He was a kid."

Poker man punched him twice in the gut. Ricardo moaned but fought against the searing pain. "I don't need you telling us how to run our damn business. That kid cost us a lot of money by trashing those drugs. A lot of time and money. He refused to sell the rest of the drugs to his school buddies. No one gets away with stealing what belongs to us."

Ricardo remained silent, watching Gael grimace. He turned away, as if he didn't want poker stick guy to see him. *Interesting!*

"Anyway, the boss believes you know more about the cartel."

Again, he decided to hold back what Manuel had given Kim, and those documents. Hopefully, she would hand it in to the right people. "I know nothing. Like I said earlier, I only know what Angel and I found out about that shipment. Nothing more."

Poker guy retrieved a knife from his back pocket, flicking it open with the press of a button. He touched the tip to Ricardo's throat, trailing it down until he pressed the blade into his chest, scraping it against his flesh. The subtle pain made him gasp. "Only a graze this time," said Poker Man. "Next time, you might not be so lucky. Do you want more damage, 'cause I can inflict that?"

"I told you I don't know anything."

Poker Man turned to Gael and pressed his lips together. "You know, Kim's a beautiful woman. Sexy as hell. I bet if we paid her a visit, she might get pleasure from a real man, not a loser like you."

Ricardo's heart raced and his throat shrivelled. "You stay the hell away from Kim. She has nothing to do with any of this."

He put up his hands. "Oh, no? She was Manuel's ex-girlfriend. I wonder if he told her anything about the business."

"She knows nothing. This is your beef with me. Leave her out of it."

Gael intervened. "Listen, Arturo. We can't do anything without the boss's orders. Let's wait and see how this will pan out. One step at a time."

Arturo! This was the guy who might have killed Alejandro. Ricardo's eyes blazed in his direction. "I will kill you with my bare hands. You killed Alejandro yourself, didn't you? It was just you. No one gave you the order, did they?"

Arturo leered at him then faced his partner. "I'm my own boss. I don't need any order if it affects the business, moron."

Ricardo had bile in his throat, wishing he could wrap this cord tightly around the bastard's neck. "I will kill you nice and slow, you child-killer."

Arturo scoffed. "Bring it. Now, about Kim. I am going to pay her a visit."

Gael shook his head. "We wait for the order, Arturo."

"You shut the fuck up, Gael. Do you always have to be like a girl? I can do whatever the hell I like. The boss doesn't have to find out."

Gael stepped forward. "I hear you, but the boss doesn't want Kim yet. He has a plan. Let's wait." He sipped lemonade from a glass bottle.

Arturo sighed. "Fine, but once we get the order, I will have my fun with Kim first. She has one fine ass."

Ricardo thrust his chest forward and pulled at the rope. "You fucking bastard." He had to get out of this damn rope, but it was secured too tight.

Arturo elbowed him in the chest. "Shut the fuck up. Let's go, Gael. I will get my satisfaction with this loser later."

As he watched them leave, Ricardo's body tightened at the idea that Kim was at risk. He had to fix this, but how?

Chapter 50

BREAKING FREE

Ricardo pulled at the rope, attempting to untie himself as he clenched his teeth, the cut in his wrists getting deeper. It was futile. He had the feeling the next time Arturo arrived, he'd put a bullet in his head.

He looked at the glass bottle. Gael must have left it behind, but was it on purpose or accidental? Throwing himself back hard, he fell on his back, his feet up in the air. The wooden chair split with a loud *crack*. He lay on the floor with one half of the chair behind him, wincing in pain. Quickly, he slid over to the steel shelf where the bottle sat beside a cardboard box, huffing and puffing, ignoring his aching joints. Dizziness set in, but he pushed on until he reached the bottle. He reached up with his right arm, but the bottle was just out of reach. He could do this. He had to do this before they decided to kill him. If he were to die, he'd rather die trying than not try at all.

Taking a deep breath, he positioned his body close against the post of the shelf and stretched his arm out even further, his face sweating and his wrist numb. Just a little further and he would make it. Another centimetre. He shifted his body higher up, continued to extend his arm. *Come on. Come on. You can do it.*

After another two minutes of stretches and curses, Ricardo knocked the bottle off the shelf and watched the shards spread around him. Moving on his back, he grabbed a shard and rubbed it as hard as he could against the rope behind him. Back and forth. Back and forth until he could break free. He was nearly there. Kim would be in his sights again, and he would tell her how stupid he was and how much he loved her. If he died without telling her he loved her, he couldn't bear to think of her grief if she felt the same way.

With bloodied wrists and grazed fingers, Ricardo cut himself free. Sitting up, he shook out his aching back and wrists then made his way to one of the boxes. He was curious about what was stored in them.

Ripping the tape off one of the boxes, he found buckets of breadcrumbs. Dipping his hands inside, he spotted bags of white powder underneath, most likely fentanyl or methamphetamine. Another box had more breadcrumbs and more bags of drugs. One beside it carried ammunition, guns, and rifles. This was a policeman's dream.

Running around the warehouse he stayed alert for any visitors and sounds of car engines, but it remained silent. More and more boxes and crates held nothing but hidden drugs or weapons. At the other end of the warehouse was a small truck which he assumed would load the contraband for transportation.

As he considered his next move, the rev of an engine made his skin crawl. He grabbed a Glock and a box of ammunition from one of the boxes. Ejecting the magazine, he loaded it with bullets before making his way behind a stack of boxes in the back. He couldn't leave without being seen, so he had to fight it out with whoever was coming in. It had to be Arturo and Gael returning to finish the job, but he was ready and willing to fight to get justice for his friends and family.

He held his breath and stood as still as a post when the door slammed. The muffled voices sounded like Arturo and Gael. Bracing for more, he took, slow deep breaths, on high alert. They might be thinking he had left.

From where he was positioned, he couldn't see them.

"Shit! Shit! Where the fuck is he, man?" said Arturo. He scanned the area at the shards of glass and broken remnants of timber from the chair.

"How the hell should I know," Gael said. "He must have left, but where would he go?"

Arturo scoffed. "You were the one that tied him up. I guess you need a damn lesson in how to secure a tight knot, don't you? Bloody hopeless you are."

"Hey, I did my best, Arturo. Don't forget he was a detective and would have a few tricks up his sleeve."

"Fuck, fuck. We are dead meat, you know that. Deader than dead."

"Relax. We'll find him. He can't have gone far. We haven't been gone that long. Come on. Let's split up and search. He'd be on foot."

"No, man. If he's still got police blood, he'll be inside this warehouse, waiting for us. Probably wanting to fight us, but we won't let him. You go that way and I'll search the back. Well, fuckin move or I'll shoot you, *cabron*."

Silence. *What's going on?* As they moved, Ricardo was able to see them from his position. Arturo pulled at Gael's sleeve. "Wait one fuckin minute. Where did all these pieces of glass come from?" Gael shrugged. "Weren't you drinking from a bottle earlier? Did you leave it behind?"

Ricardo's adrenaline escalated. *Oh, no!* If Gael was his ticket to survival, he had to make sure Arturo didn't kill him. If the bastard wanted a fight, he was ready and willing to give him one. He could take him on. *Easy peasy.*

Chapter 51

LUCK RUNS OUT

K im closed the car door and stepped out of Angel's car. Walking along the uneven, cracked ground, she stared up at the small stone house. It had a heavy timber door in the middle and bars over two windows. Behind it spread with a vast backdrop of the green hillside. A rickety timber fence stood to the right of the house.

She followed Angel inside the safe house, carrying her overnight bag. "Why are there bars over the windows?"

Angel glanced over his shoulder, then inserted the key in the lock. "For safety." He beamed. "This will all work out. Do not worry, Kim." He waved his hands around. "I'll leave as soon as the police guards arrive to keep you safe."

He opened the door and instantly, the musty smell of debris filled her nostrils. The dark, narrow corridor made her claustrophobic and the white-washed walls looked dirty. She wondered how long it had been since someone had needed to take refuge in this house.

Angel led her to the kitchen, which was windowless, with dishes on a rack. A set of keys hung on the wall, and a round table with a crooked leg stood amid cracked plastic chairs. She almost slipped on the shiny, stained floor tiles. "Let me give you the grand tour." He led her through two bedrooms, a spacious laundry, and a living room with a small smart TV on a cast-iron stand. A bookshelf stacked with novels stood in one corner, with a green cotton sofa on the opposite side. She wandered to the back of the house to find a padlocked door. "Why is that room locked?"

Angel's phone buzzed. He retrieved it from his inside pocket. "Hold on." He held the phone aside. "It is the basement. Nothing to see in there. Let's go to your room." His eyes lit up. "Unless you think there's a dead body in there." Kim's stomach churned. "An inside joke. But seriously, there are only boxes of junk from the previous owner." He put the phone back to his ear. "What is it?" His face paled as he shook his head. "Fix it." He nodded while forcing a smile on his face. "Assess the situation and if required, resolve it. I will be back shortly." He ended the call and looked at his watch.

"Is everything all right?" Kim asked.

He nodded. "Yes. A police matter that needs to be dealt with. Sometimes I wonder why we get transfers from other regions when they are not willing to conform to our processes." He took a breath. "I will not bore you with such trivial matters. Now, let us get you settled into your bedroom." He led her into a third bedroom they had missed earlier. The room featured a small set of shelves and a laminated dressing table, with a single bed and a floral quilt cover. The white, lace curtain at the window had frayed and turned black at the ends, in need of a wash. "This will be your room for the next few days. When we deem it to be safe, you will return to Ricardo's house. When you are ready, I assume you will be heading back to Madrid?"

She nodded. It struck her right in the heart to consider returning to Madrid when she had fallen in love with Ricardo. How would she live without him?

As if on cue with her emotions, Angel touched her gently on the shoulder. "I know how you feel about Ricardo and how he feels about you. I am sure you will work it out. You and Ricardo will see each other soon." He thrust out his chest. "The guards will be here shortly. They will take care of you, Kim."

It was encouraging to hear those words, but until it happened, it sounded hollow. "I do hope you find Ricardo, Angel. I miss him."

"I know, and believe me, we will find him. Do not worry." He put his phone inside his jacket. "I will come back with food and stock the fridge, but in the meantime, help yourself to water from the tap. Let me deal with this situation." He grinned then opened the front door, locking it behind him.

Ricardo moved left. He moved right. He was ready and could take them on individually and incapacitate them. He didn't want to kill anyone unless he had to, but he had to defend himself. Luckily, Gael managed to convince Arturo he had forgotten to bin his glass bottle, and Arturo was dumb enough to believe him. Was Gael the cartel member they could trust? He knew that the Madrid and Patones police worked closely together and would most likely have other informants. Was Gael working with the police?

Spinning to his left again, he paced his steps slowly behind the shelves, as he watched for any signs of the men.

Swallowing and darting from one side to another, he crept around a crate, catching sight of Arturo, who gripped a gun in his right hand and a knife in the other. Ricardo slowly raised his gun, ready to aim when Arturo moved into the open. A shot whizzed past his ear and he realised he'd been seen. *Damn! That was close.* Ricardo aimed and fired but missed Arturo by an inch. He was only getting warmed up, as he dodged behind a forklift. Looking over his shoulder, he spotted Gael between shelves and boxes.

"Come out from your hiding spot, *Cabron*," Arturo called. "We are not here to kill you. Just wanna talk. We can cut a deal. Our boss wants you to join us. Thinks you'll be a great addition to the team. With your skills and intel, we can go places beyond your wildest imagination."

Ricardo shook his head at the lies. Or did they truly believe he would turn and join them? "You would never have to worry about money again. Think about it. Your every need satisfied. Don't you want that?"

He shook his head, gripping the gun. "I will never work for scum, and for people who kill innocent kids. Never."

"Oh, come on, you don't mean that. We can talk terms and then decide."

Ricardo remained silent as he noticed Arturo shifting in the other direction. What was he doing? Was he setting a trap? No, he wouldn't fall for that and let his guard down. But he had a shot until he snuck closer to the entrance.

As Ricardo concentrated on Arturo in front of him, a tap on the shoulder alerted him. *Gael!*

The man grabbed him by the shoulders and shoved him to the floor. Despite holding a gun, he used his fists to pound into Ricardo as he lay helplessly on the floor and dropped his own weapon. Ricardo covered his face to avoid further punches and kneed Gael in the groin. It sent Gael a metre away and he moaned in pain. He dropped his gun, giving Ricardo enough time to pick it up and retrieve his own from under the shelf. "Stand back or I'll shoot." Gael winced and held up his hands. He stepped forward. "Stop! I will shoot."

Gael ignored him and inched forward again. "Sure you will." He ignored the gun pointing in his face and lunged for Ricardo.

Ricardo fell back as Gael punched him again, but he held on to the butt of his gun and struck Gael in the forehead. It knocked him out.

He stepped forward and gasped when spotting Arturo. He had ended a call. *No!* Was he calling in reinforcements? He had to finish him. He couldn't fight the army the goon had most likely notified.

Ricardo lunged forward and met him face to face. Arturo glared and pointed his own gun at Ricardo, and they had a stare-down.

"Drop the gun. I won't hesitate to shoot. Your friend over there is knocked out, so you're on your own."

Arturo smirked, raising an eyebrow. "I am impressed. But this won't last, *Cabron*. You don't know who you're dealing with. People in high places, and shit. You're a dead man. You just signed your death warrant."

Ricardo shook his head. "Put the gun down or I will shoot."

He threw his head back, laughing. "No, you won't. You're too gutless." His eyes darkened and one of them twitched. Arturo took aim but Ricardo ducked and ran behind a barrel. Turning, he fired but missed the man. He nearly had the bastard and now they were playing cops and robbers again.

Ricardo snuck around a stack of boxes, creeping slowly as Arturo fired several shots, missing him. His heart raced, his hands sweating over the two guns. He had to finish this before reinforcements arrived. He could do this.

Further shots yielded nothing until Ricardo spotted him again and shot. Arturo went down. Now he could call the police. He ran to his enemy, who held his leg, blood seeping between his fingers. "You bastard. You...will...pay for this."

Ignoring him, Ricardo rushed to the broken chair, picked up the rope that had bound him, then used it to secure Arturo to one of the shelves.

Rummaging in the man's pocket, he pulled out Arturo's phone as well as his own. From another pocket, he grabbed a set of keys. This phone was gold, but for now he had to get out of here before his thugs came. "Who did you call?"

Arturo scoffed. "Wouldn't you like to know?"

"You are going away for a long time, loser. This is for poor Alejandro." Ricardo pressed hard on his leg and Arturo screamed in pain.

"I will kill you!"

Ricardo turned away, thinking about Gael. He didn't have time to tie him up more tightly nor question his motives. He had to get out of here, and fast. Once he was safely away, he'd call the police.

He pulled open the heavy door and rushed out of the building, a blast of fresh air making his cheeks tingle. He saw a black SUV and tried the button on the key fob to hear a satisfying click. He set the two guns on the passenger seat and started the motor.

A sudden noise jerked him to the side. A bulky man pointed a gun at him through the window. "Don't move or I'll kill you."

Ricardo swallowed, his heart racing when he noticed in the corner of his eye a man he didn't recognise. He must have been hiding on the other side of the car. *Not again!*

Chapter 52

THE TRUTH

Ricardo woke, his back aching and his arms sore as he slowly opened his eyes. He was in a small bedroom with bare walls, a barred window, and beige shag carpet flooring. He was lying on a single cast-iron bed, covered with a stained quilt cover underneath him, his wrists chained to the bed head. At least his legs were loose.

As he pulled on the chain, it cut into his wrists, making them bleed. Ignoring the pain, his eyes scanned the room as if it could give him a clue about escape. Those bastards had got to him again, and this time he might die. He wondered if Kim was okay. Surely, Angel would be looking after her and keeping her safe. He could trust the guy to watch her, and hopefully they'd find him.

If they were going to kill him, he could only hope that Angel would get to them and let Kim know he had loved her. Even though he had never told his friend how he felt, he knew that Angel would come to that conclusion.

The sound of a lock in the door made him hyperalert. He shifted in the bed to look at the door. Who was behind that door? Were they going to kill him?

Ricardo's eyes lit up at seeing his friend. "Angel. You found me. Thank God!"

Angel's eyes darkened. "Hmm." He stepped into the bedroom and drew away the curtain as if he was in deep thought.

"Aren't you going to release me? Come on, man. They might come back soon. Where's the team? My wrists are killing me."

Angel pressed his lips together and approached, standing within inches of him. He leaned forward and glared. "I am not here to rescue you, my friend."

Ricardo's heart thumped. What the hell! Did he hear correctly? "What?" A bead of sweat trickled down his neck, not wanting to believe that Angel was a traitor. His own friend was a part of all this? How the hell did he not see it? Was he that stupid? Had he lost his touch after working diligently at the hotel? "Please tell me you're not involved in this?"

Angel chuckled. "Okay, I won't tell you." If only he could escape these chains, but he couldn't break steel. "I always did like you, my friend."

"Why in the hell are you involved? I trusted you." He clenched his hands. "I thought you cared about people. Cared about me, and here you are, killing everyone."

Angel stood there as if sizing him up, saying nothing for one minute. He crossed his arms and walked closer. "This is nothing personal, Ricardo. It is business, and you are a threat to that business. I refuse to let you shut us down when we are running a fruitful establishment. You are in the way."

He scoffed. "Establishment? You make it sound like you're running a legitimate business, but you're a murderer and a sadist." He wasn't sure he wanted the truth from Angel right now, but he had to steel himself. "Did you kill Manuel?"

Angel rubbed his hands together. "Now is not the time for questions. I suggest you savour your last moments while you still can." He ambled out the door and closed it behind him.

Ricardo clenched his teeth, shaking his head. The bastard couldn't even admit that he had killed his brother, and most likely ordered the hit on Alejandro, a mere child. He hated himself for not figuring it out sooner. His own so-called friend had been a traitor all this time, but for Angelo it was about business. It had nothing to do with the multiple lives he had destroyed and the bodies he'd buried. It wasn't personal. Just business.

After napping for two hours, Kim got out of bed and walked to the kitchen. She poured herself a glass of water then wandered around the house, curious about the police guards. They weren't in the living room nor in any of the other rooms. Where were they? Shouldn't they have been here by now?

Curious, she went to the padlocked basement door. It would probably be full of mice and rats and nothing of much value. But the padlock made her wonder whether there was something valuable down there.

Kim remembered the set of keys hanging in the kitchen, so she walked back and retrieved five keys joined together by a steel ring. She tried each one until the fifth turned. She slowly opened the door and climbed down the stairs, into a dark, cramped space exuding smells of body odour, dust, and soil.

Turning on the light from her mobile phone, she saw stacked boxes. Stepping in further, piles of old toys and books with torn dust jackets lay inside large clear crates. Were these toys for children of families in the witness protection program? She shuddered at the thought of staying locked up for your own safety.

The hairs on the back of her head stood on end. Was that due to anxiety, or the chill in the damp space? She slowed her breathing down as she stared up at the ceiling, cobwebs hanging down while each corner featured more boxes of knick-knacks and old books inside boxes scattered across the floor.

Approaching another door, she turned the knob, wondering what was inside this room.

Kim flinched at the sight before her. She ran towards Ricardo on a bed, her eyes searching his as he jolted upright. Her hands quivered and her vision blurred. "Ricardo. Oh my God! What have they done to you?"

His eyes brightened. "Kim. You have to leave. Please go. I don't want you involved in this. Go now!"

She shook her head firmly. "You have rocks in your head if you believe I will leave you here to rot. I will be back. The kitchen might have something to get you out of these chains."

"Wait. You have to know something. Angel. You can't trust him."

Kim swallowed hard. "What?"

"Angel's the traitor. He's been part of the drug cartel all this time, getting inside information and turning it against innocent people."

Her body shook and she was speechless. She had trusted the man. Given him Manuel's evidence and here he was lying to her face. "I cannot believe this, Ricardo. He is supposed to be your friend."

Ricardo's eyes darkened. "I know, and that's why I want you out of here. Angel might come back any time soon. Call the other policemen. If you contact the Civil Guard, they'll come here."

"I will do that, but first things first. We need to get you out of those chains. I will be back." Before he could argue, she rushed up the steps. But the door at the top would not budge. It was locked. *No! No! No!* Had Angel locked her in here? There was obviously a reason why those police guards never showed up. He had managed to make her curious about the basement, hoping she would come inside so he could keep her prisoner. How could she be so stupid?

She returned to the bottom of the stairs and began searching through the boxes. Nothing useful. All she found were more toys and books, and loose-leaf papers with children's drawings.

Scurrying back into the bedroom, she sat at the edge of the bed and gave Ricardo a reassuring smile. "The bastard has locked us in here."

Ricardo knit his brows. "Who did? Angel?"

She nodded. "He told me this was a safe house, but it obviously isn't. I cannot believe Angel's involved with the cartels."

"The creep fooled me, too. We've been friends for years. How could I not have known he was involved? I've been an idiot."

Kim rested her hands on top of his, feeling the coldness of the steel chain around his wrists, noticing flaky skin and dried blood around them. "You could not have known. He is obviously smart, knows the system well and how to cover his tracks. Being in law enforcement, he gets to play both sides so nothing ever gets solved because he knows about the leads and sabotages everything. I can understand why Manuel's murder hasn't been solved."

Ricardo bowed and averted her eyes. "He arrested men, made out he was doing his job to get people's trust. Then he'd get rid of evidence so the system would be forced to let them go. Reel in the criminals but make sure they didn't get prison time. I would say he's threatened families, particularly with the drugs that were distributed here by helicopter. He most likely arranged for that man in custody to be killed."

Kim pulled at the chain and searched inside the bedside cabinet for a key. She rummaged into her back pocket and retrieved her mobile phone. Her heart thudded. "It's dead."

"Oh, great!" said Ricardo.

"But how? The phone was fully charged from this morning. How could it go flat by this afternoon?"

Ricardo scoffed. "Angel must have hacked into your phone. He cut off your communication to the outside world."

Kim leaned in and stroked his face. "Oh, Ricardo. What are we going to do?"

Ricardo pressed his lips together. "I don't know yet. But I'll figure something out."

Chapter 53

TRUE LOVE

Ricardo woke up with a jolt, suddenly remembering where he was. Kim stood by a dirty wall in quiet contemplation, her long hair flowing beautifully down to her shoulders, her gentle energy calming his own rampant thoughts. The way she licked her bottom lip when focused; the way she drew in her eyebrows when she was scared, and the way she kept a calm head despite the danger. Her spiritual, calm nature was something he needed in his life, and now they might never get the chance to be together. He realised it was not too late to share how he felt about her.

Kim turned. "You're awake."

He had to tell her everything as he had the uneasy feeling that this might not work in their favour. If he were to die, he had to die with no regrets. "Come here, Kim. We need to talk."

She strolled to his side and sat beside him. "What is it?"

"It's not looking too good for me right now, but I think they might let you go. If they do, I want you to leave and never look back. Do not play hero, but just leave."

Kim laughed. "You are funny, Ricardo, aren't you? I am not leaving here without a fight, and you cannot give up. We will find a way."

He shook his head. "No, you need to save yourself. I can't lose someone else I...I love." He couldn't believe he'd said that out loud.

Kim's eyes widened and her body froze. "You love me?"

He nodded, shifted closer towards her, while Kim moved to meet his lips. He kissed her with tenderness, then with deep-seated ravenous hunger as his tongue delved deeper inside her mouth until they pulled apart. "Yes, I love you more than I have ever loved anyone before. If I die, I want you to know that, Kim."

She drew in her brows. "But you hurt me and said you didn't want a relationship. I thought you only wanted fun, nothing more. Or was that a lie to keep me safe?"

"I am so sorry I hurt you, Kim. But I wanted to protect you. The cartel members threatened to hurt you, and I couldn't let that happen. My fiancée died because of me, and I didn't want the same thing to happen to you. Please forgive me. I was stupid and not thinking straight. I know

now that I love you so much, it hurts." He had realised that communication and honesty was what strengthened a relationship. "I wanted you from the start, Kim, but I had to make the tough choice to fight for Manuel. Now I realise that I should have been honest from the beginning."

She looked away. "I understand, but how do I know that this isn't only a phase because of this situation? When we're no longer in danger, how do I know you won't leave?"

How much clearer could he make it? "Because when you're in a life and death situation, everything important in your life becomes clear. Like I said, I pushed those feelings aside to focus on this mission with the cartels. But I will never leave you, Kim. If we get out of this situation, I want us to build a life together."

Kim rose, her shoulders hunched for a moment. "I never thought I would love anyone more than I loved Manuel. I love you too, Ricardo. With all my heart." She sat back down and his eyes lit up.

"If I die, I will die a happy man."

She shoved him on the shoulder. "No one is going to die, Ricardo. We will think of something."

How he wanted to make love to her right this minute. One last time before he might die. Was it crazy to be thinking of his love and her body when they were in such a dire situation and might never get out of it?

She gently rubbed his wrists, reducing some of his pain as he winced. "We have no way to communicate with anyone, no equipment that will release you from these chains and no way for us to get out of this house."

A big thump made him jerk, and Kim turned sharply to the open door. *Oh no!* Why were they bringing in barrels? *No, no, no!*

A tall thug came in, pointing a gun at Kim. It was Arturo, his leg bandaged from his gunshot wound. He yanked Kim by the arms. She attempted to push him off, but he was stronger. "No, leave her alone!" Ricardo yelled. "You bastard. I'll kill you."

Arturo scoffed. "Nice to see you again, Ricardo. You won't be leaving this time. But this bitch has to be tied up in here." He slapped her hard and she moaned in pain, then pulled her out the door and shut it behind him.

"No, please let her go. This is just about me," he shouted. "Please, Kim is innocent in all this. Please. Please." Ricardo's breath slowed, but the sudden silence was a concern as he didn't know what was happening. He had to find a way out of here. *Think, Ricardo. Think.*

They would most likely transport him somewhere else to kill him. No doubt in a deserted place, but he would be ready to fight. He had taken down a few men on his own in the past and wouldn't go easily. Reminding himself of his skills, he had a semblance of hope that he could fight his way out of this. He had to, and refused to have more bodies on his watch, especially the love of his life.

His reverie broke at the sound of a scream. *Kim!* "Leave her be, bastard," he yelled. "Let's make a deal. Please, I will help you." His words were ignored as she kept screaming.

"No, please, don't," Kim cried. "No...no..."

Ricardo couldn't breathe, his body freezing as he listened with a prickle of terror down his back. Sounds of a chair and a thwack made him close his eyes as he pushed hard against the chains, making his wrists bleed. "No, you bastard. No, please. Leave her alone. Take me. Torture me."

He could hear Arturo's voice through the door. "Do not fight me or I will cut your damn eye out, bitch. Sit back and enjoy the ride."

No. The bastard was going to rape her. Surely, Angel wouldn't allow this to happen. It wouldn't be his style.

Sounds of tears and sniffles made his body shiver and a lone tear streamed down his cheek. His mouth turned dry and his head hammered hard with intense pain. He vowed to kill every one of these bastards.

Then he heard another voice. "Fuckin get off her, you prick. The boss wants you to leave her for now."

"Shut the fuck up, Gael. I'm allowed to have my fun. She's a hot piece of ass."

A punch and shuffling sounds made his chest rise. Scuffling, shifting of boxes and more punching sounds gave him hope.

"Arturo, if you don't back off, I will call Angel. He won't take kindly to your shit."

"Fuck you, man! Let me go."

"Angel said he wants you to watch that civil guard, Marco. He seems to be snooping around. Needing surveillance. More money in it for you than staying here. I'll watch over the bitch," said Gael.

"Fine. I'll go, but she is mine later, Gael."

"Whatever, man. We'll see, but for now we have priorities." Stomping lessened at the sound of a door closing. Ricardo sighed with relief. He had found something different about Gael. It was possible they could turn him. He had just saved Kim from being raped, and he was pretty sure he had lied to his colleague.

Chapter 54

FORCING HIS HAND

Kim shivered in her chair, her hands bound behind her back and a piece of cloth stuck in her mouth. She grunted in Gael's direction, but he ignored her and pulled up his own chair, pointing a gun at her. Why do that when she couldn't attack him? This man had saved her from rape. He had to have some humanity.

The side of her eye throbbed after the creep hit her with a baseball bat. The pain had been unbearable, and now she had the urge to scratch it.

Gael pointed the gun away as he glanced at his watch, then stared into the distance. She kept grunting underneath the dirty cloth, but he ignored her. Kim would not stop until he took this damn cloth off. It was her chance to convince him to let her go. If he saved her from creepy guy, then she might be able to reach him. He appeared to have more humanity than that loser, Arturo.

Kim shifted in her chair, tilting herself to the right. Abruptly, she fell on her side, injuring her arm. Gael rushed to her and she moaned in pain.

"Oh, shut up, bitch." He pulled her back upright and shook his head. But Kim kept swaying and crying out in agony after her wound had touched the cold ground. "Stop swaying. You'll damn hurt yourself." He walked back to his chair and huffed.

Kim had to keep trying. If he shot her, then so be it. At least she had died with strength and persistence.

As she grunted again, he turned to her. Shifting her body left tilted her back to the ground, but she ignored the searing pain in her left arm. She didn't care about injuries. All she cared about was their safety, and in this moment, she had to convince this man to let her go.

He glared, then scoffed. "We can keep doing this all day. It's your problem if you want to keep injuring yourself. I will keep propping you up." He pulled her back up. His arm knocked the cloth, pulling it down slightly.

"Please help me," Kim said.

Gael shoved the cloth back inside her mouth. "I said, shut up. If you keep this up, Arturo will come back and put a bullet in your brain."

Kim found it futile to keep falling to the floor, but she didn't know what else to do. She wondered how Ricardo was doing. No doubt he must have heard what was going on with Arturo and would have felt helpless.

Gael's phone buzzed in his pocket. Pulling it out from the back, he answered. "What?" His face paled and his eye twitched. What was the news that made him shiver? "An hour. Right. I'll wait for you then." He glanced past her and put his gun down, then paced up and down the floor, bumping into a box. "Shit! Shit!" Swallowing, he kept pacing in his small space and put his hands on his hips. Staring over at Kim, he approached and pulled down her cloth. "Talk, bitch. Say what you gotta say because you'll be dead soon. I'll give you your last words."

"No, no. Please, Gael. You have to let us go. Please."

He leered. "And why would I do that?"

Kim cleared her throat, speaking softly. "I can see you are different, Gael. You're not like the others. I have a lawyer friend who can help you, give you immunity. If you tell the authorities everything they want to know, you won't have to do prison time. I am sure you have family you'd like to return to. Please. You help us and we will help you.

Please, Gael. We don't deserve to die." She took a breath. "I don't believe you will stand there and watch it. I can see how young you are, and most likely haven't killed anyone."

"And how the fuck would you know that?"

Hope rose in her chest. "I can see you might have been forced into this. Did they threaten your family or someone else you love? Please, let me help you. Do you truly want to live this way? Not having control and taking orders from a madman. Please, Gael."

Kim waited for something, but the man returned to his seat, his eyes roaming the space and his hands fidgeting. Time was running out, and he would watch her die within the hour. She couldn't breathe and closed her eyes to shut out her pain. Time stood still as she floated on a cloud and put her dire situation out of her mind. When she opened her eyes, at least twenty minutes had gone by.

Gael stared into his lap, his eye twitching again. Gasping, he turned and got up when footsteps originated from the entrance. Arturo walked down the steps with a wide grin, his stained teeth showing.

In an instant, Arturo lunged at Gael, throwing him hard against the wall. Gael went down, rubbing his head. "You prick. Sent me on a wild goose chase, didn't you? You'll pay for that."

Gael got up but Arturo kicked him a few times in the stomach and stomped hard on his hand. "Oww...Christ, man." He slid back on his bottom and covered his face with his right arm.

"Leave him alone," shouted Kim.

Arturo turned to Kim. "Well, aren't you the caring one. Why the hell do you care if I punch his lights out? He's been instructed to kill you with one of our friends who will be here in less than an hour. Then Ricardo'll be next." He scoffed. "And why the hell are you talking, bitch?" He stormed over and shoved the cloth back over her mouth.

Kim lost hope, her heart hammering in her chest. She had to get Gael to help her. He couldn't fail her now. She had seen his human side, and before Arturo had arrived, he had softened in his attitude. She could see it in his eyes.

Arturo ignored Gael and rushed towards Kim, his face inches within hers as he licked his lips, devouring her with his eyes from top to bottom. "God, you are yummy. Sexy, too." His hand trailed down her chin, throat, then the centre of her chest. Kim shivered and shook her head, closing her eyes to shut out the shame. His finger found her nipple and he caressed it roughly, then pinched it. She bit her bottom lip and ignored the pain.

When his hand reached behind her head, he pulled at her scalp and kissed her around the neck, his mouth reaching the base of her throat. He pulled down the cloth and stuck his tongue inside her mouth, but Kim grunted, her head shifting in all directions. With the foul taste of his mouth, she smelled whisky and cigarettes. She wanted to vomit. Abruptly, it stopped. Arms behind him pulled Arturo away and Gael pounded into him. Arturo struck back, then reached into his side pocket. The steely glint of the pocketknife flicked open while he swung it up in the air. Gael moved to avoid the knife, but Arturo managed to graze his neck, exposing a bloody gash.

Gael screamed in pain. "Bastard."

Arturo turned back to Kim, whose bottom lip bled from biting it too hard. Frozen with fear, she awaited her fate as he approached her again. The dirty look in his eyes made her shake and she looked past him as Gael reached for his gun underneath his chair. He pointed it at Arturo, his hand shaking as he squinted. *Hurry up, Gael!* Kim said with her eyes. *Hurry!*

"Stop or I will shoot, Arturo. Leave her alone," said Gael.

Arturo glared at him. "You don't have the balls and I'm going to rip your heart out after I've had my fun with this bitch." He turned back to Kim.

The blast of gunfire reverberated in her ears as she watched Arturo fall forward and into her lap. He'd been shot in the back. "Bastard," said Arturo. Seconds later, he fell to the floor, dead.

Gael rushed forward and pushed him off. "Shit. Shit. Shit. I'm dead. Dead." He shook his head. "They're going to kill me. Kill me."

Kim swallowed. "Listen to me, Gael. If you want to stay safe, you need to get rid of the body before your friend gets here. You need to untie me and help Ricardo. There is no time to think. Hurry up."

With Gael frozen for a moment, she waited a minute for him to process the situation. Arturo was dead, and that made their lives easier. But at any moment, another thug would arrive and would surely kill them all.

Chapter 55

A TRACKER

Gael stood in shock. "I have never killed anyone. He's dead because of me."

Kim had to make him see sense as they were running out of time. "Look at me, Gael. You were protecting me. Protecting yourself. If you didn't shoot him, he would have stabbed and killed you." She sighed. "It was survival." She shifted in her chair. "We need to get out of here. Now. Or we will all die. Process this later. Please. Untie me."

Gael swallowed, took a deep breath, and nodded. Quickly, he pulled at the rope and untied her, then dragged Arturo's body into a corner and draped an old sheet over it. Blood was smeared across the floor. The tangy smell made her nauseous.

Kim rubbed her red-raw wrists. Abruptly, she stood up and helped Gael wipe off the blood with another sheet, her hands quaking. She opened the bedroom door. "We need to get Ricardo out of those chains. Would your gun work?"

He nodded. "Of course. We had better hurry."

Kim rushed into the room, with Gael following. Ricardo's eyes widened at the gun. "He's going to release the chain," she said.

Gael held the gun at an angle and shot through one of the links binding one hand, and then freed the other.

Ricardo flexed his arms. "Thanks. Do you have a spare weapon?"

Gael nodded. "Arturo had both a gun and knife. They should be here somewhere."

"I take it you shot him?" Ricardo scoured the basement floor for any sign of the gun and flinched at seeing drops of blood staining a white sheet. No doubt that was Arturo's body underneath.

"I had to. He would have hurt Kim, otherwise." Bending low, Gael checked underneath Arturo's body but found nothing.

"I found it," Kim said. She picked up the gun from under her chair and handed it to Ricardo. "Shouldn't I have a weapon, too?"

Ricardo searched the floor until he found Arturo's knife. "Take this." He handed it to Kim.

"Let's go," Gael said. "We can go to the police and stay there until they're caught."

Kim ran behind Ricardo and Gael, who stopped at the front of the house, scanning the area outside before going any farther. They all ran into Gael's car parked by the kerb. Dust permeated the air and the chilly wind scraped her cheeks.

Gael sped through the town she didn't recognise, with mansion-like homes on hilly terrain. They passed through the quiet town of Torrelaguna and its centuries-old church, hiking trails, the dips of the mountainside, and a large reservoir.

The drive ahead was quiet for the next ten minutes and Kim hugged her body tight, watching Ricardo in the passenger seat.

He picked up her hand with a smile stretching across his face. He turned back around and focused on the driver. "Listen. We shouldn't take this road. We're too exposed. Take the next turn a few streets away. I'll tell you when."

"Okay. I don't know this area that well. But if you think..."

Kim felt a jolt and realised that a car had hit them from behind, sending her falling forwards against her seatbelt. "Oh, no. They found us. Drive faster."

"Get down, Kim." In that moment, a spray of bullets shattered the windscreen from behind. Kim bent down low to avoid the bullets. She couldn't breathe with the noise vibrating all around them as more bullets rained down on them.

"Shit. Those bastards. How did they find us so quickly?" Gael said.

Ricardo sighed. "They must have tracked you somehow. Or Arturo might have put a tracker on you when you were fighting."

"Of course. Damn. We're toast," said Gael. He accelerated, the car skidding around a sharp turn, narrowly missing cars coming in the opposite direction. He zig-zagged between them while the car behind continued to pursue them.

Ricardo held on to the dashboard, his body swaying hard to the right while Kim watched him bend down low. "Take this turn here. We might lose them. "He turned to look through the back window. "Get rid of that tracker or they'll know where we are."

"I don't know where it is, Ricardo. Why don't you search for it while I try to get us as far away from them as I can?"

Ricardo neared Gael and patted him around his legs and feet, then moved his hands up to his chest. Another hail of bullets flew past him, embedding in the dashboard. "You need to stop somewhere and get rid of this tracker. It might be underneath the car."

"I've got a better idea," he said. He accelerated around a roundabout, down a narrow street and managed to lose the pursuers. He stopped in front of a café. "You guys run and I will bait them. If I stay here, it'll give you time to get to the police. Just take a taxi there. You won't be seen."

Ricardo shook his head. "No, you saved our lives. We can save you." His eyes lit up. "It's a Sunday and the youth club I work at is closed today. It's not far from here. But before we stop at the club, lose them. We need to stop to find that tracker. Once we do, we can head to the club and contact the police from there."

Gael made a number of quick turns and finally stopped at the kerb. Ricardo turned to Gael. "I'll check for the tracker." Gael nodded, then Ricardo opened the passenger door and disappeared from her sight. She hoped he found the tracker. Otherwise, it wouldn't be long before shots were being fired in their direction. This was like a movie she didn't want to be in. Her heart pounded and her breath hitched.

How long would it take to find this tracker? She believed in Ricardo, but surely it shouldn't take this long. What if they didn't find it? The only solution was to head straight to the police, but they couldn't do that until the shooting stopped.

Finally, Ricardo came back into sight and Kim sighed with relief.

He displayed the tracker. It was a small black, square box with wiggly lines on it. "Here it is. Give me a second to run as far as I can from here." He raced down an alley and threw the tracker into a rubbish bin. He entered the car. "I'll tell you where the club is." He recited directions to Gael.

Kim looked over her shoulder as the car moved again. What if the cartel found them at the club? Hopefully they'd be distracted by the tracker back near the strip of shops.

Chapter 56

A DRIVE TO SAFETY

R icardo held on to the dashboard as Gael finally reached the large, grey building with its many windows, displaying the sign, *Club Juvenil de Espana*. As he drove into the concrete drive on the side of the building, Ricardo said, "Let's go around the back. There's a bench we can sit on and contact the police. Can I use your phone?"

"Sure, but how do you know who you can trust over at the Civil Guard?" Gael said.

Ricardo sighed. He could only focus on enlisting the help of a team for now. "Do you happen to know if anyone else is working with Angel?"

Gael shook his head. "Not as far as I know, but I'm just a lackey and don't have much importance in the organisation. Angel won't tell me everything."

"It is a risk, but if they tell the whole team, we'll be safer in numbers." Ricardo placed the call and waited. "Yes, hello. Listen. I need to report a crime."

"What do you wish to report?" the officer on the other end asked. Ricardo explained their circumstances.

"Okay, I'll need to get a few more details from you, then we'll send a team over. Do you know where Angel might be located?"

"At least ten minutes from this location in the east. There was a tracker, but we got rid of it. We should be safe by now."

"I would prefer you go inside the club rather than stay outside. You are less vulnerable in there. Hide and wait for us." The officer asked a few more questions.

"Thank you. We'll head inside." He ended the call. "I need a pin or a piece of wire to get inside. I don't have the key."

Kim pulled out a pin from her hair and handed it to him. "Here you go."

"Thanks." He took the pin, straightened it by pulling its ends apart, then went to a side door to pick the lock. "It's been a while since I've done this, so if it doesn't work, I'm sure Gael knows how to do this."

"Sure I do," he said, winking at Kim.

"Of course," said Kim.

Ricardo pushed through the heavy door and made his way into the kitchen with Kim and Gael following close. He filled three glasses with water into them and gave one to Kim. "Here you go." Gael took the other glass and guzzled it down.

They sat at the table, prickles of unease permeating Ricardo's spine. "Let's hope they don't take too long. We're sitting ducks if Angel finds us and decides to call up a larger team of henchmen."

Gael wiped the back of his mouth with his hand. "I can't believe I'm on the other side."

Ricardo squeezed his shoulder and briefly watched Kim, whose eyes darkened. Were they thinking the same thing? "We can get you into a deal with the police. Your intel in exchange for immunity."

Gael scoffed. "Right. So do you think I'll live long enough to give you that damn intel, Ricardo? I'm toast."

"We can get you a new identity and you can disappear." Ricardo frowned, wondering if it would go in his favour. He was taking a huge risk, having betrayed the cartel. "If we can break the cartel you've been associated with, you don't need to worry about other cartels. They won't know you."

He shrugged. "Maybe." He rose. "I need some air. Give me a few minutes."

Ricardo shook his head. "Stay inside. We need to be together, Gael."

"I will be back soon. Don't worry. I can take care of myself." Gael ambled out of the room with a deflated posture. Ricardo understood the man's predicament but it was better to be on the side of good than evil.

Ricardo leaned in closer to Kim who sat beside him. He kissed her hard on the mouth. "God, I love you so much. When I heard—"

Kim put a finger over his lips. "Sssh...we don't need to rehash that. Gael saved me, and I am fine." She swallowed. "I was worried about you, Ricardo. Seeing you tied up that way, the torture. Are you okay?"

He nodded. "Better than okay now that I have you by my side." His gun and her knife rested on the table as their eyes locked. "Come here."

Kim inched closer and wrapped her arms around him. The warmth of her embrace made him realise he couldn't let her go. One way or another they would work out how to be together despite living an hour away from each other. Could they have a long-distance relationship and commute? But this wasn't the right time to be thinking about such things, when they were still in danger.

He pulled away from her. "Promise me something, Kim."

She knit her brows. "What is it?"

He hesitated, knowing she would not agree to his terms, but he had to keep her safe. If something happened to her, he would never forgive himself this time. He was willing to make sacrifices. "If something happens to me, I want you to leave this place, forget about me, and never return. Live your life." He couldn't fathom a life without her, but they were dealing with the cartel. "Make sure the police keep you safe, but if you're still in danger, I want you to go to Australia. I have connections over there. Will you promise me?"

She shook her head. "I will not promise any such thing. You are going to be fine. Nothing will happen to you."

Ricardo pressed his lips together. "Promise me you will find someone else and live without me."

Kim stood up. "Fine, Ricardo. I will live my life, but it will be with you."

Ricardo bowed his head, hoping they would both get out of this alive. "What's taking Gael so long?" He rose too and looked out the kitchen window. "It's quiet outside." He turned to her. "You stay here and I'll make sure he's fine. He's worried about his future and that's understandable, Kim."

His back to the door, he faced Kim and wondered why she was staring at the door with dilated eyes, her body flinching. "Kim?"

"Freeze, or you both die."

Ricardo's hair stood on end. Angel had found them. Maybe it hadn't been such a great idea to come to the club.

Chapter 57

FIGHT FOR FREEDOM

Ricardo slowly turned to stand in front of Kim to shield her. She wasn't going to die on his watch. Not this time. If Angel wanted to kill her, it would be over his dead body.

"Did you honestly believe I would not find you, Ricardo?"

Kim reached for his hand, and it warmed his heart. She moved beside him, but he turned to her and shook his head. Ignoring him, she said, "Please Angel. Let us go. If we promise to leave this alone, will you let us leave?"

He scoffed. "I am sorry, dear Kim. I liked you. I truly did, but you and Ricardo are too involved in this now, and I cannot go to prison. You know too much."

Ricardo steeled himself, the gun pointing in their direction. Two men stood on either side of his old fake friend, aiming two more guns at them. "This doesn't have to end this way, Angel. If you cared a little, let us go and we will forget all of this. Admit you killed Manuel."

He glared, appearing to consider a response. "My connections with the police force in Madrid explained how Manuel was an informant for the police, working undercover to bring the South American cartel down. He was a fool if he believed he could do that after his long, trivial involvement in drug possession and dealing. He was a small-time member who got released from prison. My police connection arranged a meeting for us to meet in Madrid. He explained how he wanted an important role in the cartel. He wanted to learn about the larger drug shipments and weapons control, but he was stupid enough to believe he could get away with it when I had a few policemen in my pocket." He gripped his gun. "Yes, I killed Manuel after visiting Madrid, my friend. I ordered the hit and watched him die. I was his boss, and he betrayed us."

Ricardo winced, not surprised by the admission. It took all of his energy not to risk his life and lunge for the bastard, but he had Kim to worry about. She was in the line of fire and he needed to keep her safe. He had no options. He was a sitting duck and knew that Angel would shoot him.

Could he stall him until the police arrived? "What about Lorenzo in custody. Did you kill him, too?"

Angel chuckled, then nodding. "Loose ends are loose ends, my friend. Alvaro was my hitman and tied these matters up nicely. Not long later, he went after Kim, but she was too smart to die in the woods."

Kim squeezed his hand. "Was Alvaro the man who got inside the club, too, knocking over our plants?"

"He had to send you a message to scare you before the kidnapping. He wasn't a man who did anything for the sake of it, dear Kim."

"Please, Angel. Don't do this. Let us go and live our lives. We can forget about Manuel."

"Get on your knees, Ricardo," said Angel.

Kim's face paled and she tightened her grip even further. "No, please. Don't do this. Ricardo has done nothing wrong. He will leave this be. Please, Angel."

Ricardo intervened. "Before you kill me, I need to know one thing."

Angel squinted. "I can allow one last question before you die."

He swallowed, thinking about his parents in Greece who would most likely never know what happened to him. A second son they were going to lose. How could he do this to them when they didn't deserve it? If only he had a way out of this. Most likely, they had killed Gael outside, so he couldn't protect him now. "Did you get Alejandro killed?"

Angel's eye twitched. "I am sorry about Alejandro, but I never ordered the hit. Arturo has always been a hot-head, and ignored my instructions when I explained how Alejandro was not a threat. That he had never even laid eyes on Arturo. But the man got a thrill out of impulse killing. Now he is dead. You got your revenge there." He took a breath. "I do not condone killing children, but Arturo was volatile, and thought that by killing Alejandro he would teach the other teenagers a lesson."

Ricardo scoffed as he got to his knees opposite the table. "No, but you still have the youth involved in your damn organisation. How is that any different from signing their death warrants?"

"I am not here to debate the issue with you, my friend. It is what it is."

Ricardo shook his head. "You bastard." His glare could shatter glass. "Lowlife. I could kill you with my bare hands." His rasping breath impacted his thoughts. He crumpled to the ground, a single tear ran down his cheek, but new reserves of energy pumped into him. *No, history was not going to repeat itself.*

"I would say you are in no position to fight me," said Angel.

Ricardo stared down the barrel of his gun, images of Manuel and his parents giving him strength. He hoped with all his heart that he could at least save Kim.

Kim's cheeks dampened with tears as her body quaked and her breath stopped. She had to do something. She couldn't watch Ricardo die like an animal. A beautiful man with a warm soul and a mind to match. Her love for him would never die, but she would gladly die with him in physical form. How could she move on without a man she loved so deeply and completely? A man she refused to live without. *Think, Kim. Think.*

Ricardo eyed Kim saying, "I love you, Kim with all my heart."

No, she refused to say goodbye. She wouldn't. *A stalling tactic.* "What would your kids say about what you're doing, Angel? I know they would be disgusted with your work."

He shrugged. "They are separate from this part of my life, Kim." He tilted his head. "I know what you're doing. Stalling. Even if the police arrive, it'll be too late for Ricardo. He'll be dead and you won't get far." He chuckled. "I have two other men in hiding that will take them down as soon as they arrive. They will not live to save you."

Kim couldn't breathe. "You will not get away with this, Angel. The police will catch you, and you'll spend the rest of your life in prison. Potentially, coming face to face with prisoners you might have helped put away. How would that make you feel?"

He chuckled. "I do not need to be educated about the horrors of incarceration, and I am too smart to get caught. I would be dead before I go to prison. That much I can tell you." He took a breath. "Now, Kim. I want you to kneel next to Ricardo here. I promise I'll make it quick and painless." He turned to his henchmen. "You guys go outside and check for any visitors. Help the others. I have this all under control." The two bulky men strolled out of the room and made their way outside. "Close your eyes," he said.

"I'm fine with my eyes open," said Ricardo.

"Me too," said Kim.

"Suit yourselves," said Angel.

Ricardo gazed into the distance as if to alert Angel to a new presence. "Well, hello there." When his nemesis turned, he took the split-second to lunge forward, wrestling for the gun. It slid across the floor and Kim lunged for it, but Angel shoved her into a corner. Ricardo ran at him and elbowed the man into his eyes and he fell back. *Where is the gun?*

"No, you won't get away with this, Ricardo," said Angel, who kneed him in the stomach, causing him to wince. But Ricardo persisted, as she knew that Ricardo wouldn't want another girlfriend of his to die.

Angel bent down low and reached for the gun underneath the table, a satisfied smirk splashed across his face.

A gunshot resounding near them made Kim jolt, but before she could see who it was, Angel's body fell backward, his gun flying across the room. *Hugo!* Recovering quickly from a graze in his shoulder, Angel lunged towards Hugo and punched him in the eyes until Hugo used the butt of his gun across his forehead. He pointed the gun at Angel. "Do not move, you bastard," said Hugo.

"I won't go to prison."

"I said, do not move an inch." Hugo turned to Ricardo with a half-smile.

Kim felt the discomfort of the knife in her back pocket so pulled it out. Ricardo quickly took it from her, his eyes telling her something." What's wrong?" Ricardo ignored her as he edged closer to Angel and Hugo.

Angel raised his body and sneakily reached for something in his sock. *Christ! Another gun!* This time, he aimed it towards Kim as she sank to the ground, realising she had reached the last seconds of her life. She didn't want to die.

Ricardo leaned forward and plunged the knife into Angel's side. He bowed over and screamed in pain, his eyes drooping and the gun falling out of his hands. Her hands shook as she stared at the blood streaming down the floor.

"You're finished," said Ricardo.

Chapter 58

POLICE ARRIVAL

Ricardo grabbed the gun, found Angel's phone in his pocket, and called an ambulance. When he ended the call, he turned to his lover. "Are you okay?"

"I'm...okay," said Kim. She stared at the bloody knife.

He stroked her face and couldn't stop a lone tear from falling down his cheek. He had nearly lost her. "I didn't kill him. He will survive to face the consequences."

She gave a dull nod. "I hope so."

Hugo patted Ricardo on the shoulder. "I am sorry I didn't get here sooner."

"How did you know how to find us?" Ricardo asked.

"I was with Marco, trying to find you guys. I was worried, and when they got your call, I rushed on ahead. I couldn't wait for them to assemble their team. If I'd waited with them, you'd be both dead."

Ricardo beamed, comforted by Kim's warm hand in his. "Thank God you did. I appreciate you saving my life, man."

Hugo nodded. "Any time."

Kim wrapped her arms around him. "Thank you, Hugo. You are a life-saver."

"What about the men outside. Angel's goons?" Ricardo asked.

"I had my own knife and incapacitated them. I took their weapons, too. The two other men that were in the building are secured inside a room. I distracted them and they were dumb enough to rush inside the room when I secured it."

"Thanks, man. Your military skills came in handy. What about Gael? Is he dead?"

"I didn't see anyone else out there. Sorry," said Hugo.

A loud commotion resounded outside. Doors slammed and loud footsteps echoed. The police were finally here—or was it more of Angel's goons? He aimed the gun towards the approaching moving bodies.

"What is going on here?" said Marco.

Ricardo handed the gun to him. "It's a long story."

The ambulance arrived and tended to Angel's wounds before placing him on a stretcher and putting him inside of it.

Marco stared down Hugo. "I will deal with you later." He faced Ricardo. "Are you or Kim hurt?"

Ricardo shrugged. "A few grazes and bruises, but we'll survive. Hugo was hurt, too." A paramedic worked on his wounds, and the stinging disinfectant across his face made him wince. "Angel has to face the consequences of his actions, Marco."

"I hear you, which is why I'll need your statement." He exhaled. "We've arrested those henchmen outside who are injured, as well as those other men you knocked out, Hugo."

He nodded. "What happened to Gael?"

Marco scoffed. "That low-life was shot, but he's alive. He was hidden behind a tree, so we barely saw him. The paramedics will transport them all to the nearest hospital."

"Gael helped us. He wants immunity in exchange for his intel," said Ricardo. The paramedics rushed out. Ricardo felt like his knees were about to buckle as he stared at Marco. "I'll explain everything, but you need to know there might be other men out there. Even more traitors in the police force. You need their intel, Marco."

Marco pulled out his notepad, jotting down notes. "Start from the beginning, and we'll go from there. We have strong leads."

As he recounted his story, he realised he had to make his life count with Kim.

Chapter 59

GOOD NEWS

A few days later, Kim's chest tightened at the thought of returning to Madrid. Could they have a long-distance relationship? Not that Patones was too far to travel, but it wasn't a place she could visit every day and be with Ricardo most nights. She would miss him.

She sat across from Marco at the station as she waited on the latest news. Hugo and Ricardo sat on either side of her. Would they need to enter the witness protection program? "What happens now?"

Ricardo squeezed Kim's hand. "Did you get intel on those thugs at the club or with Fuentes?"

Marco nodded. "Better than that. We are in the process of arresting all those involved in Manuel's and Miguel's deaths, not to mention countless others. The man who killed poor Miguel will hopefully never see the light of day. A volatile man who appears to be calm and measured but is extremely dangerous. Let's just say, he was a replacement for Alvaro. Another hitman, but we have him."

"That's good news," said Ricardo. He frowned. "Who killed Alvaro near the club?"

"Angel's men," said Marco. "According to Fuentes they had a falling-out, and Alvaro wanted to retire after his plan to kill Kim. Angel couldn't have him as a risk he'd talk to the police, so killed him as a safety measure.

"We are far from dismantling the South American cartel, but those relevant to Manuel are either dead or have been arrested. They'll never get out. You are both safe to live your lives as you wish."

Kim's heart lifted. "We don't need to go into witness protection?"

"Not at this stage. We are in the process of preparing more undercover agents to infiltrate the cartel's leadership, starting with Angel's boss who knew nothing about you or Manuel. Certain decisions could be made by Angel, and from what we have ascertained, he would only contact his boss on business matters relevant across the networks. Angel was in charge of the matters of recruitment and informants or leaks in the business. Not to mention, the law enforcement intel."

"That is good to know, Marco." Ricardo shifted in his seat. "What happens to Gael?" Ricardo asked.

"He was a worthy adversary," said Hugo. "You guys got lucky with him." Ricardo and Kim nodded in his direction.

Marco's eyes peered past him. "We are using him as our informant. Nobody else in the cartel knows he's turned. Only Angel and his henchmen knew. Arturo is dead, so he should be safe to fake being in the organisation." His eyes darkened. "Arturo was the one who killed Manuel. I am sorry we didn't get to him sooner."

Ricardo scoffed. "That bastard deserved to die after what he did to my brother, and to poor Alejandro. One less piece of scum on this Earth."

She touched Ricardo on the shoulder. "I am sorry, Ricardo. Justice has been served now." He nodded. She turned to Marco. "Please keep Gael safe," said Kim. "Manuel risked his life as an informant."

"As they all do, but the corrupt policemen have been apprehended. We are squeaky clean for now. Back with Manuel, we didn't know about Angel and Officer Fuentes."

"For now," said Ricardo. "How long will that last until another police officer or civil guard gets itchy feet and decides he wants a fancy boat or a fast car?"

"Everything is a risk, Ricardo. But we need all the intel and help we can get. We are taking these low-lives down."

"What about Hugo? Did you find out who shot him, and why?" Ricardo asked.

Marco nodded. "It was Sara's father, Andres, who despised Hugo for taking her away from him. A revenge action. He will be in prison for the foreseeable future. It had nothing to do with the cartel."

Kim had more questions. "Hugo, when you were at Ricardo's house and you were checking in, who were you talking to on the phone? I wondered then if you were involved with the cartel. You mentioned something; *she needs to pay.*"

Hugo stared past her. "I'm sorry. It had to do with my wife. I had an investigator check in on her because I suspected she was having an affair. He wanted to stop watching her, said she was innocent, but I didn't believe it and told him to keep going. We're separated now because she was having an affair discreetly, and now I'm fighting for custody of my baby boy. I was angry at the time and didn't mean to sound like a jerk. In spite of her mistake, hopefully we can do what's best for our son."

"I am sorry, Hugo," said Kim. "I hope it all works out."

"Thanks, but I'll be fine."

Kim was thankful to Hugo, and hoped that Gael would be safe, but she was also worried about her and Ricardo's future.

Chapter 60

EPILOGUE
ONE MONTH LATER

Kim packed the last of her belongings into the travel bag and dropped it on the floor. She took one last look in the mirror. The black lines underneath her eyes were a sign that she hadn't been sleeping well, pondering the possibility that more cartel members might be out to get them. The police wanted to make sure she was safe from any surprises from the cartel, so she had not left Patones earlier.

It was safe for her to leave, but Ricardo had not said one word about their future. The last month had been mostly about him watching over her and getting Hugo to babysit her, too. She had visited the club and wished the teenagers well, particularly Luciana, who had decided to leave Patones to be with another aunt in Bilbao. She couldn't stay in a place that reminded her of Alejandro, but she had mentioned wanting to be a police officer as an adult. Good luck to the poor girl.

Kim had been offered a position in a drug rehabilitation centre, counselling and case managing youth at risk in Madrid. The role wouldn't start for another two weeks, so she had a bit more time to enjoy her lady-of-leisure status. Part of her work would involve providing well-being activities such as yoga, meditation, and stress management techniques post recovery, as well as in the early stages of withdrawal. She would be selling her yoga business.

Ricardo ambled inside her room. "Is that everything?"

"Hmm. Thanks for everything, Ricardo. I appreciate all you've done."

His head tilted, his eyes questioning her. "You make it sound like this is the end of us. I don't want that, Kim. I cannot breathe without you. I cannot live without you. You make me complete, and I refuse to let you go." He wrapped his arms around her and caressed her upper back. He pulled away. "Why do you think I've been having those late nights?"

She shrugged. "I don't know. I thought you were busy at work."

He sighed. "I was interviewing my replacement at the hotel, and I have a potential buyer for this home. Hugo's going to be my advocate on the future sale."

Kim's heart was about to burst. "But why didn't you tell me, Ricardo? Why the secrecy?"

"I wanted to surprise you, beautiful. I am coming with you, but we'll have to drive in our separate cars."

Her body became alive as she hugged him tight. "I was worried you wouldn't want to leave. I know your life is here."

"My life is with you, Kim. That's all that matters to me. A job and my other affairs can be done in Madrid. I've been offered a position at a prestigious hotel in the centre of Madrid. Not far from where you live."

Kim's heart rose. She couldn't remember a time she'd been happier. "That's amazing, Ricardo. When do you start?"

He stroked her cheek. "In one week. We have that time to get up to crazy, crazy things." He ran his hand down her breast. "I am going to do things to you that you thought were never possible."

She chuckled, loving this man more with each minute. "I love you, Ricardo. I cannot wait to live my life with you."

"My life has just begun," said Ricardo. "My car's mostly packed."

He grabbed her bag, put his arm around her and together, they walked downstairs and out the door to begin their new lives together.

Reviews are gold to Authors, and allow me to keep writing. You can write a review of *Secrets In The Shadows* here: https://books2read.com/u/ml88kv

Check out Book 2 of the Women Of Strength Series, featuring Daniela in *Shadows Of The Past*:

https://books2read.com/u/3y1yAl

ABOUT THE AUTHOR

Lucy Appadoo is a prolific reader and author of the Friends In Crisis and Women Of Strength Series. After a childhood spent reading and imagining escapist worlds, Lucy has put her imagination into stories. Her work as a rehabilitation counsellor, and former work as a counsellor in private practice, have led to an interest in writing inspirational stories about authentic, driven women who manage adversity with strength and heart. She writes in the genres of romantic suspense/thrillers with significant life themes and contemporary romance.

Lucy's interests include researching crime stories and news to inspire her work, watching crime thrillers and suspenseful movies, travel, exercising, reading for entertainment or knowledge, meditation, and spending time with friends and family. She also appreciates her Italian background and culture, which has inspired her to write imaginative stories about her parents' childhoods, leading to The Italian Family Series novels.

Check out Lucy's website and sign up for a free suspenseful book:

https://www.lucyappadooauthor.com.au

ALSO BY LUCY APPADOO

<u>FICTION</u>
Women Of Strength Series — Romantic Suspense/Thriller
In Rio's Shadows (Book 1):
http://mybook.to/InRiosShadows
Shadows Of The Past (Book 2):
https://books2read.com/u/3JZe1X

Friends In Crisis Series - Romantic Suspense/Thriller
Haunted By The Past (Book 1):
https://books2read.com/u/bw2ZeY
Twisted Obsession (Book 2):
https://books2read.com/u/4DW8pk

Web Of Lies (Book 3):

https://books2read.com/u/3JXazE

Love-Obsessed (Book 4):

https://books2read.com/u/4jPKGX

The Hearts Series - Romantic Suspense

Rising Hearts (Book 1):

https://books2read.com/u/mZwpoE

Forbidden Hearts (Book 2):

https://books2read.com/u/bQBKr7

Kindred Hearts (Book 3):

https://books2read.com/u/4AJKQK

Broken Hearts (prequel to Forbidden Hearts):

https://books2read.com/u/mgrnOD

Short Story Thrillers

Evening Interrupted:

https://books2read.com/u/3yZDjZ

The Dreamcatcher: https://books2read.com/u/bzaLxn

Red Flags: https://books2read.com/u/bWZ9W1

Collection of Short Story Thrillers:

https://books2read.com/u/bP5vwj

**The Italian Family Series - Coming of Age Family
Drama/Romance**

A New Life: https://books2read.com/u/mqqwZm

The Beauty of Tears: https://books2read.com/u/bpqwk3

Dancing in the Rain:
https://books2read.com/u/bOr7LA

A Life By Design: https://books2read.com/u/3J8ene

NON-FICTION

Grief & Loss

Moving Beyond Grief - How To Shift From Grief & Loss to Joy & Peace: https://books2read.com/u/mVNzDA

Stress Management & Anxiety

Holistic Spiritual and Mental Health - Building Resilience and Creativity by Conquering Anxiety and Managing Stress: https://books2read.com/u/47kG8A

Career Guidance

Your Holistic Career Path - Create Career Change, Satisfaction, and Work/Life Balance: https://books2read.com/u/bzYDz4